UNPLUGGED

UNPLUGGED

Vol One

SIGAL EHRLICH

Cover designed by Matthew Phillips (http://thecoverlure.com/)
Cover art:
Copyright © Shutterstock 120919477
Copyright © TA/Taivo Aarna (http://www.taivoaarna.com/)

Editing by
Nicole Hornbaker
Jenny Sims of www.editing4indies.com

Interior Design and Formatting by
www.emtippettsbookdesigns.com

Published by Sigal Ehrlich
http:// www.sigalehrlich.com

Visit the author website:
http://www.sigalehrlich.com

Version 03102017

For my Liis, ma armastan sind . . . so much!

Also, for Tartu, you'll always feel like home.

CHAPTER
One

"Oh, no, sir. I don't get intimidated easily."
Ivi, first interview

I toss and turn in bed, plagued by vile jetlag and, to a certain extent, the intimidation of this mansion where I'm shacked. Throwing the blanket aside, I get out of bed. I smooth my white, oversized tee over my thighs and pull my pink knitted socks up to my knees before navigating to where, as far as I can recall, the kitchen is located.

I hold one of the monstrous fridge doors open, taking inventory of the profusion of goods on display. I twitch my lips, moving them from side to side, as I muse what can best serve as a natural sedative. *Bingo.* My eyes land on a milk carton. Warm milk. Mom's never-failing insomnia medicine. I stoop slightly forward for the carton and stop dead. More precisely, I find myself being stopped by an iron grip. Instinctively, I suck in a breath as a firm arm slides to wrap around my waist. A warm, hard body presses against me in tandem to someone's lips nuzzling me right below my ear. A momentary stupor enfolds me as a few things register concurrently. The prickly feel of the scruff on my neck, and the smell hovering near that is a mixture of part masculine, part alcohol. Heavy alcohol. The most tantalizing fact, though, would have to be that the body pressed against my back is very much naked, as I can distinctively feel every part of the firm torso through my thin, cotton tee.

Still utterly startled, I chance a hesitant glance at the strong arm embracing me. Suntanned and large, it could be easily mistaken for a canvas crowded with colorful, detailed illustrations. The other hand, the one not holding me firmly, is another art creation in the form of a human limb extended toward the OJ carton.

"Open that for me, babe," a raspy, low voice demands. And I do. The carton is lifted above my shoulder, and right after a pause, it is set in my stunned hand. Lightly moist, cold lips, bordered by a prickly beard, kiss my neck next. "Come back to bed, babe," says the utterly seductive voice. A light smack on the butt jolts me, and I'm left by myself. My heart is beating in my ears, and my lips part in shock. I swallow hard and slowly turn to see who just groped-spanked me. There's so much to take in. The lion's head tattoo covering the right shin, the dark hair messily knotted, the toned arms, the musical notes tattooed on the left shoulder blade. But one thing calls for my full attention. A delectable, as in an award-winning, butt.

Gape-mouthed, I turn back to the fridge and open the freezer door, shoving my heated face inside. *Fudge warm milk.* I snatch one of the many vodka bottles. Unscrewing the cap of the clear, frosted bottle, I take one generous sip that scorches all the way down to the pit of my stomach. I wipe my lips with the back of my hand and murmur, "Kurat!" on a jarred exhale. An Estonian cognate to damn.

Welcome to your new home, Ivi. Cheers!

CHAPTER
Two
CHAPTER

"Strangers – you'll never truly know the immense impact they'll have on your life, or you'll have on theirs. To what extent the people we meet will change the direction of our lives and the decisions we make." About Us section, Youth with Purpose Organization website.

I sit on the bed and look around me, heaving a troubled exhale. The singular midnight encounter that only fueled my insomnia plays in my head on repeat. Sighing once more, I grab my phone, plunge the earbuds in, and drop my head to the headboard. Closing my eyes, I wait for the first tunes to fill my ears. Coming to terms with the sleepless night ahead, I reach for my needles and the baby-pink wool. An easy smile loosens my face as I study the wooly socks I'm working on. Rhythmically, I work the needles and yarn while my mind wanders to the whirlwind that this day has been. Back to this morning when the plane had finally touched American soil and the awkward introduction that came right after.

For a span of some good tense moments, we study each other in silence.

Me, bloodshot blue eyes, weary as only one can be after an endless flight, yet excited and somewhat tense.

Him, brown eyes staring from behind navy rimmed glasses, guarded and somewhat timid.

I break our gaze, turning to glance at the hard-jaw gentleman in the expensive suit sitting between us with his chest pressed to the back of a chair. The personal manager of my new boss, my new boss whose kid I'm supposed to nanny for the next six months. A man I'm supposed to be meeting for the first time. I can't help but wonder who I've agreed to work for? A man who sends his personal assistant in his place to meet the person who will be caring for HIS child.

"Ivy," Eli, the personal manager, says.

"Ivi. It's pronounced Eevie," I correct him.

He offers me what I believe is a smile. A tight, amused twitch of his lips. Chewing on his gum in rapid tempo, Eli runs his eyes back and forth between the kid and me. The kid's stare casts down to where his hand circles the band of his oversized blue watch around his wrist. Eli taps four fingers on the table and rises to stand.

"I'll give you two a moment to get acquainted. I have some calls to make, so I'll be over there." He tips his chin to a table by the window. "If you need anything . . ." His words linger between the three of us until he turns on his heel. I'm not sure to whom in particular that was directed — me or the sweet, coy-looking kid.

The boy's stare follows Eli's dark suit as it goes a distance away, and I take the chance to study him. Olive skin, big, clever eyes, and a few scattered, tiny beauty marks. He is a bit lanky in a "young kid starting to knock off the growing charts" kind of way. When he pivots to return my stare, I smile at him.

"I'm so happy to finally meet you. I'm Ivi."

"Jeremy," he murmurs, giving me a fleeting glance.

His eyes drop to the large soda glass before him.

"This is awkward, huh?" I say on an amused accord. Finally, I get a smile, which is directed at the straw. Sweet, full-lipped, crooked smile. "How about I tell you a bit about me, and then you can tell me about yourself?"

He nods. I'm pretty positive the murmur that just left his mouth was something along the lines of a confirmation.

"So I came from this tiny, cold country in Europe called Estonia."

Jeremy perks up. "Yeah, it's bordered by the Gulf of Finland and the Baltic sea. Skype was developed in Estonia."

I gape at him, blink once, and frown. There's a lot to be said about the charming little country I call home. One of them is no one knows it even exists! Unless you're from Europe and watch Eurovision, and even then . . . I wouldn't put my money on it.

"It has two independence days, and it's the least religious country in the world. And oh, did you know it was the first country ever to have a Christmas tree?"

Through a chuckle, I say, "No, I didn't know that." My brows sink together in charmed curiosity. "Um, wow. I'm impressed."

Jeremy shrugs. "I read . . . a lot."

That's refreshing.

"I guess it runs in my blood. My mom's a professor. An anthropology and human genetics professor."

My eyes crinkle at the sides when a virtual fence seems to lift, and a stream of information about Jeremy flows my way. The kid resumes, telling me more about himself, and I listen engrossed with a supple grin. "I don't have any brothers or sisters. It's just my mom, Melena, and me. My mom is great, a bit of a space cadet, but she is really awesome. And smart. She's incredibly smart. She teaches at Caltech. We live near the campus. She says it's easier that way, to manage and all." He shrugs again. "I also go there from time to time for some courses."

"Come again?"

His eyebrows rise a little. "I'm in this Academic Talent Development program."

"You're ten, right?"

"Yeah . . . " He sends me an "is there a problem with that" look. I just shake my head, my thin smile growing with every passing moment and the *torrent of words gushing my way.*

"Sounds very interesting. I'd love to hear more about that. And what do you do for fun?"

"Growtopia."

"I'm sorry, what was that?"

"Grow . . . topia." Jeremy annunciates with a hint of a mocking smile.

I shake my head, signaling that I'm not familiar with whatever this "grow" thing might be. "It's a multiplayer platform where players can create a world, chat, and trade," he explains enthusiastically.

"A computer game," I state.

He rolls his eyes. "It's so much more. You basically start off with nothing, and you have to trade and stuff. You have to build new worlds. Just make sure you're not mistaken for a noob. I can show you if you want."

"I'd love that." I can't stop beaming; he's super adorable. "And how about sports, the outdoors?"

"Nah." Another shrug, which seems to be a theme with him. "Not the biggest fan of sports." He pushes his glasses up the bridge of his nose. "There's nature in Growtopia, though." He grins, and my own smile widens.

"I'm actually a big fan of both nature and sports. I used to ice-skate, and I love nature. I go hiking every chance I get," I say, and we continue to amicably exchange information about ourselves. To my utter contentment, as the minutes tick by, we feel more and more comfortable in each other's company.

"You have a funny accent." Jeremy gives me a boyish smile.

"Thank you, I guess." I beam at him.

More than twenty minutes later, just before Eli heads our way to take us both to our new home, Jeremy appears to step into his own mind. His brows wrinkle, he licks his lips, he squirms in his chair, and he raises coy eyes at me. "Did you meet him . . . my father?"

"Not yet," I say. Inching to stand, I cock my head, trying to decode the sudden change of demeanor.

His awkward smile withers, replaced by unease. He murmurs, "Neither have I." My eyes widen drastically, darting his way. He doesn't know his dad? He shoves his hands into his pockets, and his stare wanders to his green sneakers. "Promise you won't leave us alone?" He raises his eyes to mine.

And with the bonding stare we trade, this kid seeps right into my heart. It's at this moment I fall in love with a boy.

Thoughts of Jeremy and our conversation about his father don't help me relax either. The poor kid isn't sure he even wants to meet this father, who apparently chose to never reach out to him till now. *What have I gotten myself into?*

In the same breath, I remind myself that this is just a stop before the journey I plan to take to pursue my dream. In six months, I'll be going to South Asia—more precisely, Nepal—where together with other volunteers, I'll be building homes and a new school for a small community severely injured by both natural disasters and poverty.

To be able to do that, I need money. The greater part, the travel and accommodation fare of our missions, is sponsored. However, we still need to have some cushion for necessities and emergencies. It's not a lot, but it's still money I don't have. Which brought me to *this* place where cha-ching can be found in abundance. Los Angeles. The city of the rich and famous and those who require household help. More accurately, help and discretion, aka me, the foreigner nanny.

So here I am, venturing toward my dream with no clue as to whom will be signing my paycheck. What's more, I know that whatever happens, I mustn't fail either of them, my employer or his son. Whatever happens, I must hold on to this job. But that's okay because I'm a believer. Not a believer believer, as in religion, cults, or any modern stream people nowadays think it's cool to follow. At the risk of sounding naïve, I'm a believer in all that's good in this world. I believe in karma. I believe that every one of us possesses at least an ounce of good inside. I generally believe in nobility. To some people, it may sound as if I'm either a Krishna chick or high as a kite. Well, I'm neither. I'm just a person who honestly believes this world is not as bad as it seems sometimes.

CHAPTER
Three

"Take my hand, hold on tight. I'm taking you on a wild, wild ride. Don't close your eyes, baby. Run away if you can."
"Run if You Can," Tyler Lee Adams' first number one hit.

"Have a great day, kiddo," I tell Jeremy, nudging his arm.

He responds in a drowsy nod before following Victor, the driver, who's taking him to school. I wave them a final good-bye and make my way back into the kitchen for breakfast.

With my teeth sank deep into butter and honey toast, I raise my eyes toward the kitchen door at the sound of heavy steps shuffling my way. I freeze mid-chew when my stare meets the person who just entered through the vast double door. With my cheek gracefully filled like a chipmunk, I gape at the six-foot-something man who scratches his bare abs and yawns.

What the what?

Before me, tall, groggy, tattooed, blinking away sleep, stands *the* Tyler Lee Adams. As in the rocker god, Ty Lee Adams. All glorious, barefoot, and worn jeans, the first button undone. I try to swallow the contents in my mouth and "elegantly" choke. Coughing a couple of times, my hands dart for my teacup. I gulp half of the warm liquid and cough some more. At my salvation attempt, Tyler Lee Adams' eyes narrow my way. For a few long beats, he just stands there, watching me as I attempt not to die.

"What you doing here?"

"Excuse me?" I cough once more while patting my chest.

"How'd you manage to stick around? Fun is over, babe, you have to leave now."

"Um . . ." *Wha*? I blink.

He produces a hundred-dollar bill from his back pocket and slams it on the table in front of me. "Order a cab, get your stuff, and leave."

My lips part, and I blink some more. "What? Cab?"

His eyes twitch in annoyance. He shakes his head just as the bulb in my head lights up with last night's midnight encounter.

Kurat! He thinks we hooked up!

"Hold on, you think we . . . you and me, we . . . in which universe, exactly?" I snicker and light heat covers my cheeks, a product of the implied subject and, to a greater degree, irritation. His intimidating stare deepens. "Um, sir, believe me, you got it all wrong. I, well, sort of work here."

It's his lips turn to twitch in irritation. "If I had a penny for every time I heard that." He shakes his head again. "We both know you don't. So grab your shit and arrivederci, bella." He heaves loudly in frustration.

"I . . . Work . . . Here, Bello. I'm Jeremy's new nanny," I retort.

"Say again." He folds his arms over his bare chest.

"I'm Jeremy's new nanny?" My voice takes an insecure lilt, and my brows almost meet. All of a sudden, I feel less than confident about my current employment situation.

He gives me a one too scrutinizing, too disconcerting once-over that results in a shout that makes me jolt in my chair. "Eli!" And shortly after, louder. "Eli! Get over here."

I gape at him dumbfounded.

Eli, seeming not the least bit fazed, casually walks into the kitchen. He nods at me, "Good morning, Ivi," and turns to Tyler Lee. "Tyler."

"What's that?" Tyler Lee tips his chin my way. Arms still folded on his chest.

I glare at him.

"Miss Kert. Your new employee." Eli's voice is methodical and flat.

"Ivi," I mutter quietly, wrapping my hands around the mug.

Eyes hard on Eli, Tyler Lee says, "Pay her whatever we agreed on and get her the fuck out of here."

Ah? No, no, no, no. This cannot be happening.

"Tyler." Eli exhales, appearing almost bored. "She was the best candidate. In fact, she's the only one who actually met all the strict requirements *you* came up with."

"I don't need that" — Tyler Lee throws his hand my way — "around here."

I flinch. Hot irritation pooling in my stomach.

"All right, then. But just so you know, we probably won't find anyone else that meets *your* requirements on such short notice . . . there's no one to take care of your child till we do." The stare-off between the two men is a third presence in the room. A scary, buffed, badass third presence. I hold my breath, fearing to make a noise. My trip to South Asia, my dream, is on the line. And the odds don't seem to be in my favor. And for the life of me, *I have no idea why.*

"Fuck this," Tyler Lee growls before sauntering to the door. I watch him leave with wide eyes and a dropped jaw. He throws back an inscrutable look my way and walks out.

"Congrats, you just got his blessing," Eli deadpans. My gape turns to him as he grabs an apple from a fruit basket and rubs it against his sleeve before bringing it to his mouth for a crunchy bite. "He's not a morning person," Eli says through the bite and leaves the kitchen where the remnants of anger, astonishment, and attitude are suffocating.

I stare at my half drank mug.

Tyler frigging Lee Adams is my new boss. Grabby at night, crabby come morning, Ty Lee.

Jeremy is Tyler Lee's son! Tyler Lee has a son!

Wow. Tyler. Lee. Adams. *Tyler Lee Adams is a world-class jerk.*

CHAPTER
Four

NAME: JEREMY NATHAN BROWN
DATE OF BIRTH: MARCH 8, 2007
PLACE OF BIRTH: PASADENA, CALIFORNIA
NAME OF FATHER: N/A
NAME OF MOTHER: MELENA
WITH WHOM DOES THE CHILD LIVE: MOTHER

- Forest Crescent Elementary, Pupil Registration Form

By the time Jeremy is back from school, I've already unpacked most of my stuff and settled into my new room. If an enormous suite with a walk-in closet and a master bathroom could be called such a thing.

My room. A vast space with industrial concrete walls and reclaimed wood furniture, luxurious drapes, cozy chaise, and soft, upholstered bed with a wall-to-wall headboard. A spicy twist in the form of a gigantic circular sculpture takes the main focus off the overall mellow décor. And my favorite part—the panoramic windows overlooking the black, reflective infinity pool in the middle of the backyard.

Prone at the edge of my bed, Jeremy asks, "Would you come with me to meet him?"

I knit the last stitch, set my needles and yarn on the nightstand, and watch him for a stretch, contemplating. "I think that's something you should do by yourself, Jer. I'll wait for you right here."

Jeremy grabs one of my needles and pokes the air. "Did you know that stress is called a silent killer? It can cause brain damage. You know that adults normally can't comprehend the amount of stress children experience in their life? Some researchers say that even in the stomach a baby can pick up its mother's stress."

"Jer, I think you should start reading more children books." I smile at him. He gives me a half-smile, holding the needle from both sides. "I understand your concern, and I'm guessing you're nervous. It can be a stressful situation to meet your father for the first time. But I'm sure he's excited. I bet he really wants for you to like him."

When apprehension veils his face, I take the needle from his hand, set it aside, and squeeze his hand. I keep his hand in mine. "He's waiting for you. Let's go. I'll take you there, okay?"

Jeremy is a tight ball of edginess and fidgeting by the time we take the last steps to the third floor of the house. Encompassing Tyler Lee's bedroom, a home recording studio, and an office, it's a level best described as Tyler Lee's kingdom of luxury and music.

I knock on the wooden door and wait. Jeremy bites on his fingernails by my side.

"Hey, it'll be okay," I say, rubbing my hand over his tensed arm.

"Yeah," Tyler Lee's raspy voice resonates from behind the door.

Slowly, I slide the door open and am momentarily taken aback by the simplicity of his office. It's in such glaring contrast with the opulence dripping from any other space in the house. White walls, simple wooden furniture, wide panoramic windows, and a few guitars leaning against the wall. Tyler Lee is slouched on a wide leather armchair, black tee, beard, jeans, and a man bun. Casual, natural, and nothing but impossibly attractive.

"You asked to see your . . . um, Jeremy, when he is back," I say, not sure how to even approach this . . . unification. It feels so unnatural for a ten-year-old to meet his father for the first time. And for the new nanny to be the one making the so-called introduction.

At the same instance that Jeremy takes a step forward from his hiding place behind my back, Tyler Lee rises to meet him. For a space of a moment, I'm lost, sunk into the emotions conveyed by his eyes. I can't look away. They both eye each other in a palpable daze.

"Jeremy." The undercurrent of emotions bound to Tyler Lee's voice trickles all the way to my core. Tyler Lee takes a couple of steps to reach us, his stare glued to his son. Jeremy swallows, looking at his dad with no less awe.

"I'll leave you two alone then," I say in a soft voice. Not sure if either of them even heard me, I turn on my heel, closing the door behind me.

As I make my way back to the first floor, many questions run through my mind. It doesn't make any sense to me. Why are they only now meeting for the first time? What kept them apart? How could he not reach out to his son until now? Coming from a tight and loving family, this situation leaves me beyond troubled.

Hearing Eli's voice coming from the kitchen, I head there, opting to try to get some answers. At first, both Eli and the older lady who's talking to him don't seem to notice me. As I take another step into the kitchen, the older lady turns my way. Eli's gaze follows suit.

"Hi." I greet them both with a small wave.

Eli nods while the lady studies me in overt curiosity.

"Adina, this is Ivi," Eli says, pocketing his phone.

The lady with the low gray bun and black pinafore keeps eyeing me before sending me a polite smile. "Ivi, it's nice to finally meet you."

"Nice to meet you, too." I take a couple of steps to shake her hand. When I do, her smile grows warmer.

"We're glad to have you here. I'm the house manager if you need anything."

"Thank you. I'll keep that in mind." I mirror her kind smile.

"Dinner will be served at seven. I hope you like roast chicken."

"That sounds great."

She smiles again and turns to nod at Eli before heading toward the pantry.

"Eli, can I bother you? I, um, have a few questions."

Eli gestures for me to follow him.

Walking beside him toward the main living room, I ask, "Is there anything in addition to the instructions on the agreement you expect me to do with Jeremy?"

"What did you have in mind?"

"Should I go with him to his after school activities, for example?"

"Whatever you decide. I don't think it's necessary, though. Victor covers the commuting part."

"What about the mornings when Jeremy is at school? Is there anything you expect me to do around here? Is there anything I shouldn't do? Um, parts of the house that are off-limits? Um, can I use the gym?"

He purses his lips for a pensive moment. "Feel free to use the gym. About all the rest, don't think so. You'd better talk to Tyler about that," he says and calls out to a heavily pierced guy who just entered the main door.

————◆————

A knock on my door makes me jolt in my seat and thrust the laptop's screen down. The last thing I need is for someone to see my cyber stalking. There was nothing on Tyler Lee having a ten-year-old son.

"Come in," I say and swirl in my chair to face the door. Jeremy's untamed mane pops in the room. He closes the door behind him and walks my way, his eyes trained on his shoes. He leans his hip on the desk I'm sitting by and tucks his hands in his somewhat retro corduroy pockets.

"Wow," he says, urging my eyes to fixate on his baffled expression. He tilts his head for his eyes to meet mine. "I just met my dad for the first time." He pushes his glasses up his nose.

"How did it go?" My eyes run over his face.

"Awkward." He frowns. "I kind of made it hard on him. I think. It's just . . ." He huffs. "I expected my mom to be around whenever that happened. But well, she wasn't."

"Why wasn't she?"

"Something about her schedule, the project she's involved in. She wanted to, I know that. But it was a last-minute thing. She had to go or lose the funding for her project in Africa. She said she trusted me to handle it well." His lips twitch into a grim smile that disappears just as it appeared. "Did you know that one out of three kids don't live with their biological father? It's mostly common in low-income homes." His stream of facts speeds up. "Kids that grow up without a father are at a greater risk of drug and alcohol addiction. Also, mental illness, suicide, they usually suck at school, and are more likely to become criminals."

"Jeremy, Jeremy!" I take his hand in mine in comfort. In a calm voice, searching his eyes, I ask, "How do you feel?"

"He is Tyler Lee Adams, Ivi." Another frown contracts his face. "My mom told me who he was when she told me I had to stay with him till she comes back. And I knew who he was, but . . ." Jeremy trails off. He looks up, meeting my gaze. "He has no clue how to deal with kids. I think he was even more nervous than I was."

"I guess he was overwhelmed." I keep my voice level. "Obviously, you both were. I'm sure he wanted to meet you more than anything." Jeremy sends me a scorn coated glance. "Um, did you ask him why you haven't met till now?"

He shakes his head. "I guess I was, I still am, too . . . shocked?" He blinks at me and shrugs. "I don't even know what to think. I was too nervous to ask anything. I barely spoke. I guess we both need more time. It's not a very easy thing to meet someone for the first time, especially when you didn't even know he existed."

"You're a smart kid, Jeremy. You're very mature for your age."

Jeremy's contagious, crooked grin makes an appearance. He shoves his navy glasses up the bridge of his nose and says, "Well, I'm special like that. I'm a mix of an anthropology professor and a rock star. I'm gifted, you see."

"That you are." I ruffle his hair and curl my arm around his shoulder.

"Let's go have dinner."

CHAPTER
Five

CHAPTER

"The prince approached her, took her by the hand, and danced with her. Furthermore, he would dance with no one else. He never let go of her hand . . ." Cinderella, read to six-year-old Ivi by her father at bedtime.

I follow the soft tunes and the enticing, rough baritone voice coming from down the hall. Nearing the open door of Tyler Lee's office, I stop to lean against the wall. For some long moments, I just stand in place and listen. Melodic sounds seep all the way to my bloodstream. I've listened to him sing so many times before, many of which his voice led me to sleep. But something about hearing it in person, up close and personal, raw and bare, that filters my soul and keeps me glued to my spot.

When the music winds down, I finally take the last step to reach the threshold. Tyler Lee's face turns my way. He is slumped in a wide, brown leather armchair; his legs are propped on the coffee table, and he has a guitar cradled in his arms.

"Hi," I say.

"Hey," he answers, his eyes unnervingly running over me.

"Can I bother for a sec?" He tips his chin up in what I assume is an affirming gesture. "Um . . ."

"Take a seat," he says, turning to lean his guitar against the armrest. He spreads his thighs and braces his elbows on his knees. Leaning forward, he follows my every motion as I settle on the tan sofa facing him.

A light heat crawls up to my cheeks when his eyes pause on my chest. I fold my arms over my braless chest. I never wear bras at home. I can't stand bras. It always feels like they restrict my breathing a little. But it's the first time in forever I wish I had one on.

His eyes finally lift to mine.

"What's up?"

"Ah?" I ask, after a short lapse in which I've drowned in his dark eyes.

"Miss Kert, how can I help you?" he asks next with an impatient bite, still overtly scanning me.

"We didn't get a chance to talk. I wanted to ask if there's anything you'd like me to do with Jeremy, or around here, or . . ."

"Make sure he's happy."

"Oh. Sure, I fully intend on doing that. Also, is there anything you want me to do while Jeremy is at school? My mornings are pretty free, so I thought . . . if you needed anything?"

"Like?"

"If there's anything I can do to you, um, for you?"

A hint of a smile plays on his lips, but he covers it with two tattooed fingers. "What is it that you think you can do to me? I mean, for me." A wicked glee adorns his stare.

"I just thought maybe help around here. If not, and if you don't mind, perhaps I could take on another job during the mornings?"

"Need more money?"

"Oh, no, it's not about that. What you are paying me is more than enough. Thank you by the way. I just thought I might make use of my spare time, help in the organization I volunteer at, Youth with

Purpose."

He eyes me. "Don't see any problem with that."

"Good, thank you. Also, are there any restrictions?" His brows furrow, and I elaborate. "Any place around the house that's off-limits."

His lip lifts an inch. "My bedroom." To the horror in my eyes, he adds with an easy smile, "Feel at home, at least for the next six months."

"Thank you." I rise up to stand, and his eyes roam over to my chest again. I inhale, willing to stay poised. Tyler Lee sends his hand to his guitar, his eyes still on me, thankfully back to level with mine. I glance at the guitar. "It was beautiful, the song you played before."

He nods.

"Well, all your music is beautiful."

His eyes meet mine again. "My music reached — where did you say you're from?"

"Estonia." I smile.

"My music reached all the way to Estonia?"

"Apparently, it did."

We trade an amused gaze.

"Which one do you like best?"

His question catches me off guard, but I don't have to think much about it. "It's one of your older ones, 'Unspoken Words.'" As soon as the name of one of his less popular songs leaves my mouth, Tyler Lee's expression softens.

His brows sink in. "Why?"

"Why?" I repeat somewhat perplexed.

"What makes it special?"

I think for a beat. "The lyrics, the melody, and mostly, your voice when you sing it. The emotions you convey through this song seem so real, to me." Our stares are tightly locked, and it feels like we're having a wordless conversation. One in which I'm not sure what's being said.

"*It is* a special one," he says, breaking our stare.

"Oh," leaves my lips, but he is not with me anymore, his fingers already strumming the guitar. I watch him in fascination for one last beat before catching myself and leaving the room.

CHAPTER
Six

"Boys suck. Boys suck. Boys suck. Boys suck. Boys suck. Boys suck. Boys suck. Boys suck. But Evert Arma is sort of cute. Boys suck!" An entry in sixteen-year-old Ivi's diary.

"Good morning, dear. Would you like me to fix you breakfast, tea?"

"Good morning. Thank you, Adina. No need, thank you. I'll get it myself."

All the people around this place! Having someone clean after me, wash my clothes, and prepare food for me is too much to get used to. It couldn't be more different from my life at home. I still can't seem to wrap my head around this lifestyle. I'm having a hard time getting used to it. My mom would probably smack me upside the head if she knew I allowed an older woman to cater to me.

Adina, holding a tray with a coffee pot and fresh pastries, leaves the bright kitchen toward heavy voices coming from the main living room, voices brimming masculinity.

I stir sugar in my self-made tea, thank you very much, and wait for my toast to jump when the loud voices grow louder. I turn around as Eli, Tyler Lee, and a darker, handsome guy storm into the kitchen, arguing.

"Tyler, one time, one night, it's not a big deal," Eli says in his authoritative timbre.

Tyler Lee burrows his head inside the wide fridge, throwing a resolute, "No," over his shoulder.

"Dude, it's just one night. We'll be back the next morning," says the dark guy with the mischievous green eyes and the long dreadlocks.

"Not going to happen," Tyler Lee drawls, holding a beer bottle in one hand while using the other to shut the fridge.

Green Eyes and Dreads shakes his head. Along the way, his stare lands on me. His lips tip up into a charming smile. "Oh, hi."

"Good morning," I say, subtly checking him out.

He holds his hand out. "I'm Jay." I send mine for a shake. Instead, my hand somehow ends up with Jay's lips attached to it. "I'm a member of the glorified entourage." He winks at me, releasing his hold on my hand. Wicked smile intact.

"Ivi, I'm the nanny." I return his cheerful glee.

His smile grows wider, much wider. "Oh, what a lovely coincidence. I have a very, very special place in my heart for nannies."

I smile at him, but my smile fades when I hear Eli's snort followed by a head shake and Tyler Lee's bothered expression.

"Out," Tyler Lee snaps, looking at Eli and Jay.

The men grin in unison, heading to the door. Jay sends me another smile, and Eli calls after him. "One night, Tyler. One damn night."

Tyler Lee, appearing spiked, says, "I'm not going to say it again. I'm not going to be away while Jeremy is here."

My heart swells at hearing Tyler Lee's reasoning. I send a gentle glance his way and am countered by furrowed brows above an irritated stare. For a span of a whole second, there's a warm fuzzy feeling in my stomach. But it dies quicker than I can say "royal jerk."

Tyler Lee takes a sip of his beer (at ten a.m.!), shoves his hand into his back pocket, and produces a black credit card. "Here," the card lands on the island next to me. "Get some bras."

"Pardon?" I choke on my own question.

"Cover them, for Christ's sake." He gestures with his free hand to the direction of my torso. "Your nipples are all over the damn place. There are enough dickheads around here; I don't need a lawsuit on my hands because someone popped your precious cherry while working here."

No, he did not just . . .

A flash of exasperation blooms inside me, unleashing my reservations and generally controlled behavior. "Thank you very much for your generosity, boss, but I have plenty of bras. And just so you know, I'm no Patron Saint of Virtue. So you can rest assured, there aren't any impending *cherry popping* lawsuits."

His eyes morph from alluring brown to pissed as he glares at me for a charged beat before turning around and exiting the room.

Wow, what an ass.

———◆———

It's only much later, after a checkers game with Jeremy—in which he totally kicks my ass—herbal tea, and a long, warm bath, that my exasperation subsides. However, said exasperation turns into a nagging, unsettling sensation. Have I crossed a line? Yes, I did. After all, Tyler Lee, a prick or not (which he obviously is), is the boss. I'd never dream of speaking the way I spoke to him at any other workplace, unconventional as it may be.

Dred crawls in at the realization that he might sack me after less than a week on the job. I *cannot* lose this job. I should get a grip, grit my teeth, bite my tongue, and just cope with whatever he dishes out going forward. I wonder if I should apologize before I get canned.

Seven

"When a boy pulls your hair, it means he likes you. But still, if he does so, stomp his toe. No one should ever hurt you!" Marrika, Ivi's mom, in an educational insight to her eleven-year-old daughter.

"Homework?"

"Duh." Jeremy gives me a cheeky grin.

I fold my arms across my chest, my legs slightly parted in a drill sergeant stance. "Duh as in yes or duh as in no?"

"Duh, as in I always do my homework first thing when I get home." A sassy eye roll under thick-rimmed glasses follows.

"So let's go outside. You can't be glued to the screen for the rest of the afternoon." I slip my feet into ballerina flats, tucking my tank top into my cutoffs.

Jeremy holds the wireless mouse as though holding onto dear life. "Hold up, I'm in the middle of a trade. I'm getting *the* cape!"

Of course, he is. Whatever that means. I wait patiently for a moment and not as patiently when more than a minute passes by.

"Jeremy . . ." When he lifts one finger at me, I grab it and swirl him in his chair to face me.

"Hey!" he protests.

"Don't hey me. Either you're coming with me, or I pull the plug." I narrow my eyes at the wall where the PC is plugged in.

"Don't!" He holds a hand up. "Jeez, I'm coming. You're so annoying."

"I'll take that as a compliment," I say with a grin, and he rewards me with a boyish smile. "So why don't you teach me how to play football?"

"Do I look like someone who plays football?" The kid has a point; he looks more like someone who can teach me all the secrets to Dungeons and Dragons rather than anything sport related.

"C'mon, I'm sure you can teach me."

"Whatever."

Jeremy and I are on the verge of hysterics, what with our lame attempts at throwing the ball, when Tyler Lee saunters toward us.

His lips jolt at the sides, watching us. "What you guys doing?"

Jeremy gets this expression on his face, the same one he gets every time his father is nearby. A blend of awe, twitchiness, and excitement. His head is slightly tilted sideways, his eyes open, and his eyebrows an inch higher, making me think of a sweet puppy begging for attention.

"Where did you learn to throw like that?" Tyler Lee asks his son.

"Um, PE?"

Tyler Lee shakes his head in fondness. His lips tip higher. He motions for Jeremy to go back and throws him the ball. The ball flies right between Jeremy's flailing hands, and they both trade amused stares.

"I'm getting drinks," I say and turn on my heel, letting them be. Something I've been doing for a while now. Whenever there's a spark of bond forming between them, I make sure to make myself scarce.

———— ◆ ————

"My favorite nanny." Jay's voice reaches me before his handsome face graces my peripheral view. Soda can in hand, I turn to him.

"My favorite glorified entourage member." He grins with a wholehearted, fabulous smile. "So how's La La Land been treating you so far?"

"Pretty fine, getting used to, well, all of this." I gesture with my hand to the space around us. "La La Land, as you put it."

"Jeremy seems to really like you. It's cool, what you're doing for them."

I lift an eyebrow, gazing at him from above my drink.

"Helping them get tight."

I nod.

"Hope the father person won't scare you off, though. I love him like a brother, but Ty is not exactly Little Miss Sunshine all the time."

I laugh, somewhat stunned by the openness. "Well, I'm not easy to scare off."

"You're not, huh?" Jay's green eyes lit up. "So you won't be scared off if I asked you out?"

I blink at him and blink again. Jay wants to ask me out? Caramel gorgeous skin, long dreads, and a smile to die for? Hell to the yes. "Are you kidding me? On the contrary." I send him a flirty glance and watch as his grin widens.

"How about tonight, when the little human hits the sack?"

"I guess it should be okay. I'll just check in with Tyler Lee and make sure he doesn't need me."

Jay's eyes roam over me. "I can do that."

"No, that's fine." I tip my chin to the sweating sodas on the counter. "I'm going to get these to the players, okay?"

Jay nods with a wink.

A smile hovers on my lips with the thought of tonight as I get back to Tyler Lee and Jeremy, who seem to have moved to tackles. I lightly giggle at Jeremy's attempt to tackle Tyler Lee. It reminds me of

David and Goliath, albeit sans the powerful stone. Jeremy's cheeks are pinkish, his forehead glistens between clusters of dark hair, and the rise and fall of his chest is evident. And Tyler Lee? Not even the least bit affected.

At my light giggle, they both turn my way.

"Ivi, help me out here." Jeremy feigns a begging expression.

"Hey Ivi, catch." Tyler Lee throws the ball my way. Instinctively, my hands fly up, and I catch the shooting football. Not long after, I squeal when Jeremy, with utter determination, runs my way. I start running backward while wiggling my eyebrows, tangling the ball in my hands with the widest grin. I dodge Jeremy's attack and run toward where we've set our imaginary touchline. I sprint en route to the guesthouses at the back of the patio, and before I know it, I find myself on the grass with a heavy mass of deliciously masculine smelling Tyler Lee on me. When I turn my head, a tense silence swallows my flit squeal. For a long moment, everything around me stills. The sudden unexpected weight and warmth of him are so inexplicably wonderful, eliciting a yearning for him I never knew existed. It's literally physically impossible for me to attempt to wiggle out from under him.

As I turn my head to look up, my lips accidentally brush against his slightly moist ones. The brush of our lips feels like a short circuit. Like ten thousand little electric currents running under my skin. One that's so short lived yet resonates. For the next sluggishly passing seconds, I sink into his eyes with an irresistible, forceful adhesion. Nothing but the distinctive beat of our hearts beating against each other, our breaths mixing, and the currents looping between our eyes exists. I can't unglue my gaze from the tiny golden flakes hidden in his brown irises. Breathing is the greatest challenge.

"Wow, great tackle." Jeremy's voice bursts the alternate universe I've just been teleported into. A universe where I lock eyes with Tyler Lee Adams and our lips brush. A universe where my mind is swimming in a pool of confusion, and my heart rate is beyond racing.

A frown settles between Tyler Lee's brows, and not a second later, he rises to stand above me.

"Yeah, it's all about tackling," he murmurs as he extends his hand to help me up. Once steady on my two feet, I gape at him, heady. "I'm going to get back to the guys." Tyler's thumb aims at the house, his expression no less confused than mine is. Jeremy nods, and I order myself to get back to the present.

Jeremy tells me something I fail to hear given my full attention is on his dad's departing back. My chest tightens when Tyler Lee sends me a glance over his shoulder. One I can't begin to decode.

———— • ————

Although I stand before the bathroom mirror, applying makeup for my evening with Jay, he is *not* the one dominating my thoughts.

"Tore, just tore." *Great, just great,* I murmur in Estonglish and throw the liner to the vanity in frustration. I need to kill these thoughts here and now. I had given the lip brush with the boss way too much thought throughout the day. I'm attracted to Tyler Lee Adams. Big deal. Who on the planet isn't?

However, it's something I should get under control and the sooner, the better. It's not a good thing, any way I look at it. I take a deep breath and turn to apply my mascara. Well, anyhow, soon enough he'll remind me just how "sweet" he can be. Which I'm pretty sure will eradicate any bud of anything involving my hormones and him. God, his body felt so good on mine. And his warm man smell!

I give myself another look in the mirror, fixing my lipstick with my pinky. A loose polka dot halter-top tucked in on one side of my jeans and red kitten heels complements the casual theme. Classic cat-eye and red lip combo for the evening look. Not too trying; however, it definitely has the right effect. Taking the stairs to the first floor, I realize

I haven't told my boss that I'm going out. Having him occupy my mind in the most wrong way for the better part of the day, I decide to look for Eli instead.

"Who's *that*?" I hear a bass voice ask as I take the last step and lift my eyes in search of the orator.

Tyler Lee and Jay's voices mix as they answer in unison.

"Miss Kert," Tyler Lee says flatly.

"The *nanny*," Jay declares in utter enthusiasm.

What can only be described as a *Rolling Stones* magazine centerfold packs the living room. Crammed around one of the sitting areas in the grandiose living room are badass rock-ish men in all shapes, colors, and sizes. The only person appearing completely out of place but somehow the one setting the tone is Eli.

"*I* want a nanny like this one," mutters a lanky guy with longs strands of ginger hair and a nose ring.

"I've been a bad boy," says the guy next to him with the tribal neck tattoo.

Jay chuckles and jovially tells them to can it. I send him a thankful smile, but the weight of Tyler Lee's eyes on me pulls my attention. His jaw is locked, and his eyes are trained on mine. I can't decide what they hold. They are narrowed and profound and unreadable. I break away from the intensity.

"Eli, can I talk to you in private?" I ask.

All eyes in the room are on me. I chance a glance Tyler's way and am left in greater unease.

"Sure." Eli stands up and motions for me to follow him.

"What is it, Ivi?" He turns to face me once we're far enough for our conversation to remain private.

"We haven't set any rules for my evenings. I just wanted to make sure it's okay if I went out after Jeremy goes to sleep."

"Yeah. You can do whatever you want in your free time. Just make sure whatever you choose to do won't affect your work."

For a short beat, I remain frozen. The insinuation that I'd be doing something un-kosher pokes at me.

"I'd never do anything that will conflict with my job."

"I'm glad to hear that," he says solemnly.

When we return to the men, Eli and Tyler Lee exchange a look that seems more like a brief conversation.

Eight

CHAPTER

"Alcohol! Because no great story ever begins with a salad." An inspirational
sign on the wall behind the bar.

"Cool place," I say, admiring the cozy bar Jay chose for our date.
It's small, not more than six tables. A rug of peanuts shells covers
the floor, and black and white framed photos of different bridges
and some funny, inspirational prints decorate the walls.

"What can I get you?" Jay asks, looking exceptionally good in jeans,
a gray tee, and a leather jacket.

"Appletini." I give him another appreciative glance before resuming
my visual tour of the place.

"One appletini." Jay sets my drink on the table. "Not even sure if it
constitutes an adult drink." He takes a drink of his scotch with a smile.

"Alcohol and I have a history. We don't get along too well. It has a
tendency to turn me into an idiot. And I'm not a cute idiot, so you see
. . ."

Jay's eyes crinkle at the sides. "Filed, saved, and will be used in
relevant occasions." He turns the chair parallel to mine around and
straddles it with his chest pressed to the back. "Anything serious?"

"Almost, though I didn't let it go too far. Lesson learned. I try to limit it to a glass at a time, preferably nothing too lethal."

"Appreciate the honesty." Jay takes another quick drink that ends with a twist of his mouth. "So, beautiful Ivi, tell me your story."

I smile at him. "Why don't you tell me yours first? I bet it's much more interesting than mine is. Small town girl vs. music kingdom figure, it's a no-brainer."

Jay chuckles, brushing a sheaf of dreads over his shoulder. "Sorry to disappoint; the only connection between me and the music kingdom is Ty or the furniture I make for him and his sorts." He chuckles again. "I'm a simple laborer, a carpenter. No stardust here, beautiful."

"Oh, I thought you mentioned you were a part of the, how did you call it? The entourage. And believe me, there's no disappointment whatsoever. Nothing better than a man who's good with his hands."

The wicked smile that spreads across Jay's handsome face triggers mine to heat up. "So you like your men good with their hands?"

I roll my eyes and take a sip of my drink. "A man who creates things with his hands, beautiful things." The sinful smile grows and grows. "Oh, come on; stop taking it to shady places. You know what I mean. And stop with that smile. It's distracting!" Said smile turns into a charming chuckle. "So how did you guys meet, you and Tyler Lee?"

Jay sets his tumbler on the table and rests his veined arms on the chair. "A few years ago. To make a long and boring story short, he came into my store looking for a chair and stayed for a drink."

I take a bite of the decorative slice of apple. "Sounds like the perfect beginning of a beautiful love story."

Jay's lips stretch. He leans his chin on his crossed arms. "Let's just say neither of us was in a good place in our lives. He bought one of my armchairs and stayed for a drink that led to him joining me the next month to hike the PCT."

"You guys seem so different, Tyler and you."

"That's not completely true. It depends on which side of Ty you get to know. The first week of hiking stripped him of the rock star. Nothing but a hundred percent Ty, and that's when he became my people. He's a good person and a great friend; the kind who'll always be there for you, no matter what."

I can't help but think about the Tyler Lee that I know so far. It doesn't sound remotely similar to the person Jay is describing. "Which armchair is it? The one he bought from you?" I say, needing a change of topic to get me back to our date and away from Tyler Lee land.

"The one in his office. The brown leather one."

My eyes lift up to Jay's. "You made that one? It's so beautiful. It's the kind of chair you want to curl up in and never leave."

He nods a humble thank you. "Your turn now," Jay says, his lips tipping up. "I showed you mine . . ."

We exchange a flirty stare. I clear my throat as though I'm about to deliver a lecture. I tell Jay a little about my family and home. My smile and my excitement grow as I continue discussing my volunteer work. "The name of the organization is Youth with Purpose Organization. I've been actively volunteering there for the past six years. We work together to help minorities across the globe. We deal with human trafficking, disaster-stricken areas, poverty, and orphanages. Wherever our help is needed."

"Lo and behold, humans, we've got a twenty-first-century saint over here," Jay says to no one in particular, gesturing his hand my way.

I twist my lips and nudge his arm. He grabs my hand and squeezes lightly. I look at him from under my lashes. His smile softens. He keeps my hand in his.

"I think it's incredible, what you do." His voice is tender.

———◆———

"When do I get to see you again?" Jay says, killing the engine of his pickup truck in front of Tyler Lee's mansion.

"Soon?" My smile echoes his.

Jay sends his hand to open the door. "Hopefully," he murmurs, standing up. I wait in my seat, watching him as he circles the car to open the door for me. "How about Thursday?" he asks, taking a step closer and reaching for my hand.

"I'll just have to check with . . ." I tip my chin toward the house, surprised to find someone peering out one of the windows of the third floor.

"'Kay then, let me know." Jay hugs me.

I return his easy hug. He kisses my cheek and draws back.

"Nighty night." I wave my hand.

He nods with a side smile, and I turn to the pathway to the house.

CHAPTER Nine
CHAPTER

"Mommy, do fairy tales happen in real life?"
"No, honey. Now, finish your dinner."
Ten-year-old Ivi's first (of many) reality checks.

"So let's see, do we have everything?" I ask Jeremy, rereading the list of items for the "science experiment" we're about to conduct.

"Like I said, I'm the mad scientist. You're just the adult in charge," Jeremy says, pouring baking soda into a clear container.

"Don't put too much, it'll . . ." I don't get to finish the sentence with the rise of Jeremy's finger my way. I nod in submission and take a step back.

When a string of creative swear words reaches our ears, Jeremy pauses and grins at me.

"Not okay," I murmur, wincing when a few more c, f ,b and many more bombs continue to assault our ears. I shake my head. "Hold on, okay? I'll be back in a minute."

Jeremy runs a hand through his messy hair and grins wider. "It was never proven that bad language can harm children. I don't think any studies show that a word in itself can cause harm. So you don't need to worry. I'm safe."

"I told you to start reading books appropriate for your age. How about *Harry Potter*?" I say already heading toward the verbal filth-producing gang. Halfway through my stride, I turn back to get a mason jar.

"Oh, hi, gentlemen, may I have your attention for a few minutes?" I say to the group of men dotting the living room. All eyes rise to me. It's not the usual kit and caboodle, but I recognize most of the faces.

"You can have anything of mine you want," says someone, strumming on a guitar. "Hell, I'm already at attention."

"Cute," I say in a dry tone with a matching overly sugared smile. Tyler Lee's eyes twitch at the corners. "So I couldn't help but notice that you lovely lot are quite the aficionados of the word fuck and its deviations. Now, I'm not sure if you've noticed, but we have a ten-year-old living in this house. Who also happens to be within earshot. And though I'm sure he's quite fascinated with the word, it's not exactly appropriate for his age, agree?"

They all look at me amused. But at least I have their attention. Or maybe it's my free-range bosom that has it. Whatever it is, they seem focused.

"So in order to give you the extra push you need and remind you that said word or any of its associates shouldn't be used around a child, here's your motivation jar." I put forward the empty mason jar.

"I'd be more than glad to fill your jar, sweet thing," says the guy who told me he was a bad boy a week ago.

I bite on my smile, seeing Tyler's heavy work boot meet his shin. I inwardly snort at the "ouch" that follows.

"Hey, Mary P?" Max, the bassist, calls as I'm about to leave the room.

"It's Ivi, Flea." I turn to him.

His grin tips higher. "So, Ivi, you coming to the shindig tonight?"

"Um, I wasn't invited." I smile at him.

He gives Tyler Lee a questioning look. Tyler Lee shrugs. "Some people are coming over later. Come hang out with us," says Max.

"Fuck, yeah," says a guy with dark sunglass. I turn to him and extend my hand, holding the jar. He laughs and puts a buck inside. "So you coming tonight?" he asks next.

"I'll see." I give a little curtsy. "Thank you for your cooperation, gentleman."

I manage to catch a glimpse of Tyler Lee's lips jolting before turning to go.

"Ivi." Tyler Lee's voice stops me this time. I try to make sense of the little pang in my heart caused by him saying my name as I turn his way.

I gaze at him in question as he grabs his phone from the table and holds it up. "Here, add your number."

The confusion only deepens. I do as said with puckered brows.

On the way back to the kitchen, I entertain a ridiculously heady feeling of a cute boy asking a girl for her number. I shake my thoughts away before they take the liberty of writing my boss's name inside a red heart. It's only natural for an employer to have his employee's number. Reality check, Ivi.

"Oh, Houston, we kinda, ah, have a problem," Jeremy says with a mischievous grin.

I feign a frown at the homemade volcano dripping white frothy substance all over the long kitchen counter. "I told you to take it easy on the baking soda. You're cleaning this mess." I fetch a roll of paper towel and hand it to the boy. "Here you go, Mad Scientist. Clean it up."

"I shouldn't be touching vinegar; it's a very acidic substance, and I might be allergic to it. I can get a stuffy nose and clogged head, or in severe cases of . . ."

"Use gloves."

Jeremy huffs and turns to fight the foamy waterfall dripping all over the place. And that's when my phone pings with an incoming message.

Oh, come-freaking-on, Ivi, it's just a text. That tingly sensation in my stomach is ludicrous.

Unknown: Wear a damn bra.

The tingly feeling hides under a rock embarrassed.

Ivi: I don't remember this mentioned in the employment contract.

A response never arrives.

———— ♦ ————

I'm showered, snuggled in bed, and glued to the screen when a knock on my door has me sending it a stink eye. Who has the audacity to interrupt my quality time with Jax Teller? I pause the video and call out, "Yeah?"

Jay's smile greets me as the door cracks open. "Hey, beautiful, can I come in?"

"Sure." I get out of bed.

He takes his time running his eyes over my knitted knee-length white socks over black yoga pants and spaghetti strap, tank top-clad body appreciatively before reaching my eyes. "What are you up to?"

"Just chilling." I give him a scan in the same fashion as he did me. Jay, in general, is a sight to behold. Jay in a black tee and ripped jeans is a meal fit for kings. His mocha skin, those long, wild dreads, and green eyes—dang . . .

"In that case, you're my date to the unofficial hangout going on downstairs."

My eyes drop to my pajama-ish attire. "I need to change into something more . . ."

"You kidding me? You look *hawt*." A warm fuzzy feeling powders my stomach, only to intensify when Jay takes a couple of steps forward, releases my hair from the knot on my head, and watches the heavy fall of my golden-brown locks make their way down to my waist. "Beautiful," he murmurs. His eyes drop to my lips. The air I'm breathing thickens. "Let's go," he says in a low voice, taking my hand in his.

"Shoes. I need shoes," I say, still soaring back from the moment we just had.

———————◆———————

With a bottle of beer in hand, I enjoy light conversation with Jay and Zen, another friend of Jay's who's not a member of the music realm. A couple of dozen people are scattered around the living room, engaged in conversation with light music in the background. The men-to-women ratio is three to one, and a few ladies look like they were designed by a horny male artist with a Playboy Bunny in mind. The fact that the majority of the bunnies delegation is giving Tyler Lee the eye can't be missed. I feel a little uncomfortable with the disapproving frown that forms when I notice the beautiful blond twins practically throwing themselves at Tyler Lee. When his eyes catch mine boring into him, my frown morphs into an uncomfortable flush. I bounce my eyes back to Jay, not looking back.

Elated greetings, followed by a ruckus of high-fives, semi-hugs, and "dude"/"man" draw my attention to the main door. I do a double take when I realize who just stepped in. I guess I should get used to this; a famous person visiting this house is obviously the norm. But holy schnitzel, the Dante! No last name, he doesn't need one. Another music industry immortal. An all-American, blue-eyed, blond hair Manhattan royalty heir who turned to the music dark side. At twenty, with a badass prison tattoo on his neck, alcohol, women, and enough other scandals, he was crowned the next rocker bad boy. When his eyes target me, and he gives me his trademark sinister smile, I'm both jarred and a little swooned, what with the flock of bunnies pecking around looking to conjugate with his kind. This is not a self-conscious bitter thought. I know I'm pretty. My dad's thick, tawny hair and mom's delicate features and huge blue eyes spawned an easy on the eyes production. However, put me in a lineup with the rest of the women in the room and, um, well . . .

"Get you another one?" Jay asks, tipping his chin at my beer.

"One drink limit, remember? And I still have some, thanks."

He smiles. "Be right back."

"Hey, don't be shy. Mingle. Some of them are idiots, but they're mostly cool people." Tyler Lee's voice alone brings back that strange feeling that hovers over me since our accidental tackle.

I look up at him for a short moment, sucked into the irresistible allure that is him. My lips pull up a little. "Oh." I smile. "Don't confuse me as shy. I'm just holding it all in, all my awesomeness." His lip twitches at the side. "Don't want to outshine you. You know what they say about rock stars and their egos." I pat his chest and start toward the bar for some water. When I turn my head to give him a flit glance, all I see is a gigantic, heart-melting smile.

With a bottle of water in hand, I stand by myself. Feeling a little out of place, I observe the unfamiliar, to put it mildly, and intriguing scene. It's like watching *TMZ live*. One of the bunnies whines about the indie music playing in the background, making sure that everyone is aware of her displeasure. She pouts and strides to the stereo, her curves swaying from side to side. When she pushes on random buttons, trying to figure out what to do, my eyes meet the lighting fixture of their volition. I close them next and inhale.

My eyes flick open to the lips lightly grazing my ear and the message they whisper. It takes me another moment to make sense of what was whispered. Did I hear right? Did someone just suggested we "go upstairs and fuck?!" My heart is beating a little faster as I turn to face the hustler.

Shock. I'm still.

And then I'm not anymore.

"You are incredible, you know?" I say to the cocky smile on Dante's perfect face. He leans against the wall, his eyes unabashedly stripping off my clothes. His perusal comes up to gaze intently on my lips. "What did you think? That looking at my lips for more than two seconds and whispering some oh-so-sexy words next to my ear will make me voluntary take off my panties?" I grab his drink and down it. "So, okay, you're Dante, and you might have one hell of a product in your pants. Stuff made for legends, I bet." The last sentence comes out in blunt scorn. "So help me out here, why don't you? What now? Am I, like"—I bat my eyelashes exaggeratedly—"supposed to stop my life, quiver inside, bite my lip, and *let you inside*?"

His grin grows so big and sleazy it prompts an urge to wipe it off with a punch. *The nerve!*

"Excuse me." Attempting to get away, I stop short and swallow hard. Apparently, the bunny-idiot who tried to change the music killed it all together, and the entire room just had a front row seat to my little conversation with *the* Dante. A couple of snorts and masculine laughter, an "ouch," and a "burned!" pop my uncomfortable lapse. Straightening my posture, I fabricate coolness and make my way to Jay, trying to avoid Tyler Lee's amused eyes on me. *Trying* being the key word.

CHAPTER
Ten

CHAPTER

"They say it's more than your music. They call it the Tyler Lee Adams magic. That all you need to do is smile a little to turn a girl's world upside down. Is that true?"

Through a light chuckle, "Next question, please."

Tyler Lee Adams, Cosmopolitan *interview.*

I climb up to my room on the second floor. Jay tried to persuade me to stay but relented when I told him I needed to wake up early to see Jeremy to school and promised we'll see each other again soon.

I stop with my hand on the knob to, "Hey, Ivi, wait up." Trying to disregard The Feeling in my belly, I turn around. Watching Tyler Lee close the distance between us in a V-neck Henley, layered with a white tee, worn jeans, and combat boots, I take a step back till I come in contact with the doorframe.

"Everything okay?" he asks a step away, tucking a loose strand behind his ear.

My brows slightly furrow. "Um, yeah. I'm just going to sleep. It's late, and I wake up early with Jeremy."

He nods, doing his unnerving, intense gaze thing. He lightly scratches his trimmed beard. "Dante upset you?"

"Oh, that." Why does my voice sound so breathy? "He has very unique pick-up lines." At unease with the whole having Tyler Lee near, I mumble, "Not that I think he tried to hit on me. That would be incredibly presumptuous of me. It's just, his way with words is . . ."

"Why wouldn't he try to hit on you?"

I gape at him, not sure what to answer. Instead, I say, "I think I handled it myself just fine. It's okay, really."

A low chuckle rolls out of his lips, firing up whatever is happening in my stomach. "Oh, that I saw."

I lightly smile, finally having the strength to look him directly in the eyes. For a few beats, we stand in silence with our eyes locked.

"You got a . . ." His voice comes out mildly raspy. And as if in slow motion, his hand lifts up to my face. The pad of his finger touches my cheekbone. I can hardly breathe. His finger on my skin, his body about to fill my personal space.

He brings his finger close to my lips. "Make a wish."

I blow on the eyelash resting on his long finger, my heart thrumming in my ears.

"What did you wish for?"

Through the frenzied, unanticipated sensations taking over me, I manage to utter, "That would be telling." To be honest, even if he insisted on knowing, I wouldn't know the answer for my brain is a mash of heartbeats, lips, gazes, and proximity. Incredibly unnerving, wonderful proximity.

When his lips tip at the side, a light smile stretches mine. A little wrinkle forms between his brows when his eyes fall to my smiling lips.

He slightly leans in. His finger comes back to my face, only this time to gently brush my upper lip. My smile, together with my breath, disappears. With his finger still hovering over my lip, he says in a low voice, "Your lip, it curves so deeply when you smile."

Involuntarily, my lips gap. It feels like butterflies are dancing pogo in my stomach.

His frown deepens, and his finger keeps caressing my lips when his face slowly dips closer. It feels like my heart is trying to fight its way out of my chest.

Tyler Lee Adams is about to kiss me.

I feel like crying but in a good way. A heartbeat and his lips near mine. Our breaths mix. His scent baths me. The warm air traveling from his mouth to mine brings in a heady lungful of seduction, man, and alcohol. His nearness — what's happening — is too much.

I expel a shaky breath, sobering us both up. As though shaking out of a trance, we both jerk back. For a confusing stretch, we stare at each other. And then he leaves. No words. No backward glance. He walks away.

My hand is still shaky when I dab a cotton with toner on my face. As I blink, all I can see is Tyler Lee's face so close to mine. His pouty lips slightly parted amid his beard, a few loose tendrils that escaped his knot brushing against his strong cheekbones. I squeeze my eyes tight, reasoning that what almost happened could be explained by the noticeable level of alcohol on his breath.

Think about Jay. Think about Jay. But the only thing that comes to mind is how he didn't make me feel the tension and the headiness I felt with Tyler Lee.

CHAPTER
Eleven

"I think I deserve something beautiful." A highlighted sentence found in an
Elizabeth Gilbert novel resting on Ivi's nightstand.

"You look great," Jay says, opening his studio door wider for me.
"Come in."

"Wow, I'm in love," I say, spinning in my spot as I take in
his workspace. "This place is incredible." I run my hand over a long,
sturdy table with more than a few work tools scattered on top. A chisel,
a hammer, sandpaper squares, and other carpentry doodads. The floor
is a carpet of sawdust and woodchips; a couple of unfinished chairs
stand next to the work area. There's a bit of an industrial feel due
to the unique suspended metal ceiling in the otherwise warm rustic
atmosphere.

"This is what you're working on?" I run my fingers over the
unclaimed wood chairs.

Jay's eyes echo my excitement. "Yeah, it's a part of a farmhouse
style dining set piece I'm creating. I'm going to finish it with a distressed
veneer that'll give it a lightly aged character."

"You're so talented."

He shrugs, his eyes descending to the floor in a humble, sweet way. He takes my hand. "Let's go into the store. I promised you dinner, didn't I?"

I follow him into the adjoining showroom. It feels like stepping into a cozy country house. A vast room encompassing a wide variety of rustic designs, distressed woods, a mix of patterns, and soft color palettes. Next to an electronic fireplace, on an oriental rug, our dinner is waiting.

"I'm impressed." I settle down crossed-legged next to the little dishes of tapas. "And a little swooned." We smile at each other, and Jay shrugs again in that modest way of his then sits next to me. He pours us a glass of wine.

"I'm sorry this didn't happen before today, us hanging out, but work got in the way and . . ."

I shake my head, touching his hand. "You were busy. I get it, really. And in general, don't ever apologize for something you don't need to apologize for to begin with."

He nods. "What you been up to besides minding that lucky, lucky kid?"

I smile, telling him about meeting up with local YWPO volunteers. "I'm going to start helping with some projects, you know, admin stuff, in my spare time when the lucky kid is away."

"So I hope you haven't been seeing Dante behind my back," Jay teases me.

I roll my eyes. "I bet he was totally wasted that night."

Jay shakes his head. "Innocent looking fresh meat is his kryptonite." I poke him with a fork. He rubs his forearm, laughing. "He has a tendency to go after the unattainable . . . the forbidden."

"He's a bit of a smug . . ." I search my mind for subtle wordings to endorse Dante's assholery.

"A smug prick?" Jay offers casually.

"Sort of, yeah. But if he is a douche, why do you hang with him?"

Jay reaches for an olive. "You could say it's Ty's way of burying the hatchet."

"Oh," I say, surprised by both the revelation and my reaction to Tyler Lee's name. It's as if the mention of his name alone has a direct effect on my stomach, peppering it with something warm.

"Yeah, there's some bad blood between them. Dante sort of hurt Brooklyn, and Ty wouldn't have it. It was messy, but since they have a few projects together, Ty decided to be the better man."

"Who's Brooklyn?"

"Brooklyn Mars. Her and Ty, they are . . . tight," Jay clarifies, and #Brookty jumps to my mind.

Disturbingly, something in the vein of poking jealousy nestles in me. Brooklyn Mars, singer/actress/fashion icon, Tyler Lee's on and off—never officially confirmed by either side—girlfriend.

I'm busy scheming how to get him to elaborate when Jay says, "Enough about that. Tell me something no one knows."

My smile grows. Something about Jay makes me feel like we've known each other forever. "No one knows how I'm enjoying myself with you."

He smiles softly. A smile that slowly flattens into a serious line. Jay's eyebrows lightly furrow, as his stare on me grows profound. And then he leans closer. And closer. Stare searching mine. Closer. The space around us grows tense. Closer. His lips meet mine.

I close my eyes, absorbed in his touch. Warm and soft. His scent masculine and outdoorsy, like pine and earth. His hand moves to my neck, mine trails to his ribcage. Slow kissing deepens and our lips part together. When our tongues unite, my features furrow. On cue, we both ease off.

Our awkward smiles freeze foolishly.

"That was, ah, nice," I say, sounding even less convincing than the famous "I did not have a sexual relationship with that woman" infidelity anthem.

A low chuckle comes out of Jay's awkward smile. "Wow, it felt, it felt . . ." His lips tip higher, his frown deepening.

"Wrong?" I blush a little.

To Jay's agreeing head bob, we both crack into a free laughter.

"It felt like kissing my," Jay says, and we complete his sentence in unison.

"Sister." Him grinning.

"Brother." Me snickering. "Incest-ish."

Jay sends his hand to hug my shoulders. "Young Ivi, I think this is the beginning of a beautiful friendship."

"Old Jay, I think I just found me a bestie."

Another fit of laughter, small talk, and dessert later, we are lying on our backs, our legs up on the sofa, groaning over eating too much. After Jay tells me a little more about his business and a few snooty clients, I turn my head to study his handsome profile.

"So what's your real story, Jay?"

He cranes his neck to look at me. For a beat, he is quiet. "My fiancée passed away a week before our wedding, and a year later, I'm still having a hard time to let her go. Woodworking helps-" He trails off.

A rock free falls on my chest. "I'm so sorry."

Jay brows lift, and he exhales. "What's yours?"

"At sixteen, I somehow managed to make a total mess of my life. My low point was taking a pregnancy test on Christmas Eve while my family was caroling down the hall. But it was a turning point. I got my shit together and channeled all my uncertainties and rebellion to do good. Not long after, I met Chris. An American that, at the time, volunteered in Northern Europe, helping youth get back on track. He sort of became my mentor. He's the one who introduced me to YWPO, the organization I volunteer at, and the rest is history."

————◆————

Lying in bed, I run the evening in my head. How easy it is to be around Jay. How quickly I grew to like him. I giggle thinking about our kiss, which immediately made it to my kisses list. A list I came up with right after my very first kiss. It's a kiss by category list. Tomas is the first kiss. Allan is "I wanted to punch you in the face right after" kiss. Paul is a sweet kiss. There are many more. Jay just entered at number fifteen with an awkward kiss. I'd never admit to this because even to me it feels surreal to be putting it on paper, but Tyler Lee Adams might be at number fourteen with "an almost kiss." *Tyler Lee*. I have no business thinking what I'm thinking. I'm his employee. I'm Jeremy's nanny. I just need to stop. Stop it. Stop secretly dreaming of how it'll feel to have Jeremy's dad's body mesh with mine.

CHAPTER
Twelve

"Strip socioeconomic status, religion, gender, age, and ethnic background off, and you're left with a simple human." A pep talk by Ivi's mentor before Ivi's first mission trip.

I adjust the earbuds better, searching my playlist for something more upbeat. Breathing in and out a couple of times, I send my finger to tilt the treadmill to a Mt. Everest-like degree incline and brace myself to die soon. Peanut butter filled pretzels, also known as my new obsession, be damned.

With Jeremy over at a friend's, I decided to steal some alone time. As it happens, my days end up filled to the brim. Between Jeremy, hanging with Jay, helping at the local YWPO branch, and planning our forthcoming mission trip to Nepal, I'm left with very limited me time.

Excruciatingly long minutes later, I grab the water bottle and take a long swig. My tank top and shorts cling to my damp skin, my pulse loud and rapid. I push myself harder. Losing my interest in the reality playing on the built-in TV, trying to avoid the treadmill's clock and the remaining time, I give the indoor gym and its state of the art equipment a thorough scan. When I turn my stare to my left where a glass wall separates the gym from a no smaller dance studio, my neck remains stuck in its angle.

It's one thing to watch a Tyler Lee Adams' video clip online, but it's a completely different experience to watch him move live. On the other side of the glass, in a pair of loose, black track pants, a fitted gray, long-sleeved training shirt that wraps around his fit torso, showcasing his ripped muscles, is Tyler Lee. Man bun gone wild, trimmed beard, and light sweat glistening his features, he moves as if he is in the midst of seducing the entire female population. His instructor, a fit brunette in pink leotards and shorts, tells him something, and they restart the steps together.

Turning back from a sensual spin, his eyes dock on me. Moving like he's about to get the air around him pregnant, his eyes bore deeper into mine. As a response to my overt gaping, a flirty grin touches his lips and shorts out my brain-to-feet communication. With a surprised yelp, I find myself flying back, hands flailing in the air only to gracelessly land on my bum. Hard.

For shame. I want to die.

As I attempt to rise to my feet, a firm arm encircles my waist and pulls me up. Catching his breath, Tyler Lee asks with utter embarrassing concern, "You okay, Ivi?"

"Sure, it's only a part of the routine. I call it the 'fall on your butt' drill." A beautiful sound enriches the room. Tyler Lee's genuine chuckle. "I can teach you if you want, but I'm not sure you'll be able to handle it. It requires an abundance of talent, you see," I say and start toward the door. His easy chuckle resonates in my head long after I leave the room.

———◆———

"You ready, young Padawan?" I ask Jeremy, who's sitting on the sofa beside me in gray and black striped pajamas holding a large bowl of popcorn on his thighs.

He shakes his head with a scornful twist of his lips, causing his damp hair to fall lower on his eyebrow.

I frown at him. "What you're about to watch is a sacred cinematic piece. You cannot mock it nor take it lightly." Then, "I can't believe you haven't watched it till now."

"You're so lame, Ivi." His cheeky smile makes an appearance as he throws a kernel at me.

"Sit back and enjoy the perfection, young Padawan," I say, bringing the kernel to my smiling lips.

Jeremy sinks his hand in the bowl for a fistful of popcorn, his eyes trained on the bazillion inch TV. With his hand next to his mouth, Jeremy turns to me. "Did you know that movies can affect kids' health and mind? Studies say that over fifty percent of kids had trouble sleeping or eating after watching films with scary or violent elements. It can cause feelings of hostility."

"Jer, survive it, you will. Come out stronger, you will. Now, the movie, shush and watch!"

He grins at me, shoves a mouthful of kernels into his mouth, and turns back to the movie. I reach for my needles and yarn. Sliding back on the sofa, resting my purple knitted, sock-covered legs on the table, I slip the first stitch then knit to the middle of the row. I tug on the yarn and resume knitting, splitting my attention between the movie and the pink sock in the making.

By the time Luke Skywalker makes his way to the top of a rock ridge and scans the canyon with his binoculars, little snores intertwine with the dramatic background music. I glance over at Jeremy, who couldn't look more adorable with his glasses slightly crooked, eyes shut, and his hands still holding the bowl. Carefully, I remove the bowl from his hand and cover him with a throw. I gently pull off his glasses and set them on the table. When I brush the hair off his forehead, I sense someone behind me. My hand darts to my chest as I spin around.

A few steps away, Tyler Lee stands with his hands in his jean pockets, watching me with an unfathomable expression.

I shrug with a little smile. "I guess *Star Wars* didn't leave such a great impression on him." Tyler Lee's lips twitch. "I tried . . . and crashed and burned," I add, mirroring his amused air.

To my surprise, he walks over and takes a seat next to Jeremy's free side. Casually, he takes possession of the half-empty bowl and extends his legs on the coffee table, settling in.

I furrow my brows, considering what to do. Do I just lie back and chill with the boss? With my boss who happens to be one of the world's most famous rock stars? My boss, who makes my body hum in a strange, disconcerting, and overwhelming way? For a span of a very awkward moment, I sit straight, not sure what to do next. Until a pep talk Chris gave me funnels through my thoughts. It came long ago, before my first mission trip, when I was nervous about how I'd be able to communicate with people I had no common background or language with. "Strip everything away," Chris said with his trademark fatherly expression. "Strip socioeconomic status, religion, gender, age, and ethnic background off, and you're left with a human. We are all, after all, the same. Flesh and blood. Flesh and blood and oh-so-much drama, kid. We're all equal; we all wake up each morning and deal with whatever life has in store for us. Some of us have it easier, some don't. But yeah, we're all the same, so that's where you should be coming from." Those words lead me to decide that Tyler Lee Adams is, after all, a human being. Superior talent and hotness aside, Tyler Lee Adams is just another human who rests his legs on the coffee table and eats popcorn while watching *Star Wars*.

Just when my heart settles down a little and my fingers pick up a knitting rhythm, he turns to me. "So what is it that you do at YWPO?"

My features set into baffled query. Where is this coming from? How did he even remember the actual name of the organization or the fact that I told him about it? "How did you . . .? You remembered the name of the place where I volunteer?"

It's his turn to look mildly confused. "You told me the name." A little spark lights his eyes when he says, "I even read a little about them," making my jaw slightly drop.

"How? You . . .?" I'm having a hard time wrapping my head around, firstly, him even remembering something I've mentioned as a side note, but then actually taking an interest in it and reading about it? Where? Where's the candid camera?

Tyler's lips twitch; he sends his hand over the sleeping Jeremy to rest on mine. Slanting his head my way as though revealing a secret, he whispers, "People from all walks of life have access to Google."

He's just a fellow human, Ivi, isn't he? Time to start acting accordingly.

I grin at him. "Fancy that!"

His lips lift into a little grin.

"I mainly volunteer in helping with children, orphans, human trafficking." My focus wanders to some indistinct point ahead while my mind takes a brief jaunt down memory lane. Visiting with events from my volunteering chapter that have left a mark on me, I muse aloud, "Our world is divided in so many ways. Geography, economy, gender, ethnics. Most of us, though innocently, are utterly blind to what goes on in less privileged societies. It's so much more than just a disaster here or there that the media chooses to put in the spotlight for a minute or two. There are so many wrongs in this world, so much to mend. So many people struggling to survive that we aren't even aware of." As though shaken out of a trance, my eyes slowly climb up to search for Tyler's. "I got a little carried away here, ah? It's just this subject . . . It always gets me fired up."

Tyler's lips quirk up. "I like you fired up." A flirtatious gleam sparks his brown eyes.

Fighting a blush, I change the subject back to innuendo-free territory. "On the next mission trip, the upcoming one to Nepal, we plan to build a school for a small community severely damaged by the last earthquake. It depends on donations and the number of volunteers, but we might be able to do more than that."

"Like what?" The intensity of his stare makes my heart beat a little faster.

"A nursery, maybe fix some private houses that were damaged."

He purses his lips in an impressed expression. A light beam tickles his eyes on me. "You have the skills for that, the building part?"

"Hey, don't judge a book by its cover. I can hammer a nail with the best of them."

"Respect." His amused expression fades. His eyes hold mine, and something shifts between us, something that brings back that humming in my body that his presence seems to regulate. "Yeah, don't judge a book by its cover," he says in a breath.

Needing desperately to break the tension, I say, "Hey, give me some of that," shifting my eyes to the popcorn bowl in his hand. When Tyler passes me the bowl, Jeremy stirs in his sleep, letting out a soft snore. We both drop our eyes to him, matching fond smiles on our faces.

"Amazing. I have enough fans to make a country, and it's this little person," Tyler tips his chin at his son, "who, in a matter of weeks, I'd do anything just to have him look at me proudly."

His words are like a glowing red-hot needle puncturing my skin, making its way into my heart. Poking, in a good way. In a way I have no business feeling about this man.

"He does look at you that way."

He nods. "It's the impending backlash I fear. It's been going on too smoothly with him. I'm not that experienced with kids, but something tells me a blowout is a natural part of the process. He seems sort of reserved as if he's restraining himself around me. He's more open and carefree around you."

I glance at Jeremy's serene face and look up at Tyler. "I can't really blame him. There's the getting used to a new parent thing that by itself is momentous and then . . ." I bite on my lip, considering how to convert my thoughts into words. "There's the whole Tyler Lee Adams concept which could be sort of intimidating."

He nods again, seeming to consider my words. He turns to me. "Thank you for being there for him. I'm sure it hasn't been easy on him."

Silence embraces the room as I resume my knitting and Tyler checks his phone. After a moment or so, we turn to each other at the same time, our questions colliding.

"Do you mind if we change to *The Tonight Show*?" Me with a smile.

"What are you making?" Him tipping his chin at the pink knitted patch I'm working on.

"Villased põlvikud! Socks. Estonian sheep-wool socks." I lift my legs a little from the table. Tyler's eyes roam over my lilac, knee-length, wooly socks. His eyes slowly trail higher to the patch of exposed skin between my knees and my long nightshirt. I'm glad the heatwave on my skin is an internal one, and that he's unaware of what his stare is causing. "My creation!" I add with a grin, hoping he didn't notice the hitch in my voice.

His eyes lift to mine. "Fabulous." It's casual but with the right amount of tease.

"Do you want me to knit you a pair?"

He lets out an easy chuckle. "But of course. Maybe in a different color, though."

"God forbid; I'd be damned before I put your badass rock n' roll image at risk. I got your back; you're safe with me, Tyler Lee Adams."

"Am I?"

I need to swallow hard because that flirty smile of his just caused a drought in my mouth.

When *The Tonight Show* host challenges his guest to a lip sync battle, we both turn to the screen. I don't get to see the end of the show. Somewhere between the last song and the headlines, my heavy eyelids give in.

I wake up to the ruckus my alarm is producing, tucked under my blanket, after a deep, serene sleep. When I realize how I must have ended up in my bed while falling asleep on the couch, the waking up process is not as serene.

"Roller coaster, I want to go on a roller coaster. Go up, up, up, and then fall down, down, down." A young orphan's answer when asked about his dream during one of Ivi's mission trips to South Asia.

I try to extinguish the little buzz in me I woke up to, one that kindled to the notion of Tyler Lee carrying me to bed and tucking me in, all through the day. Trying to smother it as I help Jeremy get ready for school, during my lunch meeting with the YWPO people, and even now, as I talk to Jay on the phone.

Jeremy is sitting at the kitchen table doing his homework when Jay tells me about an eccentric customer who came into his store today and asked for a double cappuccino and a Babka cake.

I laugh. "What did you tell him?"

"That I'm out of cake and made him a coffee to go."

I laugh harder. "No, you didn't."

"Oh, I did," Jay answers over a chuckle.

I lower my elated tone a little when Tyler steps into the kitchen, talking on his phone. My buzz, like a reflex to his presence, builds up.

"Jay, seriously you're the bestest," I say, still grinning.

"Ivi," Tyler's snap makes me turn to face him. "You need a reminder that you're at work? Your personal calls can wait until after Jeremy goes to bed."

My frozen, foolish smile flattens into shock as I look up at Tyler's stoned features. The buzz? Dies! "I've got to go," I tell Jay in a dainty voice.

Feeling somewhat humiliated for being scolded like an errant kid, I almost miss Jays', "What crawled up Little Miss Sunshine's ass?" before I press end.

Tyler gives me another look that makes me wince and brings the phone he was holding to his chest back to his ear. "Yeah Eli, go on."

The realization that Eli might have also heard Tyler's chastening only adds to the foul feeling growing in me.

Jeremy gapes at the two of us. I fabricate an easy smile that I hope says "That? Was nothing" and gesture for him to carry on with his homework. Busying myself making tea, I try to subordinate the anger eating at me birthed by Tyler's uncalled for scolding. Out of the corner of my eye, I see Tyler grab a beer and turn to rest his hip on the kitchen counter, still on the phone. When an F-bomb shoots out of his mouth, I flinch and squint my eyes at Jeremy whose lips are widening into a smile.e

When another expletive lands in the vicinity of the kid-inhabited kitchen, my jaw sets tightly. When the next one comes shortly after, I squint my eyes at Jeremy again. Jeremy bites on the pencil in his hand, his lips around it stretched into a smirk. I shake my head, almost causing a whirlpool in my teacup as I channel my irritation into the teaspoon. I breathe through my nose, doing my best not to snap when another obscenity falls from Tyler's lips. Jeremy snickers at his assignment. I reach for the already nicely cushioned swear jar, holding it in a death grip.

Tyler ends the call and takes a long drink of his beer. Combative expression on, I extend my hand, placing the jar right below his line of sight. He gives it a glance and raises his eyes to me. We hold a strong stare, narrowing our eyes at each other. His eyes still pierce into mine as he dips his hand to the back pocket of his jeans and produces a Benjamin.

"Here." He shoves the note into the jar. "That should damn cover it for a while."

"Five minutes tops," I murmur, stare offing my boss.

"What, no one-dollar notes?" Jeremy asks somewhat animated.

We both look his way.

An overly sweetened smile adorns my lips when I say, "No Jer, I guess your father contributed all of his one notes to enthusiastic young dancers' college education."

Tyler's eyes slice me. "Enthusiastic young dancers usually aren't interested in my financial contribution to their education; they are more into my wisdom. They'd rather suck my wisdom right out of me, pro bono."

I feel sick with the visual he just planted in my head. And maybe a little green? *I hate you, Tyler Lee Adams.*

My pissed stare bores a hole in Tyler's back as he exits the kitchen.

"The other day," Jeremy says, erasing something from the paper he's working on. "During our Healthy Adolescence unit of inquiry lesson, Miss Montgomery said that sometimes when a girl and a boy face-off, especially when it's intense, it really means that they like each other."

I nearly spray out my next sip. Opting for nonchalance, I say, "Your father is my employer. And the way, er, I spoke to my employer was inappropriate, and I'm going to apologize for that later. You should always be respectful to adults, no matter what." *Even if you're in the middle of fantasizing how you'll gladly assist them in their departure from this world.* I continue with, "Wrap it up, and we'll go for a walk, maybe get some ice cream," I say, deliberately disregarding his comment.

———•———

Sitting next to Jeremy at dinner, I try, as covertly as possible, to sneak a peek at his iPad screen. My eyes practically hurting from the sharp, strained squinting. Let's just say that I might be a little curious to see how Jeremy's mother looks. And *maybe* it's all about what the woman Tyler made a baby with looks like. *Maybe.*

"Miss you infinitely, honey. Love you to the sky and back," Melena, Jeremy's mother says. Jeremy closes the video and turns to press the Growtopia icon on his iPad.

"Uh-uh, hold it right there, mister." I snatch the iPad from under his conniving little hands. "It's A-Okay to talk to your mom during dinner. Computer games, on the other hand," I shake my head lightly, " are a big no-no."

"You know . . ." Jeremy pushes his glasses up his nose before forking a Brussels sprout. "Video games have many positive effects on kids. It hones your skill in problem-solving and logic, following instructions, fine motor coordination, strategizing, and fast thinking." I fold my arms across my chest, waiting for the clincher which I'm sure is soon to come. "By not allowing me to play, you're taking all of these away. In a way, you're slowing my development."

There we go.

"Of course, I am." I send him an amicable smile. "You'll have enough time to work on your development after dinner."

"Thank you, Adina." Both Jeremy and I thank Adina for dinner after I make Jeremy clean up after himself.

"Thanks for making me clean up," Jeremy murmurs under his breath, as we make our way to the living room.

I pat his shoulder. "You'll thank me in a few years when you don't turn into a spoiled brat."

"You're so annoying." He dips his chin to hide his smile.

"I love you too." I hug his shoulder, and he sinks into me with that endearing smile of his. I truly adore the kid. It doesn't feel like work at all. Feels more like a big sister sort of connection. Then, in a very disturbing way, it implies that Tyler Lee is my father. Scratch the siblings thought, pronto.

"It's my favorite nanny and little Ty," Max, Tyler Lee's bassist, greets us as soon as Jeremy and I enter the living room.

I lightly smile at him and the rest of the gang. On the wide L-shaped sofa is Max in a shirt that's too psychedelic for a direct look and a bulky, bold dude who goes by the name Killer. On one of the two-seaters is Eli in a charcoal suit. On the other two-seater is Jay, grinning at Jeremy and me. I return his smile before my eyes end up on Tyler. Tyler is in an armchair, looking delectable in worn jeans, loose-laced black combat boots, a beard that goes in perfect harmony with his knotted up hair, and a guitar on his spread thighs. Trailing over him, my eyes stop on his tee, and instinctively, my lips spring into a grin. Decaled in white letters across the front of his black tee is #JBiebs, have my baby.

Noticing my smile, Tyler's eyes light up. We hold an amused stare till Jay reaches me and takes me into a hug. Before turning to him, I get to see Tyler's lips morph into a flat line.

"Hey, Jeremey, wanna watch the game with us?" Tyler asks. Jeremy doesn't even ask which game, nodding enthusiastically as he takes a seat next to his father.

"How about you, Mary P.?" Max asks.

"I have a Skype call with my parents and some things to do so rain check?" I say.

Jay by my side says, "I'll come keep you company during halftime."

"Tore," *Cool*, I answer in Estonian. It's one of the few words in my mother tongue Jay managed to actually register.

"Tore," he answers in a heavy American accent and a grin.

I steal a glance at Tyler, who's watching us like a hawk. Our eyes meet, and the pull feels like a magnetic field.

"What's 'tore'?" Jeremy asks, seeming genuinely interested.

"Hold up, my darling young one," I beam at Jeremey. *"Jeremy Nathan Brown* doesn't know something?" I hold my hand to my chest and feign shock. He rolls his eyes at me. My smiling eyes echo his. "It's a variation of 'cool' in Estonian."

"Tore!" Jeremy repeats after me. I'm pretty sure that by this time tomorrow he'll be able to lecture me on the origin of the word, or maybe the entire Estonian language, for that matter.

"Yo, Mary P., can I also visit you at halftime?" Max wiggles his eyebrows.

Breaking another eye lock I find myself holding with Tyler, I shake my head in response. In my periphery, I notice Eli's gauging stare ping-ponging from Tyler to me.

Max's smile widens. "No halftime then how about bedtime?"

"Enough." It's Tyler's cold voice, holding zero tolerance.

"Lost cause, dude," Killer says, patting Max's chest, maybe a little stronger than called for. "Can't you see that her heart belongs to Daddy?" He gestures with his chin at Tyler Lee.

Don't look at him, don't look at him, I inwardly chant. My renegading eyes bounce to Tyler, though. Only to find his stare trained on me, a wrinkle formed above his nose, appearing to be absorbedly hypothesizing Killer's observation.

I breathe through the warmness threatening to wash over my cheeks. I shake it off. "Gentlemen," I give a little curtsy, tugging on my shirtdress à la Disney princess style. "As always, it's been invigorating chatting with you. Nighty night and sweet dreams." I turn on my heel and climb up the stairs to the second floor while mapping out Killer's killing.

Ending my Skype call with my parents an hour later and feeling homesick, I text Jay, telling him it's going to be an early night and that I'll text tomorrow. Seeing that it's a solo evening for me, I pull out my natural beauty kit and start applying a seaweed mask that turns my face into a lumpy, shining display of vomit-green. Next, I squirt some toothpaste on my toothbrush and top it up with activated charcoal, a nature-whitening wonder. In mere seconds, my mouth fills with blackish froth. I stick my tongue out at the mirror, snorting at my frightening appearance. A Shrek double, the rotten teeth edition.

Hopping on my luxurious bed, I rest my back on the headboard. Straightening my knee-length, stripy sock-covered legs before me, I plunge the earbuds into my ears. With my "Ivi's favorite" playlist on, I bring the Kindle app to life on my phone and get back to *The Girl with the Dragon Tattoo*. Some good few moments into the fast-paced story, I start feeling the mask on my face breaking with each little twitch of my features, and I realize I might have left it on a little longer than needed. I hold my breath, devouring the next brutal scene that has my body strung and still. When a message pops next at the top the of my phone screen, I give it a reflexive peek and then return to the story. My eyes widen as the message sinks in. With a start, I leave the Kindle app and go to my messages. Yep, I read it right.

Tyler Lee: Are you awake?

An "awake message" from Tyler Lee Adams at half past eleven?

The awakened buzz looping inside me is not to my liking, to say the least. It's as if my body and subconscious flip my brain the bird each time the man is mentioned. Hop, there goes logic.

Ivi: Yes ...

Waiting for a response while listening to the song playing through the earbuds, I glare at the phone. More than two minutes pass and ... nothing. Probably sent by mistake. If he did, then it means he intended to "awake message" someone else. Oh, how I don't like nor can I begin to understand why the notion bothers me as much as it does. Sensing a motion in my periphery, I lift my eyes and let out a choked yelp. It takes me a few frightening seconds to register Tyler at my doorframe. I inwardly curse the incredible book I'm reading. Damn you, awesome piece of frightening thriller.

When the initial shock wears off, I look at Tyler in question. Not missing the awkward way he looks at me nor the fact that his lips are moving and no sound comes out, the realization that my earbuds are still in my ears follows.

As I pull the earbuds out, Tyler says with a swift shrug, "I knocked a few times."

"Come in," I tell him, drinking in the sight of him. A few strands have escaped his loose knot, only to add a wilder edge to his already sinful appearance. He takes a step closer, his eyes running over my face. As he sits on my bed, his bottom lip is trapped by his teeth, clearly holding a smile.

Oh crap. Crap. Crap! I'm sitting in front of Tyler Lee Adams with something resembling a frog smoothie covering my face. When I give him a timid smile, and he cringes with a slightly disgusted expression, the black teeth situation ricochets into my consciousness.

I clear my throat, squaring my eyes with his. "Beauty treatments, highly recommended."

Tyler finally lets out the chuckle he's tried hard to hold in.

Not letting it rub in, I ask, "What's up, boss?"

"About earlier . . ." He scratches the side of his neck, calling my attention to where his loose hair strands hover over his beard, nearly hiding a small Coptic cross tattoo. Every bit of this man is everything women everywhere make him to be. His brows crease. "You can have personal calls whenever . . . I, my remark, wasn't cool."

Tyler just apologized, sort of? The buzz makes a comeback, healthier and keyed up.

I nod, looking at him from under my lashes. "Um, my response earlier, it was out of line. I'm sorry for that."

He holds his hand out. "So we're tore?" Smiling at his usage of Estonian and his accent, I watch as our hands connect for a shake. His large tan, veined hand just about swallows mine. A current traveling all the way from our skin on skin connection powders my stomach with warmness.

"We're tore." I smile, having a hard time collecting my hand back. But when he winces again to my smile, I do and also snap my lips shut for good measure.

"Oh, and there's . . . I have a local gig this Thursday, something intimate. I thought Jeremy could come, and you, of course," he says, averting his eyes from direct contact with my face. A ghost of a smile plays at his lips.

"That would be great. I think Jeremey will be thrilled. I sure am." When a smile starts to crawl up my lips, I kill it immediately. I've exposed the poor man to enough grotesqueness to last him a lifetime.

"I'll sing some new material I've been working on. You tired?"

Where did that come from? "Nooo?" I answer hesitantly.

"Up to listening to something new, be my guinea pig?"

"Tyler." It's the first time I call him by his name, and it feels so strangely personal and wonderful. "Nothing would make me happier than to be your guinea pig."

His amused expression gradually falls pensive as he watches me for an unnerving beat. He cocks his head to the side. "The way you pronounce my name, your accent . . . the way you roll and accentuate the R." He chuckles softly, his brows bunched bemusedly. "Sweet."

I'm afraid the buzz is about to short out and cause a fire inside me. I'm rendered speechless, though inwardly all I want to do is say his name like a mantra. I want that expression he just had when saying "sweet" on a loop.

He tips his chin at the door. "I'm getting my guitar."

"I'm just going to wash this catastrophe off my face." I tip my chin at the bathroom.

"Fuck, please." It's an exhaled, relieved, humored declaration.

Washing the mask off, I can't begin to fight the idiotic smile that spreads across my face. When I turn to brush my teeth, I can hear Tyler enter my room. I rinse quickly and go join him.

Switching off the bathroom light and walking into my room, I stop short and gape. Tyler rests against the headboard at the left side of my king-size bed, one knee up, his guitar in hand. I swallow hard. Do I just take the other side of the bed? Do I sit on a chair? Do I run out of the room because . . . Tyler Lee Freaking Adams is on my bed!

And then logic arrives to protest. This is so inappropriate, to put it mildly. But then again, this is Tyler Lee Adams, rock and roll immortal, celebrity material with a side dish of bad boy. He, for sure, has a completely different set of values. Operating to some special kind of rules. No doubt, the whole "someone on my bed" works differently for us.

A man in my bed — a rare occasion that usually leads to something in the PG-13 realm.

A woman on his bed — probably an hourly reoccurring occasion that presumably leads to some members of her flock joining to a "merrier time." After all, the more, the merrier, no?

His eyes lift from the guitar to me, a blue guitar pick held between his lips, looking like something that should be commemorated, sculpted, in bronze. "Please don't look at me like that," he says in a low voice.

My head jerks back in surprise. "How am I looking at you?"

"With the look people get when they realize who I am."

I nod slowly, twice, and claim the right side of the bed. Bringing my legs to my chest, I hug them over my thick, gray and pink striped socks.

Tyler gives me a slow once-over. Taking the guitar pick from between his lips, he sends me a little half-smile. "Ready to be my victim?"

I'm already one of your victims, Tyler Lee Adams.

But I choose to go with a subtle response. "Let's see if you're any good. I might even throw in some pointers as a gesture of goodwill." I hug my legs tighter, sending him a sass-coated grin.

The smile he radiates at me next makes the buzz perk up, up as in put on a pair of cleats and kick my heart up my throat.

He shakes his head, his smile softening as his fingers touch the strings. I watch him captivated as he plays a few notes. The first lyrics roll out of his mouth, causing an avalanche of goose bumps over my skin. He closes his eyes, his voice warm with an edge of roughness that trickles up my spine, seeping into me like a thick liquid, slowly melting my insides. It's like having an out-of-body experience listening to him sing for me in my room, on my bed. Watching him is numbly mesmerizing. All I can do is luxuriate in the moment as surreal as it feels. My eyes draw to his lips as they produce this music that caresses every part of me, externally and internally. He sings the last few lyrics and looks up at me, cocking his head.

"It's perfect." My voice comes out raspy.

He nods unassumingly.

"Tyler," I say. When his eyes meet mine and slowly trail over my face, I realize just how intimate this moment is, how physically close we are. "How does it feel to sing in front of a large audience?"

He inhales. "Phenomenal," comes out on an exhale. "When I'm on stage, adrenaline takes over, and in a way, it feels like I'm high. In a trance. Pair that with the fans' response . . . and it's incredible. It never gets old."

My features turn stern as I softly ask, "How does it feel to be you?"

He chuckles, his eyes dropping to the guitar, his lips set in a meek smile. "Like everything in life, Ivi." He lifts his eyes to mine.

"Sometimes good, sometimes less. Especially when things get out of control or became a little insane." He laughs, but it's brief and with a touch of frustration. "It can get pretty wild at times." His fingers resume strumming the guitar. I watch his fingers, as they own the strings. On his left hand, two thick silver rings adorn his fingers while the third one has a calligraphy of the letter J. His other hand has only one silver ring and two fingers decorated by tattoos. One of a cross, and the other of a Viking symbol.

"Is there anything you don't like about it?"

He keeps playing the chords. "When people think they know me . . . or own me." His eyes meet mine. "Or put me in a pigeonhole, just like you did earlier when you considered sitting next to me on the bed."

I worry my lip, not breaking our stare. "Are you always this direct?"

He shrugs, his fingers running on the strings. "I guess. Well, when you live in a world full of bullshit, the least you could do is not get sucked into it," he says to the guitar. He plays some more chords, and his expression turns amused. "Oh, and I'm not the biggest fan of those weird t-shirts with my face on it. I can understand tour shirts; I even own more than a few." He shakes his head, side smile tipping higher. "But a shirt with my face on it sort of creeps me out."

I lightly chuckle. His animated eyes meet mine. A yawn escapes my lips, and his smile grows.

"Yeah, got the hint." He straightens, dropping his legs off the bed. "I'll let you go to sleep."

I cover my mouth with my hand, trapping another yawn. "I have a busy day tomorrow. I heard Tyler Lee Adams is playing an intimate gig this Thursday, so I got to go stand in line to get a ticket."

Tyler looks at me, his lip quirk at the corner. "I'll get you a backstage pass. I know a guy who knows a guy." With a shadow of a smile, he starts for the door.

"Tyler," I say, and he halts. "The new songs, they are great, really."

I bite on my smile. "But they have nothing on your shirt. I'm so jealous. I want one just like it."

He drops his eyes to his JBibes shirt and grins. Then, without warning or as much as a blink of an eye, he sends his hand to the back of his neck and pulls the shirt up over his head. Under my stunned gaze, he wads the shirt into a ball and in a perfect shooting arc, lands it in my hands.

Holding his warm shirt in my hands, having his toned, bare torso to feast on, my mind lapses.

Lord have mercy on my poor ovaries.

"Good night, Ivi." Tyler closes the door behind him.

"Good night, Tyler," is a soft, soft murmur to the quiet room.

Fourteen

"Risk of injury or serious damage from improper use." A warning label on Ivi's pink toolkit.

"The opportunity for social interaction with others is very important for the development of all children. Through social interactions, children establish a sense of 'self,' hone their social skills and social communication, and learn how to interpret and handle singular inter-social situations." Jeremy, sitting at my desk, reads to me from my laptop.

"True and true, and you're still not having a sleepover on a school night," I say to the piece I'm knitting, my eyes crinkled at the corners. Gotta love the little brainiac and his clever ways.

He twirls in the chair a couple of times in thought. Stopping mid-spin, he folds his arms across his Minecraft tee and says with a cheeky air, "How about I ask Tyler?" His eyes challenge mine from behind blue framed glasses.

Needles frozen in my hands, I arch an eyebrow.

He counters with two arched eyebrows and a slight head slant.

"Be my guest," I say and put the yarn and needles aside, the new set of black socks I started working on. "Go ahead, ask your dad . . . And if he says no, which I'm quite positive he will, you can still visit with your friend and come back for dinner."

At the threshold of Tyler's home recording studio, I gesture with my hand for Jeremey to get in first. Tyler and a guy I haven't had the chance to meet yet, who is donning a camo jacket with a buzz cut and black stud earrings, sit by a desk that looks more like an operation room, complete with the wall-mounted screens and consoles with endless buttons. On a bulky, black leather sofa, Eli sits one leg crossed over the other, barking at someone on the phone. The song Tyler sang to me the other night plays in the background while the guy next to Tyler presses and shifts some buttons. Tyler drums with his fingers on the desk, his head gently moving to the rhythm.

"Um, Tyler?" Jeremy says, his voice slightly pitched in an effort to be heard.

Tyler turns in the chair to look at us. Camo jacket dude throws Jeremy a glance and then slowly scans me. He nods with a smile, which I return.

Leaning to rest his elbows on his knees, hands steepled ahead, Tyler raises his brows in question. "Yeah, bud?"

Jeremy pockets the little rubber ball he fiddled with coming up the stairs. "Can I have a sleepover with my friend Gaylord?"

"On a school night," I add, giving Tyler a "please back me up on this one" look.

Tyler's face screws up as he asks, "Your friend's name is Gaylord?"

Jeremy shrugs in a confirming fashion, and I stifle a snort when Tyler murmurs, "What's wrong with people." He exhales through his nose. "Sorry, bud, not on a school night."

Expecting the signature Jeremy Nathan Brown relentless facts-dropping debate, I'm surprised to watch the kid's lips shut and eyes round. I follow Jeremy's stare to check out what got little sir chatty pants quiet. Tyler's eyes follow suit. A grin climbs up my lips to the light hue tinting Jeremy's cheeks and the beautiful girl his eyes are trained on.

"Tyler, I hope you don't mind. Amelie wanted to say hello," Adina, who just entered the room, says proudly, resting her hand on the pretty girl's shoulder. The girl, who looks to be about Jeremy's age or maybe a little older, sends Tyler a dreamy, blue-eyed look.

Tyler smiles back. "How you doing, Amelie? We haven't seen you around here for a while."

The apples of Amelie's cheeks redden with her answer. "Good, Tyler Lee." She fidgets, holding her hands together. "Um, I made you this friendship bracelet for letting me take photos of you and your recording studio for Show and Tell." Amelie holds out a navy and black patterned thread bracelet. "It was really cool of you."

Tyler gazes at the offered gift with an adorable side smile, points a finger at himself and mouths, "For me?"

Amelie bobs her head with a huge smile, probably unable to form words. That Tyler Lee smile does things to you. Even at her age, I wouldn't be surprised if she remembers *that* smile long after a series of boy crushes wreaks havoc with her heart.

After Amelie ties the bracelet around Tyler's wrist, Adina says, "Amelie dear, this is Ivi. Ivi, this is my granddaughter, Amelie. She visits me at work sometime."

"Nice to meet you, Amelie," I say.

"And this is Jeremy," Adina says. "He is . . . " She turns unsure eyes to Tyler.

"My son," Tyler helps out. Something about Tyler's voice as he says it and his eyes on Jeremy have a direct impact on my belly.

"Hey, Jeremy." Amelie takes a step closer to Jeremy, which makes the poor boy's face flame up.

Stud earrings dude excuses himself while Adina and Tyler discuss something about Adina's family, and Amelie asks Jeremy if he lives at Tyler's place now. I remain close to the kids because their interaction is too damn adorable to miss.

"I'm going to stay here for a while; do you want to hang out?" Amelie says.

Jeremy's head bobs. "We can watch a movie."

Amelie grins. "Cool." Jeremy, watching her like a smitten kitten, seems a bit lost when she asks, "Do you also play the guitar like your dad?"

Jeremy looks a bit stressed out, calibrating his answer. "Yeah . . ."

I raise a doubtful eyebrow.

Amelie grins, and Jeremy returns a boyish smile. A gushy "Awww" threatens to leave my lips.

"Darling," Adina says to her granddaughter. "Why don't we let Tyler get back to work?"

"You coming?" Amelie asks Jeremy, following her grandma.

"Yeah, in a sec."

When they leave the room, Jeremy turns to his dad. "Um, D-Tyler, can you teach me to play guitar?"

"Sure, kid," Tyler says, positively surprised.

"Sweet," Jeremy says, looking like he is screeching his tires as he shoots out of the room.

"Hey, Jer," I call after him.

Breathy, he pops his head back into the room a second later. "Yeah?"

Having a very hard time covering my amusement, I ask, "What about the sleepover?"

"Some other time." And he's off.

"What was that all about?" Tyler asks.

"I think our little boy is developing his first crush."

Tyler's lips quirk at the corner. "Kid's got good taste. Beautiful girl."

"Agree. She is pretty," I say meeting his eyes.

"She looks like you." His voice is casual, in complete contrast to the stare he has on me.

My lips faintly part as his observation sinks in. Amelie does look a little like me with her heavy fall of shoulder-length, dark brown hair and big blue eyes. She even has a slight bump on her nose just like me. What also registers and has a way greater effect, is the fact that Tyler just insinuated that he finds me pretty.

"'Kay, let's get this party started." The stud earring guy returns to the room.

Putting my game face on, I nod and turn to leave, catching Eli's hard look at me on the way.

——————◆——————

"So how did you guys like the *Gremlins* movie?" I ask Jeremy as he gets into bed. Now that Amelie has left, he's finally back to a normal kid state and not a tongue protruding puppy.

Jeremy reaches for a thick Harry Potter book on the nightstand. "It was good."

The nervous undercurrent in his expression makes me cock my head sideways in assessment. "Jer, everything okay?"

He nods, but his look at me tells me otherwise.

"Are you, maybe . . . a little scared?"

"No!" His face twists.

"Okay then, good night," I say, walking to the door. "Leave the light on?" I turn to look at him. His anxious nod backs my assumption. "I'm two rooms away if you need me . . ."

Closing my room's door, I turn to the walk-in closet to change into my night gear. Shimmying out of my cutoffs and silky black button up, I keep my purple boy shorts. I reach for my new pajamas, which I managed to convince myself I wanted because the shirt was large, comfortable, and snuggly—definitely not because it touched Tyler's skin or still faintly smell like him. Rolling my eyes at my reflection in the mirror, I pull up my knitted red knee socks and head to bed.

Rereading the passage I've already read twice, I let out an irritated sigh. Though I've been trying really hard to ignore the rhythmic tapping coming from the bathroom, it still manages to seep in and play on my nerves. It sounds like water drops methodically coming in contact with a hard surface. Like Chinese water torture. I huff and get out of the warm bed. Switching the en suite light on, I check the faucet and showerhead. Finding them both dry, I stand still, waiting for the next patter. It takes me another moment to locate the mother lover.

I yank open the vanity, and another tap comes, a little louder this time. Twisting my mouth from side to side, I gauge the lack of illumination. Pulling my hair up in a messy knot, I stride out of the bathroom to get my toolkit. Yes, right, my toolkit! And it's in cute, shocking pink. I got it from my mom as a "leaving the nest" gift when I moved in with a roommate, together with a speech about how I should never, *ever* rely on anyone and get things done myself. My mom is the best kind of badass. And not the greatest fan of the damsel in distress variety.

I set the toolkit open on the floor and lie on my back beside it. Pink flashlight and pink wrench in hand, I slide back till my upper body is inside the vanity cupboard. I rest the wrench on my belly, and with the flashlight pointed at the P-trap, I feel my way to locate the leakage. A knock on my door comes just as I hit home run.

"Come in," I call out.

Pointing the flashlight at the source of evil, I hear Tyler calling my name. "In the bathroom," I say, reaching for the wrench on my stomach.

"Ivi, *what the fuck?*"

Startled by the harsh tone, I lurch up with a start, banging my forehead on the T-trap along the way. Rubbing my forehead, I slide forward to meet Tyler's dark eyes and intense expression.

"What are you doing?" He sounds pissed or . . . something. His eyes raking over my bent red sock clad legs, up to my exposed thighs, to my purple boy shorts, over the black JBiebs shirt, up to my hand rubbing my poor forehead and slowly, very slowly all the way back.

"Fixing a leak," I say, sitting up.

"What?" He fists and releases his fingers. If I didn't know better, I'd think he's about to enter a ring and beat the shit out of someone . . . or have his way with me, here on the floor. That's how he looks. His eyes burn each part of my skin as they roam all over me.

"There's a leak in the T-trap. I'm fixing it." I shrug.

He slightly shakes his head, opens his mouth to speak, and then closes it again.

"Did you want anything?" I ask, my brows slightly advance toward each other as a reaction to *his* odd reaction.

"I wanted . . ." He pauses and shakes his head again as though trying to win an internal battle. He holds the doorframe from both sides, gazing at me for a beat and then pushes himself back, murmuring something that I swear sounds like "*You make me fucking lose my mind.*" Which I dismiss immediately on a technicality because it was a mumble and I'm not in clear hearing distance, and frankly, why would he say something like that?

"Never mind." My eyebrows almost meet now upon hearing his pissed tone.

He turns around and takes a couple of steps. I follow him with my gaze, utterly perplexed. And then he turns back with a start, his steps toward the bathroom determined as if I'm his prey and he's about to drag me back to his lair. He opens his mouth again, but the chime of his phone stops him from uttering whatever was about to leave his mouth. As though a spade of ice water just sobered him up, he takes a step back and stills. He reaches for his phone and checks the screen.

Giving me another look that I can't begin to make sense of, he answers the phone. "Brooklyn." Then, "I'm coming over." And he leaves the room.

#*Brookty!* Tyler's, according to the media, girlfriend is on the phone, and he just told her he's coming over. Feels like the wicked ice-water downpour moves across the space and lands on me.

———— ◆ ————

With my eyes still shut, I toss and turn. A creepy feeling of being watched trickling in.

"Ivi." Someone says my name. My eyes rip open to a figure looming by my bed. I blink a couple of times, my heart thudding in double-time before Jeremy's alarmed face comes into focus.

"Jer?" I ask, straightening to sit, sending my hand to his forearm.

"I'm scared, Ivi."

I take a deep breath and get out of bed. I take his hand in mine. "Let's go, I'll sleep on the sofa in your room."

As Jeremey climbs back into bed, I drag the pale-blue armchair closer to his bed and settle down with my legs bent over the armrest. When Jeremy's breaths even out, I let my eyelids rest.

I'm not sure how long I've been sleeping in Jeremy's armchair when I feel someone lifting me up and carrying me out of the room. I flutter my eyes open to Tyler, and close them back again, dropping my head on his shoulder.

Drowsy, I'm being set on a bed and covered with a soft blanket. I blink my eyes open again to Tyler standing above me, gazing at me.

"You're sleeping in my shirt," he says softly.

My dozy mind has no control over my lips and "it smells like you" spills out. I try to keep my eyes open, but they fight back. And then like a dream, Tyler's scent washes over me while his fingers thread into my hair at my temples.

And then his mouth touches mine.

My eyes are still closed when his lips brush against mine in feathery waves. When my lips slightly part to his tongue, I get the first taste of Tyler. And it's so incredibly wonderful. I let out a small whimper, and it's like a catalyst to his kiss. His hands on my face hold me still as he deepens the kiss. It's so overtaking as though empowered by hunger, by unleashed craving, by raw pull. His tongue, warm and demanding, relishes me like he is starving for my taste. It's rough and forceful but in a delicious way that travels all the way down my body in warm, heady surges of perfect. It feels unreal. I feel like I'm floating. Like I'm intoxicated. Like I'm being possessed. Like I'm about to pass out from bliss.

Slowly, he eases the pace. So slowly until it's just his soft lips tender on mine. He holds me like this with our mouths pressed together for a beat in which he steadies his breath.

And then he is gone.

I don't want to open my eyes and find out if I dreamed it all or not. Because if this was a dream, I never want to wake up.

Fifteen

CHAPTER

Ivi: "Me? Pfff, I'll never be as pathetic, falling for the unattainable, bad-boy cliché. Whenever it happens to me, I know it'll be drama-free, stress-free, and sweet."

Krystina: "That sounds sooooo boring."

A transcript of a conversation between seventeen-year-old Ivi and her, at the time, "best friend forever."

"Hey Jeremy, let me just help you with this bit," Jay says, sitting next to Jeremy on a bench in his studio. Jay takes the piece of wood Jeremy has been working on to the table saw, shaping the blades at each side a little. Shaping it into a more distinctive, pixelated pickax form, he then hands it back to Jeremy for some good old-fashioned sanding labor. In an attempt to minimize the kid's screen time and also to get to hang with Jay, I brought him over to Jay's for a woodworking for dummies session.

Watching Jeremy enthusiastically work the sandpaper across the wood, Jay says in a heavy Asian accent, "Wax on, wax off."

Jay and I laugh briefly while Jeremy darts ignorant eyes at us.

I shake my head. "Kids these days have zero appreciation for cinematic classics." When Jeremy twists his lips mockingly, I add, "Next on our rapidly growing 'to be watched' list is *The Karate Kid*,

Jeremy-san."

Jeremy and I continue messing around with the wood, trying our hands at basic woodworking while Jay orders pizza.

Jay's phone rings when he's about to put it down. "Hey, you done with the interview?" he says as a greeting. After listening, he adds, "Come over, pizza is on the way." He ends the call and tosses his phone on the long worktable.

"Did you know that trees never die of old age? It's usually insects, diseases, and people that end up killing them," Jeremy says, blowing off the dust after sanding his pickax. "And also, trees use almost fifty percent of all of the sun's energy taken by all living organisms."

"Here's another fact for you, kiddo," Jay says, working the screen of my phone, connecting it to the Bluetooth speakers. "Wet wood, unlike dry wood, can conduct electricity."

Our attention wanders toward the sound of squeaking steps that lead to Jay's studio. My eyes do a double take when Tyler materializes in the room. His hair is slicked back in a knot, light-blue button up rolled to his elbows, displaying toned, tattooed sleeves, paired with gray tweed pants and suspenders. Holy suspenders on Tyler Lee Adams! His heavy brown boots carry him into the room, and all I can do is inwardly drool.

Tyler nods at us, stepping over to ruffle Jeremy's mane. "What you working on, bud?"

With that special glee of admiration Jeremy's eyes take when his father is around, Jeremy looks up at Tyler and says, "A Growtopia pickax. Cool, huh?"

Tyler lips quirk. "Coolest thing I've ever seen."

"Look at you all dolled up, Buttercup," Jay says to Tyler with a smirk.

Taking a seat next to Jeremy on the bench with a leg on each side, Tyler says dryly, "You know I always make an extra effort when I visit you, Cuddles."

I smile to myself, more than enjoying the interaction between them.

"What you smiling at, Ivi?" Tyler asks, resting his forearm on the table, his eyes teasingly on me. "Don't you think Jay is worth the effort?" He winks at me, and my smile grows, as does my pulse.

"Nah, she's just happy playing with my wood," Jay adds in an elated accord.

A piece of wood meets Jay's forehead, followed by, "You be respectful to my Ivi."

It's all fun and games till Tyler sucks the air right out of my lungs with his statement. I know it's all a part of the friendly banter going on, but I can't help the silly, silly, wonderful feeling brought on by hearing him call me his Ivi.

"Dude, the lady takes care of my kid. That's almost as sacred as a mother."

"My sincere apologies for the innuendo." Jay holds his arms up, grinning. Something in his eyes changes, as though carrying a message, when he adds, "Tyler's Ivi."

A song changes to another in the background. Tyler grabs a sandpaper square and starts helping Jeremy when Jay puts a cloth in my hand, wordlessly asking me to help polish an antique chair he restored as a personal favor for a client. We work in pleasant silence with my playlist in the background and random facts coming from Jeremy's side.

From time to time, I send unconscious glances over to Tyler, getting glimpses of him sanding the wooden piece with his son, singing along to the music. A soft hum seems to come so naturally for him. His head slightly moving to the music.

One of my current favorite songs comes next—The Killer's cover to the Dire Straits hit "Romeo and Juliet." This time when my eyes, of their own volition, draw to Tyler, he is waiting for them. He holds my stare, singing along to the music. "You and me babe—how 'bout it?"

After a short, profound look, my eyes drop to the chair I'm methodically polishing. When they come back to look at him from under my lashes, I catch the little faint smile that touched his lips before he turns to nod at something Jeremy just said.

"Booyah!" Jeremy declares, lifting up his completed pickax proudly, bringing back the light ambiance to the room.

When the pizza arrives, we wash our hands and settle at one section of the massive, long worktable.

On one side, Jeremy perches next to Tyler, his legs barely touching the floor. Jay and I sit on the other side facing them. Tyler and Jay mock Jeremy amicably, telling him that he won't be able to meet a cute girl if he's glued to a computer screen all the time. Adorably blushing, Jeremy retaliates, telling both men that the real cute girls are gamers, and the best way to meet them is over game chats.

"Hold on." I raise my hand. "I'm not a gamer girl? That means I'm not 'real cute.'"

"You're an adult, Ivi. You can't be cute," Jeremy says too seriously for my liking.

"Blasphemy," Jay protests, smacking the table. "Ivi is in a league of her own. Nothing is as cute as my dear friend here." Jay sends his arm around my shoulder and squeezes me into him.

If I didn't know better, I'd say Tyler is not the greatest fan of Jay's arm around me. His furrowed brows and piercing eyes are difficult to miss.

Jeremy takes a bite of his slice and wipes his mouth with the back of his hand. "Did you know that NASA is developing 3D printers that can print pizzas for astronauts?"

The three of us look at him with the same fond expression.

"What?" he asks with a smile. "They paid this company to develop 3D printers that will be able to print food for space missions, really!"

Comfortable silence embraces the room as we continue to eat. The cheese topping on my slice keeps stretching out as I try to bite off a piece. I send out my tongue to wrap around the string of cheese. I give it a few twirls, sensing Tyler's eyes on me. With my tongue still sticking out, I trail my eyes up to look at him. What they meet has my stomach make a little loop. His gaze on my mouth and its reaction can only be described as scorching.

"So I heard Brooklyn's back in town." Jay chooses this exact moment to bring me back from my delusional thoughts, that maybe, just maybe, that kiss the other night is not a figment of my imagination, and that maybe, just maybe, the look Tyler just had on me was a product of desire.

Tyler clears his throat. "Yeah, we grabbed a drink together the other night," he says noncommittally.

Oh, the pang of jealousy I have no business feeling. It's also a reality check pang. Realizing I'm making a complete fool out of myself, giving stage to things that exist only in my head.

Jay nods slowly, his stare traveling from Tyler to me and back. "Saw it circulating already." He scratches his eyebrow with his thumb. "Did she get her shi—" His eyes land on Jeremy, and he corrects himself. "Did she get her mind sorted out over in Australia, or she need more time to complicate your life just a little more?"

"Enough. Don't go there," Tyler says in a low, hard voice.

I pretend to be absorbed in brushing crumbs off the table, but my attention is very much in the encrypted conversation being held next to me.

When I lift my eyes from the table, it's to Jay's arms spread to his sides. "Just looking out for you, bro." He shakes his head. "Wouldn't it be nice to be able to try things you might be missing?" Jay's eyes travel to me while Tyler's follow, his jaw working hard under his skin. In a weird sense, it feels like they are having another conversation I'm not privy to yet somehow involves me.

"Jay . . ." It's definitely a warning.

I'd give anything for someone to translate whatever was just discussed between these two.

"Who's Brooklyn?" Jeremy asks.

Tyler gives me a glance that I return with a thin smile in disguise of a revelation. Because what just clicked in my recognition is so very wrong. I got it bad for him. Not for *the* Tyler Lee Adams. For just Tyler.

He exhales, and that's when I choose to make myself scarce. Stepping over to the bathroom, I still manage to hear him say, "A good friend of mine."

"Your girlfriend?" Jeremy asks.

I lock myself in the bathroom, ensuring I don't hear Tyler's response.

———— • ————

"Okay, this was the last round," I tell Jeremy, sitting crossed-legged on his bed. He closes the wrestling game on his tablet and sets it on the nightstand. "Did you brush your teeth?" I ask.

He flashes his pearly whites at me. I laugh warmly. His features flatten, and his eyes rise to me. "Will you come back after your trip to Nepal?"

Tyler steps into the room as I say, "Sometimes, I visit the States for my volunteering. No chance I won't be meeting with you when I do. Even if you forget all about me."

"I won't," he says. "I wish you could hang out with me when I visit my d —" He sends Tyler who's now leaning on the wall, a short peep. "When I visit Tyler." He turns to Tyler. "I will be visiting you when Mom is back, right?"

My heart squeezes with so much love for the kid.

Tyler pushes himself from the wall and settles on Jeremy's bed next to me, a sliver of air between us. He runs his hand over his trimmed beard. "Do you know what joint custody is?"

Jeremy rolls his eyes with a little scorning smile. "We live in L.A. Most of my friends' parents are divorced."

Tyler chuckles briefly. "Well, we are not going to do that. Your mom and I agreed to let you decide if and when and for how long you want to stay with me."

Seeing the personal angle the conversation is taking, I straighten and move a little, about to excuse myself and give them the privacy they need, but Tyler stops me. He covers my hand that's supporting me behind my back with his and squeezes it. Skyrocketing my heart along the way.

He keeps his large hand on mine, resuming his talk with to his son. "I hope you'll do that, but just know that it's entirely up to you. I know that this is all new to you, and I want you to take your time adjusting to the situation. I'm not going to force you into anything. But just know that nothing will make me happier if you choose to visit me, often."

And I fall deeper and deeper.

"I want to do that," Jeremy says in a soft voice.

And I fall deeper, and deeper, for them both.

Tyler removes his hand to take Jeremy into a quick embrace. When they ease off, Jeremy asks, "Then Ivi will come back after her trip?"

"Hey, you still have me for about four months. Who knows, I might get on your nerves by then." I try to lighten the moment as the probability of me actually coming back after Nepal is less than slim.

Tyler and I tell Jeremy good night and step out of his room.

Tyler turns to me. "Want to watch TV?"

"Sure." I nod just as I've been doing every night for the past few days. It's become a thing, us ending the day together. Him with a bowl of popcorn, me with peanut butter filled pretzels, our legs resting on the coffee table and Netflix on the TV.

CHAPTER
Sixteen

"Love, because it is the only true adventure." A message from a fortune cookie Ivi had at lunch just before leaving for L.A.

I let Jeremy play on my phone to kill time till the concert starts. We're backstage in Tyler's dressing room. It's a cozy place, nothing over the top. A couple of black leather couches, a few guitars in a special case, and snacks and water bottles on a low table. Killer is leaning on the wall, holding a set of drumsticks in his hand, talking to Max, who keeps bouncing back and forth on his feet.

"Hey." Jay enters the room, saunters over to squeeze Jeremy's shoulder, and then gives me a hug. Easing back, Jay's eyes run over me, approvingly taking in my shocking blue kitten heel slingback, black leather shorts, and a snug graphic tee. I left my hair down to caress my waist, lined my eyes with a thick, black liner, and kept the overall look toned down with a pale pink gloss. Jay shakes his head admiringly than lets out a snort. "Has Ty seen you yet?"

Hardly holding a smirk, I shake my head from side to side. "We got in ten minutes ago."

Jay's smile doesn't waver as he asks if Jeremy or I want a drink.

Heading to get himself one, he shakes his head again, that smile intact.

"I'm going to peep at the crowd. Wanna come with?" I ask Jeremy.

He shrugs his shoulders. "Get wrecked, noob!" he says to my phone's screen, seeming complacent with his achievement.

Following the excited buzz, I pass by the sound engineers waiting at their stations. Taking a few more steps, I peep at the nearly thousand fans waiting for the show. Apparently, a thousand or so people is an intimate event in Tyler's world. Intimate was how he described the concert when he told me about it.

Looking at the last few months retrospectively, it feels like I fell through a rabbit hole into a fantasy world populated by fascinating individuals of a special kind. And as different as it is from what I know, I made a smooth transition. Moreover, I even grew to like it. Not in a groupie-aficionado kind of way, but in an "I truly feel at home" sense. All the credit for making me feel as I do goes to the wonderful people I've been lucky enough to meet. Jeremy, Jay, Killer, Max, Adina, Eli, and Tyler. Tyler. Simply inwardly saying his name makes my stomach feel all warm and fuzzy.

As if the entire crowd read my mind, I hear, "Tyler Lee, Tyler Lee" as sporadic voices coming from the darkened venue gradually morph into a united wave of incarnation. "Tyler Lee, Tyler Lee." A thousand voices become one, calling for him.

Beaming, I make my way backstage, feeling blessed for getting the chance to be a part of this evening. The backstage is bustling with the stage crew, roadies, security guards, and one Eli, walking around giving orders. I follow Eli's back to the dressing room. He pops his head in. "Five minutes, people." He taps a flat palm on the doorframe. "Showtime."

Stepping into the room, my arm accidentally brushes against Tyler's who's heading the opposite direction. He halts, his eyes drop to me, sucking on a hard candy, looking every bit the rock star he is. Breathtaking, intimidating, and impossibly attractive in a black leather jacket over a tight black tee, black jeans tucked into unlaced heavy boots. His hair is knotted at the back of his head, his brown eyes gleaming with buzzing energy. He scratches his beard; the slight lift of his jacket's sleeve reveals Amelie's friendship bracelet, and something about the fact that he kept it on does things to my heart.

Sucking on the hard candy in his mouth, he lets his eyes scan me unhurriedly. When his gaze meets my shirt, they pause. Observing his own face plastered on the front, he lets out a free laugh. Smirking, he sends his thumb to gently graze my cheek, and he walks over to exchange some last words with Eli.

Jeremy and I take position backstage with a direct view to the center of the stage. Veiled by darkness, it's still clear enough to see the setting. Guitars, mics, and a drum set stationed around the stage in preparation. There's a tall stool positioned on the front center side with a mic stand in front. A guitar leans against the high chair, and a water bottle waits below the footrest.

The venue dims to an almost blackout, making the crowd hum with excitement. A beam of light falls on the stool in the otherwise darkened stage, just as Tyler passes by us, heading to take his place. He squeezes Jeremy's shoulder and sends us both a soft smile before following the green arrows on the black floor leading to the bowels of the ample stage.

Tyler takes a seat, one leg bent on the footrest, the other casually on the floor. The audience goes wild. As the first tunes fill the stage, Tyler lifts his head a little. Giving the sea of people a glance, he looks at them from under his lashes. His fans go wild in an escalating hum of excitement. Someone yells, "Tyler Lee, I love you." Tyler's lips curve into an adorable, humble smile. He bows his head and cranes his neck, looking to the side of the stage. For a stretched moment, he steals my breath and heart altogether.

He leans in and grabs the mic, tilting the stand closer to him. With both hands wrapped around the mic, he closes his eyes. His voice funnels the jazzed space, eliciting another wave of roars.

Exhilarated and embraced by the familiar music, I hug Jeremy from behind and whisper in his ear, "It's my favorite song." We lightly sway together, Jeremy and I, listening to Tyler Lee sing an acoustic version of "Unspoken Words."

Tyler leans down, reaching for his guitar. "I left you there that night, together with a part of me," Tyler sings, his fingers deftly on the strings. The fans sing along, forming an overwhelming echo to Tyler's bass-baritone that permeates like smoke. "There are a million reasons why I shouldn't," Tyler closes his eyes, taking the song to a new level. "But none is strong enough. I'll never give you up."

I rest my arms around Jeremy as we both watch Tyler mesmerized, lightly swaying together to the beautiful music when Tyler glances our way. It feels like his flit stare released a heavy weight to fall on my chest.

When the music winds down to whistles and rumbles from the crowd, Tyler grins and lifts a finger in the universal signal for "a moment please" and jogs over to where Jeremy and I are standing backstage.

He crouches a little to align his stare with Jeremy. "That one was for you. I wrote it a long time ago about you."

A spat of emotions saturates my core.

"It was awesome, Da . . . Tyler," Jeremy says, nearly choking me up with feelings.

The smile that spreads across Tyler's face together with the little scene I just witnessed makes my eyes slightly mist over. Tyler straightens to stand, and for a brief moment, his eyes run between mine. He sends his hand to cup my cheek, locking our stare.

"Love the shirt on you." He grins wholeheartedly and jogs back to his fans. Leaving my heart thudding a lot harder.

During the short pause, the band members took their places, and the high chair was removed from the stage. A new tune comes to life when Tyler takes his place at the center of the stage. He releases the mic from the stand, adjusting his earpiece. Taking the lead, Killer, on the drums, and Max, features tight with concentration as he plays the guitar, ignite the crowd with an energetic piece. The fans sitting on chairs jump to their feet. Countless high-speed lights move across the stage in sync with the music. "Let's bring it home," Tyler says, sending the entire venue into a frenzy. And thus begins the upbeat part of the evening.

It's an hour and a half of pure, mesmerizing performance by Tyler and his band. Sensual, energized, and overpowering. Tyler's fans go wild each time he teases them with his moves or when he takes his jacket off and sends them a flirty, sexy side smile or on a random "Now, me and you" and "Sing with me, baby."

But no one is crushing harder or deeper than I am. Each time he sends a look or a smile backstage directed at me, I need to remind myself over and over that this is him. This is what he does. He's a performer, programmed to make girls fall at his feet. This is his entire existence.

This is him just being . . . him.

Yet, me being me, I can't resist the immense pull and keep on free falling, falling, falling.

The crowd keeps chanting Tyler's name long after the lights are out and Tyler's back in his dressing room.

Jeremy pulls my hand. "Let's go hang with Tyler."

I let him drag me after him as I don't think I stand a chance; the kid's more than determined.

Tyler is sitting on one of the couches, gulping down coconut water as we enter the dressing room. His face glistens with perspiration, his hair is damp, and some of the darker strands cling to the sides of his face. On the table next to him is another empty bottle of coconut water. Tipping his head up as he inhales the bottle in his hand, his eyes welcome us.

"Wow, that, that was so awesome!" Jeremy hardly contains his excitement.

Tyler's lips that are attached to the bottle twitch a little.

"Thanks, kid." Tyler puts the empty bottle down, reaching for a towel on the table and towels his sweaty face.

"It was crazy! Your fans went crazy. Sweet!" Jeremy continues pouring out his exhilaration.

Tyler grins then unexpectedly peels his shirt off and shrugs on a gray thermal. For that moment his body is exposed, I swallow hard.

"Did you know that when you sing small vibrations go through you and can affect your mood? It gives you a high. It releases hormones that bring the feeling of pleasure." Jeremy starts a mini-Jeremy lecture.

Tyler and I exchange an animated stare. The light atmosphere is cut when Eli enters the room, the planes of his face tight. Tyler stands up to meet him. He draws up to Tyler and tells him something in a hushed yet hard tone. Tyler bites his cheek, a frown settling above his nose. He folds his arms over his toned chest.

"How did we let it happen?" he asks. "I thought my instructions were clear."

Eli keeps talking.

"I see," Tyler says solemnly. He unfolds his arm. "Hey Jer, Eli is going to take you to meet someone. I need to talk to Ivi, okay?"

Given Eli's tense air, and the brief, serious exchange, I tense a little.

"Close the door," Tyler tells Eli as they leave the room.

"Everything okay?" I ask, taking a couple of steps closer to Tyler.

"Nothing too serious, but" — he inhales — "somehow, a reporter managed to get backstage. I'm not sure how. Usually, I don't have any issues with it, but I don't want anyone digging around and finding out about Jeremy." He sighs again. "I know I can do only so much to prevent it from leaking to the press, but I'm trying to delay it for as long as I can. I don't want the kid's life to change into crazy zone just because of me."

I nod.

"So Eli has Ben, one of my bodyguards, waiting to take you guys home from a back entrance."

"Of course," I say. "I'll just tell Jeremy that we need to go home because it's a school night, and he's way past his bedtime."

Tyler's eyes hover over me as I talk. He sends his hand to the hem of my shirt that ends above just shy of my navel. He lightly tugs on it with a boyish smile. Accidentally, or not, his knuckles brush my skin, setting it on fire at contact. "Thanks for taking such good care of him. I don't know what I would've done without you."

"It's my absolute pleasure," I say, drowning in his dark, molten stare. "I'm more than a little in love with your boy." I shrug. And then I let out a small gasp when Tyler's fingers slowly and *deliberately* caress the slice of exposed skin between my shirt and shorts. Silence, it's only our gazes and his fingers on me.

At the sound of the door opening, we both pull back with a start. In unison, our stares arrow to where the one and only Brooklyn Mars materializes in all her platinum blond, dark flirtatious eyes, and trademark blood-red lipstick glory. She raises an eyebrow at the both of us, and from then on, everything moves forward like a fast-paced movie. I tell them good-bye, walk out, and say hello to Ben, the bodyguard. When we get home, I make sure Jeremy brushes his teeth, and then he goes directly to sleep.

I fall on my bed, and all I can think about is Tyler spending the rest of the evening with the beautiful and talented Brooklyn Mars.

After all, birds of a feather fornicate together, right?

CHAPTER

Seventeen

"Something is happening there; I'm telling you. That sparkle in his eyes. I've
never seen Tyler so . . . joyous."
"It's his son."
"It's more than that, much more. Hmm, bless his heart, the way he looks at
her."
"It's the last thing he needs. It's ridiculous. She'll never fit in."
"You're in charge of his business affairs; his private life is NONE OF YOUR
BUSINESS."
"His well-being is my business."
"Don't you dare go meddling, Eli Reuben Cohen!"
A hushed conversation between Eli and his aunt, Adina, over tea and banana
bread in the back kitchen.

Jeremy and I hold a tense stare down, both stubbornly unblinking.
He nods at me in *The Godfather* fashion, raising his Nerf gun intently.

Securing my sarong around my bikini bottom-clad hips, I say,
"You can run, but you can't hide." I make a whole production of
looking badass. Narrowed eyes and a clenched jaw complete with a
slight tip of my chin.

Gun in one hand, Jeremy walks backward, eyes pointed at me.
"Count to twenty," he commands, eyeing me as he makes his way out

of the indoor swimming pool room. Jeremy brings his other hand to hold the barrel and sprints into the hall while calling over his shoulder, "You're so going down!"

"Careful, you'll slip, your feet are still w—" *Wet*. I call after him, to no avail. Kid's probably already in an ambush, waiting to slaughter me. *Fee-fi-fo-fum, I smell the blood of a brainy-brat*, I sing, amusing myself while loading the ammo. I adjust my bikini top, making sure the girls will remain safely covered during combat. Gun pointed ahead, I go look for Jeremy.

I take soft steps, peeping into rooms, alcoves, behind the grandfather clock, anywhere the kid might be lying in wait. With my back to the wall, I slowly turn into the extensive main hall leading to the living area. To the sound of foot shuffling, I halt with my gun pointed forward, waiting.

A sparking wave washes over me to the sight of Tyler rounding the corner a few steps ahead, clad in nothing but a pair of snug boxers. The muscles in his back flex as he walks in harmony to the light sway of his rear. Licking my lips, I catalog every piece of his perfectly shaped body and the complementing tattoos.

Sighing in appreciation at the sight bestowed upon me, I bring the gun higher, highly amusing myself as I aim the barrel at his toned butt. Mimicking a shot, I bring the gun's mouth to my lips and blow on it. Grinning to myself, I take a few more silent steps and aim the gun at his advancing rear again. I wink one eye, my finger ghosting on the trigger. As I inwardly snicker and whisper "kaboom" my finger slips a little and pulls the trigger a tad harder than intended.

Shoot! No, no, no.

Horrified, I watch as the foam missile shoots out in the direction of my boss's ass. Holding my breath, I pray to all possible powers to be that it won't hit the target. My eyes grow bigger, and a shriek flies out of my mouth the moment the foam bullet lands smack dab in the middle of Tyler's left, perfect, butt cheek.

Adding insult to injury, when Tyler spins around, the gun is still frozen in my hand, aimed at where his glorious behind was just a second ago. I bite my lip, searching my mind for something intelligent to say in light of the obvious assault as Tyler watches me with bunched eyebrows above narrowed eyes.

He licks his bottom lip, running his eyes over my scantily clad body and back to the gun in my hand. Eyes zoomed in on me, Tyler bends a little, sending his hand to the bullet and grasps it between two fingers. Holding the bullet on display in his open palm as though exhibiting evidence, he takes three steps to reach me.

I tilt the gun a bit higher, and without much thought, murmur, "The sight on these little suckers is darn accurate."

For a millisecond, before bursting into a guffaw, Tyler's lips crook up so adorably. I melt a little inside. "Let me get this straight," he says with a chuckle. He gives me back the incriminating ammo. "You've just confessed to deliberately shooting my ass?"

Swallowing over the little pool under my tongue that's caused mainly by his perfect naked proximity and partly by mortification, I croak, "Um, I was just target practicing . . . That kid of yours is some vicious opponent."

Tyler's amusement softens every single feature on his face as he watches me squirm under his gaze. And then, without warning or so much as a mother-loving blink, his toned arm snakes around my waist, effortlessly scooping me up. In a tight grip, he presses me to his chest, the skin of his arm deliciously pressed against my belly. I'm flailing in the air, huddled to his side as Tyler shouts, "*Jeremy.*"

"That's not fair," I protest, airborne.

"Indeed not." Tyler chuckles next to my ear, the sound tickling all the way down my body, and calls for Jeremy again. "Jer, come over here, I've got a little something for you."

Carrying me in one arm, Tyler starts toward the living room. Fun and giggles aside, being pressed against his body does things to me. Wonderful, wonderful things. I'd let Jeremy shoot me seven ways to Sunday, with a nail gun, if it meant being held as close to a nearly naked Tyler as one can get. The hard planes of his body, his intoxicating scent warmly hovering around my nose, and the scrape of his beard on my temple feels startlingly delicious.

Alas, though, I don't get to luxuriate in the moment as long as I please. What with the battle cry announcing an exhilarated Jeremy is headed our way. The kid is one huge grin when he notices my helpless condition.

Spinning the gun around his finger a couple of times, eyes shining behind blue-rimmed glasses, Jeremy exclaims, "Booyah!" And the artillery commences. "Boom, head shot!" After emptying his gun on me, Jeremy grins at Tyler who meets him for an elated fist bump that ends with the kid screeching, "Booyah!" once more.

And the most ridiculous part? All that's happening, is happening with me still pressed against Tyler like a weightless rag doll.

"What you two grinning about?" I feign a frown at Tyler and his offspring as he finally sets me down. He squeezes my waist, giving me a half-smile. "I call for a rematch!" I narrow my eyes at the elated kid. "Let's see you win without help from your henchman, shall we?" I try to hold a straight face, but that darn Tyler Lee Adams' smile . . .

"Oh babycakes, look at you prancing around in your little undies. Cute," Jay's comment precedes him. He walks over, smirking at Tyler.

Tyler bats his lashes at Jay a few times. "All for you, schnookums. All for you." His middle finger rises up against his cheek in a covert "scratching" motion. The gesture's true nature doesn't escape me.

I stifle a giggle.

"What's up with the weapons, Bloody Benders?" Jay asks next, tipping his chin at the guns in my and Jeremy's hands.

Smartass kid smirks in response. "Ivi just got her hiney handed to her."

I shake my head. "Yeah, it takes a real hero to win with Daddy's help."

"Whiner." The little brat coughs the word into his little hand while the father person chuckles too proudly for my liking.

"I was just calling for a rematch," I tell Jay, overtly disregarding Jeremy and Tyler. "These two don't play fair."

Grinning, Jay jerks his shoulders, shrugging his tweed blazer off. Folding his jacket on his forearm, he brings his other hand forward. "Where's my weapon, kid?" Next, "Ivi, you on my team?"

I open my mouth to answer, but Tyler's quick draw leaves me with my mouth slightly agape and my happy slightly boosted.

"Ivi's with me."

Jay raises a jeering eyebrow but keeps his lips amusingly pursed.

Jeremy, too excited to catch on to the underlying exchange, runs en route to his room for extra artilleries.

Less than a moment and a half later, we each load our guns while Jeremy says, his breath still a tad labored, "Since Ivi is the weakest link, we'll give you guys a head start, count to ten." On cue, Tyler and Jay's lips twitch. I give Jeremy the stink eye, which only prompts him to add, "Okay twenty, off you go." The little brat has the audacity to add a little dismissing hand gesture, motioning for us to get going.

I aim my gun at his shoulder from the closest range and pull the trigger.

"Ouch." Jeremy rubs the place with utterly forced drama.

Shaking his head in amusement, Tyler grabs my hand and tugs me after him. We make our way toward the main door in silence. The fact that he never lets go of my hand burns in my recognition. Ready to follow him in the direction of the patio, I find myself a little confused when he opens the mudroom closet louvered doors and leads me inside.

I clear my throat, looking at Tyler. "Aren't we going to . . ."

He turns to face me, his wide shoulders barely fitting in the confined space. The curl of his lashes gleams by the soft light funneling through the slightly agape blinds. His lip twitches at the side. "Nah, let them run in circles for a while."

I let out a dainty titter, very aware of his closeness, and the warmth his bare torso radiates to my exposed skin.

Tyler begins to say something, but the sound of steps followed by Jeremy shushing Jay and then a whispered, "This way," makes me dart my hand to cover his mouth.

Tyler's surprised stare meets my eyes while his hand travels up to cover mine. I expect him to remove my hand that's covering his lips, but he stays still, leaving it palpable and warm on mine. Under our joined hands, his lips part a little, supplely caressing my skin.

I return his gaze, and my breath gets trapped somewhere near my heart as a notion sinks in. All the times we've been together alone since the alleged magical kiss happened set in my mind like moving images, creating a film that pushes my heart higher up my throat. The notion crystalizes, each time we were together, Tyler somehow had touched me. Not in an intent, suggesting way but as though he couldn't stop himself. As though, just like me, he couldn't keep a lid on restraint. Couldn't resist the pull. I wet my lip, drawn into the intensity of his eyes on me. I whisper, "That kiss. . . the other night . . . really happened?"

He presses his lips to my hand and gently lowers it to rest on his chest. With his hand covering mine, he nods a confirmation.

My voice comes out so soft, I'm not even sure if I said it out loud. "It felt surreal. It was perfect."

Holding our eye lock, Tyler leans in a bit closer. The soft rays of light coming through the blinds enlighten his handsome features. His eyes, his sharp cheekbones, the line of his square jaw under his beard, his full lips. His body tilts a little closer. And closer. His voice is a rough whisper when he says, "So this thing flows both ways?"

His question hangs heavy yet promising between us. Like a warm blanket around me. Against every possible warning bell hollering in my head, my lips part, about to confirm, about to confess, about to tell him I'm more than halfway crushing on him.

But the words never leave my mouth.

Instead, we both jerk back as light blinds our pupils when the doors jolt open to Jeremy and Jay's pointed barrels and wicked smiles.

"Booyah!"

CHAPTER
Eighteen

"An attitude of gratitude brings great things."
Yoga instructor quoting Yogi Bhajan at the end of an introductory Kundalini
Yoga lesson Ivi tried out earlier this morning. (Never to be repeated due to
unbearable boredom and a sore buttock.)

Be that as it may, regret, confusion, avoidance, the greater forces that be, or simply . . . life, a whole week passes till I get to see Tyler again after what had almost happened in the darkened closet. A week in which I tried not to read too much into the slowly burning anxiety in the pit of my stomach over how things will play out the next time we're face to face. And the greatest uncertainty of them all—are we ever going to continue *that* conversation? Six simple words have been resonating in my head like a slowly maddening chant ever since. *"So this thing flows both ways?"*

"Ivi, darling, why don't you go get ready?" Adina asks, bringing my relentless thoughts to a screeching halt.

I put another bowl in the dishwasher, raising my eyes to her.

"I'll finish up here. You go on, get ready," she encourages with a motherly smile.

I wipe my hands on a dishtowel and nod. "If you need anything else, holler."

Adina's easy smile expands. "Thank you for helping, darling."

I pop my head in Jeremy's room on the way to mine. "Jer, time to get ready."

Jeremy's brows bunch, his eyes glued to a tablet. "I am ready," he says to the screen.

"Jeremy, you're in pajamas!"

He drops his eyes to validate the claim. "Oh." The kid seems actually surprised at the revelation. Getting up, he heads to the bathroom, tablet in hand.

Three doors down the hall, I lay my outfit on the bed. A short, bottle green plaid skirt with a thin, cream cashmere sweater, knee-high crochet socks, and heeled ballerina pumps. Pleased with the ensemble, I turn to the bathroom to get ready for my first ever Thanksgiving dinner. I will see Tyler today.

———————◆———————

"Did you know that turkeys can have heart attacks?" Jeremy mutters, eyeing the huge roasted bird Adina places in the center of the dining table.

Max's brows almost meet his hairline. "Really, dude?" Fascination brims his voice.

Jeremy's ever-present, boyish, know-it-all smile widens as he turns to Max. "An Air Force study exposed farm animals to sonic booms, and they found out that turkeys fell dead on the fields!" Jeremy's eyes light up. "Booyah! Sonic booms give turkeys heart attacks!"

"Poor birds, may their little feathery souls rest in peace," I murmur, adding the final dishes to the plethora of goods on the long table.

"That's dope." Max boosts the kid's high spirit.

Both Adina and I shake our heads as we walk back to the kitchen, leaving Eli, Max, Jay, Jeremy, and Killer and his girlfriend to watch the parade on TV. I wash my hands while Adina gets her things before leaving for her own family's dinner.

"I hope you enjoy your first Thanksgiving dinner," Adina says, giving me a warm hug.

My heart takes a plunge upward as greeting sounds mixed with Tyler's voice waft into the kitchen. "Thank you. Happy Thanksgiving." I return her embrace, schooling my voice to remain unaffected by the thrill knotting my stomach.

"Oh, you're still here, good. Glad I caught you before you left," Tyler declares, entering the room. His voice alone augments the buzz in me.

Disengaging from our embrace, Adina turns to Tyler. Tyler takes a couple of steps to reach her. He squints my way as he sends his hand to his back pocket. With a thin, genuine smile, he offers Adina a white envelope. "Happy Thanksgiving."

She returns his smile with sentimental eyes. "Oh, Tyler dear, you shouldn't have."

In lieu of an answer, Tyler wraps his arm around her shoulder. "Say hi to that pretty granddaughter of yours for me."

Adina shakes her head fondly. "Thank you."

"Ready to go?" Eli emerges out of nowhere.

Adina grabs her bowler handbag and a coat. "Sure."

"If you need anything . . ." Eli turns to Tyler, waiting for his aunt to get ready.

Tyler raises his hand to stop Eli, his lips twitching at the corner. "Enjoy the evening with your family." He brings a long finger to his heart and draws a cross, his smile a display of mischief. "I promise to try to stay out of trouble."

Eli's hard features melt a degree. "I'll have my phone with me at all times if you need anything."

Unexpectedly, Tyler's arm winds around my shoulder, causing my next breath to catch in my throat. "Ivi here will keep an eye on me.

Right?" He winks at me.

I flush a little, noticing Eli's astute gaze on me, and Adina's strangely secretive smirk. Tyler squeezes me against him, and we both give Adina and Eli exaggerated, saintly smiles before they leave.

Expecting Tyler to release me next, I move my foot in an attempt to take a step back. He doesn't, and the action shifts my torso to lean deeper into him. Taking advantage of my position, Tyler turns me into a tight, frontal hug. "Happy Thanksgiving," he says to my hair. The hug outlasts my next few wild heartbeats.

Wordlessly, Tyler releases me, and we make our way to join the others. A podcast I've listened to enters my mildly Tyler-stunned mind. "Can something really exist without being perceived?" was the topic of said podcast. Or something along that line. It didn't really hold my attention at the time, yet something a guest professor had said stuck with me. With the warmth, scent, and feel of Tyler's embrace resonating on my skin and within my insides, the professor's words come back as an enlightenment. "To a blind man, things don't exist until he touches them, feels them." Something about the way Tyler just enveloped me in his arms made the constant current in me . . . perceptible. That embrace wasn't powered by any holiday spirit. And sure as heck, it didn't hold any platonic intentions. Not to mention the lungful he took while his lips nuzzled in my hair. That hug changed something in me, something that now allows me to wish for . . . a little more.

I take the vacant seat next to Jay, still high on that hug, while Tyler takes the one across the table by Jeremy's side. A sitting arrangement that "forces" us to have a direct view of one another. Something that we both seem to exhaustively exploit throughout dinner.

"So, Mary P., it's your first Thanksgiving, eh?" Max says, making me break yet another eye lock with my boss.

I smile at Max.

My smile turns into a query when he asks, "Are you ready for later?"

My intrigue deepens to the way he wriggles his pierced eyebrows suggestively. A thin, confused smile settles on my lips before I answer his question. "I'm not sure what exactly is planned for later, but I'll be washing dishes down at the Union Station over in San Bernardino."

"Why?" The question comes from Jeremy.

"I wanted to help with the Thanksgiving dinner over there and still be here for ours, so helping out with the cleanup was the solution to juggling both."

"It's for the homeless, right? Can I come with?"

I turn to Tyler, slightly thrown back by the look he has on me. "Do you—" I clear my throat, willing my voice to steady. "Do you mind?"

Tyler, as though shaken out of deep meditation, wrinkles his brows. "Sure, why not. Yeah."

"Can't you stay a little longer? You should!" Max claims my attention again. He grins with a suggestive head bob. "Whenever mini-Ty hits the sack, shit gets real."

Everyone turns to him.

"What's happening after Jeremy goes to sleep?" I ask.

Max's face shines as he leans back in his chair, steepling his fingers. I can't help my smile, what with the mischievous expression on his face and his attire. Only Max can pull off a white tuxedo jacket, board shorts, and a tattered graphic Smurfs tee. "Sit back and listen, Mary P." His crooked smile grows. "The bunnies and colored eggs are a cover-up. Thanksgiving is, in fact, an adults' holiday." He winks at me, more than pleased with himself. "Imagine the real festivities with the real bunnies and real eggs, and if you are into kinky shit, you can even be tied to a cross."

Killer frowns. "How many did you have to drink?"

"Someone shove a turkey leg down his throat." Tyler's humored voice and headshake prevent Max from spewing further nonsense. "So much talent, so little in the head. What a shame."

"Wrong holiday, dude," Jay says with a chuckle.

"Why would Ivi want to be tied to a cross?" Jeremy's expression is adorably baffled.

Sounds of chuckles accompanied by snorts roll around the table. My cheeks warm a little.

When Max opens his mouth to answer Jeremy's question, Tyler's hand comes in contact with the back of his head.

Max rubs his head. "What was that for?"

"So, Jer, did you put together that list your friends asked you to make?" I say the first thing that jumps to my mind to prevent any further discussion involving me and my bondage of preference.

Jeremy's cheeks tinge now that everyone's attention shifts to him. *Sorry, kid.* It's the people you love the most who sometimes end up under the bus.

"What list?" Tyler asks his son.

Jeremy gives me the stink eye, which, if we're being honest, I totally deserve. "The girls in our class asked the boys to make a list of the top three girls we like." He rolls his eyes as if saying: girls . . .

Max perks up. "Oh, everyone's got one of those lists. The top three celebrities they'd want to lay down and slow bon—" To my glare, he adds, "Get to know." He tips his chin at Jay. "Who's on your list, dude?"

Jay takes a drink from his glass. "There's only one for me. Only one. The legendary goddess, Kate Winslet."

"Didn't know you were into older women, Jay. Fancy that." I smirk.

Jay pats my head as if I were a toddler. "Not just any older woman, young Ivi. Just Kate. And she's definitely not old. She's perfectly and gloriously ripe."

"Who's on your list, Sir Adams?" Max's raised eyebrow is directed at Tyler.

Tyler shakes his head, a shadow of a cocky smile veiling his lips. He takes a sip of his drink, ignoring Max's waiting expression.

Killer lets out a rumbling chuckle. "You're talking to Tyler Lee fucking Adams, man. He doesn't need a list. *He is the list.* He's like the fucking benchmark for any list out there."

Tyler's lips twitch, his attention turned to the food on his plate.

"Two smackeroos to the jar." I send a feigned scowl Killer's way, which is followed by a snicker coming from Jeremy's side.

Killer shrugs with a smile.

"Mary P.?" Max says.

"Yes?"

A wicked glee adorns his eyes. "Who's on your list? Please say it's me."

I dart for my glass, taking a generous sip in an attempt to let the attention move on to some other sucker. I choke a little on my hastily inhaled drink, which, of course, does the very opposite. Everyone is looking at me now.

"Well?" Max insists.

My stupid cheeks take the liberty of warming up. "Jimmy Fallon," I blurt. Tyler's stare hones in on me. "He's cute in a dorky, handsome sort of way." Tyler's unnerving gaze makes my lips continue to vomit unnecessary information. "I love it when people make fun of themselves."

"Just one person?" Jeremy probes this time.

"Two," I murmur absently. Wincing at my little gaffe, I ask Jay to pass the salad, forcing my eyes not to meet Tyler's.

"Who's lucky number two then?" Tyler asks casually, a beer bottle tilted toward his lips.

I bring my eyes up to his. Big mistake. This time the heat reaches everywhere. My face, my ears, my neck. Everything's on fire.

Noticing my discomfort and clearly reading what I'm never going to let out of my mouth, Tyler's lips stretch into a smile around the bottle's mouth.

It seems like understanding also dawns on Jay from beside me. Being the awesome person and friend that he is, he turns to Max. "Well, who's on your list, man?" Letting me off the hook.

Instantly, Max becomes the focus of attention, reciting a long and eccentric list of actresses and singers. Relieved, I chance a glance Tyler's way. A cloud of heat explodes in my belly, its emission coursing to every part of me, to the heat in his eyes, and to that sexy smile slowly stretching his lips.

That's the last time I dare to look at him. And I mostly succeed in policing myself to avoid him until I have to change into casual attire for my late evening volunteering at Union Station.

I slip my feet into my Chucks and tie my hair up. Throwing on a red hoodie, I grab my keys and switch off the light. My hand is on the handle of my bedroom door, about to close it, when I yelp.

Tyler sends a hand to my shoulder. "Hey, I didn't mean to scare you."

I mumble something about not expecting him here when all I can think of is his hand clutched around my shoulder and the fact that it's only the two of us up here on the second floor while everyone else is a flight of stairs away.

"I'll drive you guys there," he says, retrieving his hand from my shoulder.

"No need, you have guests, we can—"

He shakes his head. "Ivi, I'm taking you."

"Really, you don't have to—" This time, it's not his words that silence me. This time, it's the way he leans closer. It's his hand making its way toward my neck that makes me freeze.

Instinctively, unconsciously, I mirror him, slightly stretching on my tiptoes, leaning toward him. With my lips a few inches from his beard-rimmed chin and my torso hovering next to his, two things happen at once. He gently pulls on my ponytail while saying, "You look cute," and I realize he wasn't about to kiss me. He's just tugging on my hair while giving me a compliment. Of the brotherly variety. Embarrassment takes over, ordering my lips to close and my eyes to snap out of the dreamy haze. Alas, though, it happens a moment too late.

When the realization of what I thought was happening sinks into Tyler's recognition, something in his stare on me alters, coloring them with a darker shade. His hand that just a moment ago tugged on my hair briskly moves to cradle the nape of my neck. Just seconds later, he pushes me back against the door. The wooden plank absorbs my collision. Tyler's lips crashing into mine steal my next breath. My wide-open eyes flutter closed to the feel of his lips, to the delicious feeling of his mass on me. It feels like I'm being wrapped in him. In his firmness. His warmness. His perfect scent. A whimper leaves my lips when his tongue touches mine. The fact that he is my boss, the fact that he is Tyler Lee Adams, the fact that there are people a floor below all vanish from my mind as I melt deeper and deeper into the heady sensation. I feel like I'm free falling into an abyss of euphoria. It has never felt as electrifying. As sensational. As perfect.

In an overpowering pull toward one another, we draw closer. My breasts mesh with the hard planes of his carved torso, his thigh wedged between mine, making our bodies perfectly connect in a human puzzle. He threads his fingers through my hair, pushing my mouth to meld with his. His other hand moves to my cheek, holding me firmly for his tongue to reach, taste, every depth of my mouth. I bring my hand to his waist. Hesitantly at first, I feel my way under his loose shirt. When the tips of my fingers encounter his smooth, warm skin, they grow independent and confident, exploring, caressing. A low growl rolls from his mouth into mine as he deepens our kiss.

Long enchanting moments into our passionate kissing, Jay's voice penetrates our sizzling bubble. "Yo, Snuggle Muffin, game's about to start."

"Fuck . . ." Tyler breaks the kiss, his breath labored. He leans back, moving his hands to either side of my shoulders, supporting himself against the wall. Dropping his head, he closes his eyes and takes a deep breath.

I watch him, my lips pulsing as I try to level my own breathing. Try to regulate my overwhelmed thoughts.

Tyler lifts his eyes to me, looking as disoriented as I must appear. His voice comes out rough and low as he says, "We need to get back."

I nod, not sure what to say or do. Not even sure I'd be able to properly walk down the stairs. I let out a muddled sigh, gesturing with my thumb at the door. "I'll, eh, freshen up."

His sinful smile makes an appearance. "Why?" and then, "You look good like that." He smirks at me and walks off. "Yo, Boo Bear, coming," I hear him call out to Jay before I lock myself in the bathroom.

Tyler's words keep playing in my head as I observe myself in the mirror. *You look good like that.* My lips are pink and swollen, my hair looks like it participated in a violent revolt against the hair tie, and my eyes . . . God, my eyes. I bet this is how they'd look if I ever got high. They look heavy and gleaming but more than that, they look satiated. I splash cold water on my face twice. Burying my face in a towel to dry off, I feel a realization drop on me. *Tyler just kissed the heck out of me.* This brings along a slew of questions that I can't even begin to answer.

With powers mysterious even to me, I somehow manage to put one foot in front of the other and make it to the first floor without toppling over. What's more, I succeed in playing it cool standing before everyone, including the person who just gave me a kissgasm.

"Jer, we should get going," I tell Jeremy, who's in the middle of a heated discussion with Jay over computer games versus sports. The kid should be on the debate team. Heck, he should run for office.

Tyler, who has his eyes trained on me, rises to stand, fisting his key fob. "Let's go."

"We can drop them off. It's on our way," says Sophia, Killer's girlfriend. Killer nods, towering above her. They look like The Thing and Thumbelina standing next to each other.

Tyler's stare meets mine. He tilts his head sideways as though asking me if that's okay. I nod, a tad overwhelmed by the nature of his expression. It's as if the subtext of his stare says: "I want to continue what we started upstairs."

On the ride, try as I may, I can't stay tuned to the conversation around me. My thoughts keep wandering to what happened merely half an hour ago. The way Tyler's lips felt on mine fades away each and every kiss I've had before tonight like waves washing away messages in the sand. Every time I see his face in my mind, I feel the intensity his eyes held. Conjuring the feeling of his beard against my skin, his full lips, pressing, touching, and tasting mine causes yet another kiss from my list of kisses to fade away. The way I felt in his arms — being pressed against him, kissed by him — wipes out every other name and leaves only one. In dark, bold calligraphy.

Tyler.

Because nothing can ever be as terrifying, sensual, and incredible at the same time. Nothing can be as perfect.

Nineteen

CHAPTER

"Hommik on õhtust targem." An Estonian proverb, frequently used by Ivi's grandma.

Morning is wiser than the evening. In other words, sleep on it.

"Jer, you okay?" I study Jeremy's strained expression as we sit on the patio. "Are you feeling well?"

He drops the pencil in his hand to the open notebook. Biting on his cheek, he disappears inside his head for some pensive seconds. He lifts troubled eyes to me. "Did you know that people can feel real ache and pain when they are depressed? And tiredness. And sometimes, they even lose their appetite."

"It's about your homework?" I ask, lifting my sunglasses up on my head.

His stare wanders toward the pool. "I try not to think about it too much. And I-I'm having a great time here. And Tyler, Tyler is cool. And you and Jay—"

"What are you trying to say, Jer?" I drop my feet from the chair in front of me, scooting closer to him.

Swallowing, he turns to me. "I miss my mom. Really miss her."

My heart compresses as I choose my next words. "That's only

natural. And it's okay to think about your mom and miss her. I miss mine too, a lot." Jeremy gives me a frail smile, remaining uncharacteristically silent. "You'll be seeing her soon. Only about a month and a half to go." I squeeze his hand. "You know, in my family, we start working on our Christmas wish list more than two weeks before Christmas. That way we have enough time to change or add things. It's like a mini-happy project."

Jeremy's smile reappears. "It's fifteen days until Christmas."

"The perfect time to start working on your wish list." I return his grin, glad to see my sad-topic diversion has worked.

"Um, maybe taking a trip beyond Earth's atmosphere is a bit too much to ask for. How about keeping that one for your birthday?" I tell Jeremy half an hour later, suggesting he might want to cross off item number eleven from his list.

He sighs. "Crossing off space tourism." Biting on the pencil in concentration, he runs his eyes over his quickly growing list. "Oh, I know, an MLG sweatshirt."

"What's MLG?" I ask, glancing at my hollering phone.

"Major League Gaming." He grins.

"Of course, it is," I say before answering Jay's call.

"I don't think I can," I tell Jay when he asks me to hang out with him at his place tonight. "It's Adina's afternoon off, and I'm not sure if Tyler will be home. Why don't you come over instead?"

———◆———

"So, Curry Beef, Ma-Po Tofu, and how many fried rice was it?" I ask Jay, who's untying his shoes and getting comfortable on the sofa.

Pointing the remote at the TV, he says, "Make it three. Oh, and get the Kung Pao chicken and shrimp for Ty."

The mention of Tyler's name and the fact that he'll be joining us for dinner makes me pause with the phone in my hand. Ever since

The Kiss, I've been in some kind of what-in-the-actual-heck limbo concerning Tyler. It's been two weeks since he kissed me silly. Two weeks and *nothing*. Zero. Nada. Besides the way he looks at me like his stare sees past my pretend calm, reaching right to my accelerated pulse that proves me a liar. Despite this, it has been nothing but polite, dull conversation between us. Besides hanging with Jeremy and sometimes his entourage, Tyler had either been out or locked up in his studio. Not to mention, our nightly TV watching on the couch had abruptly ended. Actions and facts that, in a way, brought me to my senses, and to finally read the obvious writing on the wall. The facts I've been trying to avoid ever since he asked me if whatever it is that's going on between us was mutual. The very clear message in cheerfully colored graffiti reads:

No, really, girl?

What's next? Tyler Lee Adams will ask you to be his girlfriend, hold your hand everywhere you go, and dedicate his songs to you?

Do yourself a favor, silly girl, and stop deluding yourself.

I shake my head clear of degrading thoughts and turn to Jay. "What are we watching?"

"Tonight, young Ivi, after everything you've done for little Jeremy, it's about educating you. We're watching *Trailer Park Boys*." Jay nods in elation, propping his legs on the coffee table.

Placing my water bottle on the table, I slouch back on the sofa. "Doesn't sound familiar."

Jay shakes his head from side to side as though disappointed in me. "It's a legendary Canadian comedy about three ex-convicts who live in a trailer park."

I beam at him. "Sounds right up my alley."

To the sounds of heavy footsteps, both Jay and I look over at Tyler as he enters the room. I feel like my heart tries to give the heavy timbre a run for its money.

"Poopsie Bear," Tyler says flatly, tipping his chin at Jay in greeting.

"Missed your cute, little smile, Pork Chop," Jay counters.

Looking my way, Tyler nods again, his jaw set.

Needing a little breather before a night with Tyler and actually needing to use the toilet, I excuse myself. "Be back soon." I point toward the guest bathroom.

"You rock a piss, I'm going to rock some Mitchell," Jay says, a statement that's followed by chuckles from both men.

"What?" I ask, already heading en route to the toilet.

"*Trailer Park Boys*." Jay points at the screen, which is paused on the opening credits of the alleged legendary show. "Gold." He bobs his head.

It takes me a while to get into the show, but once I get the hang of it, I can't stop laughing. Tyler and Jay repeating key gems just adds to the overall experience.

"I'll get it." Jay pauses the TV to the buzzing coming from the intercom. He fetches his wallet and leaves the room.

His absence immediately fills the room with tension.

A throw pillow is all that separates us on the sofa, but somehow, it feels like there's a wall between Tyler and me. Made out of ice. I chance a glance Tyler's way, only to find him looking at me intensely.

"You've been busy," I say. It's the first thing that comes to my mind, opting to break the unnerving vibe.

He nods slowly then scratches his beard. "Listen, Ivi, whatever happened between us on Thanksgiving." A frown settles between his brows, and he lets out a bothered sigh. "Some things are just not worth the trouble."

My eyes widen in tandem to the parting of my lips. What does that mean? I'm not worth the trouble? I feel like I don't have the context to understand what he's saying, and the one I'm conjuring . . . For a beat, before he speaks again, I'm actually offended. The reminder of the ass he can sometimes be comes marching in.

"Ivi, I didn't." He sighs again, uncomfortable. Closing his eyes, he presses his fingers against either side of his temples. "I'm trying to do the right thing here." His brown eyes open to mine, captivating and distressed.

"What do you mea—" My question is cut off by Jay's return.

Jay strolls back into the room with a large brown paper bag in his hand. Jay's perceptive eyes run between Tyler and me. "I'm going to get some plates."

"No." Tyler rises to stand. "I'm getting them." Hammering the thin nail he just stabbed into my heart a little deeper.

Placing the food on the table, Jay asks, "What did I miss? What's going on?"

I shake my head with the phoniest of smiles. "Where's my tofu?"

Peeking over his shoulder, Jay turns back to me. "I'm not buying this smile. What just happened, Ivi?"

"Jay please, drop it." He takes a deep inhale, gazing at me, assessing. "Please?" I add as the patter of Tyler's steps sounds closer.

With a frown, Jay lets it go. Tyler settles himself in an armchair, and we dig in with the show back on.

I bring a chunk of tofu squeezed between two chopsticks to my lips. "God, that's greasy."

"Sometimes, life is greasy, Bubbles." Tyler grins at me. It's another quote from the show that elicits healthy chuckles from my companions, and at the same time brings back the casual atmosphere Tyler managed to kill with two inscrutable yet upsetting statements a hilarious scene ago.

The laughter and constant banter between Jay and Tyler die, at least for me, more than half an hour later when Tyler's phone hollers and vibrates on the table with a goofy photo of Brooklyn Mars sticking her tongue out across the screen.

Watching Tyler leave the room to take the call, Jay pivots my way. "What happened earlier?"

My lips part on their own accord and, "Is Brooklyn his girlfriend?" spills out.

"No." Jay's answer couldn't be more adamant. And maybe even a little pissed. "Ivi, what happened earlier between Tyler and you? Why did you look so upset?"

"To be honest" — I fiddle with a button of the throw pillow in my lap — "I have no idea." I look up at him. "No, you know what. I think I know what happened. I think it was Tyler's way of making sure I know my place."

"What?" Jay's voice rings with surprise and a dash of fury.

"I mean he just made sure I know where I stand. We, the other night . . ." I let out a frustrated sigh. "I don't think I should be telling you this."

"Did he fuck it up?"

It's my turn to frown. "What do you mean?"

Jay leans back onto the sofa. "You'd have to be a blind, deaf chump not to know what's going on . . . the vibe you both transmit. And I know that whatever happened between you two on Thanksgiving shook him a little. And you. And as much as Tyler tends to play it cool, I know him too well. I can tell he more than digs you."

"Uh?" Could this evening venture even further into Bizarreland?

And with that, our conversation ends.

"Another episode?" Tyler, changed into jeans and a gray Henley, takes a seat on the opposite sofa. As far away from where I am sitting as possible.

"Not me. I'm too tired," I bluntly lie and stand up. "Night, boys." I give them a small, semi-fake smile.

Getting into bed after brushing my teeth and cleansing my face, I reach for my phone on the nightstand. About to set my alarm, a new text message lands in my phone.

Tyler: Can I come in?

Anxiety laced excitement gathers momentum as I get out of bed and walk to the door. Slowly, I crack it open. I raise my eyebrows in question, looking up to meet Tyler's eyes that gleam back at me through the dimly lit hall.

I swallow hard. "Want to come in?"

He nods in response. I take a couple of steps back, letting him inside my room.

Tyler leans on the wall next to the slightly ajar door. His eyes slowly run over me, across my white tank top, down to my white boy shorts, and lower to my white knee-length socks. "I think." He breathes in through his nose. "What I tried to tell you earlier didn't come across well. I don't think I was clear enough." He brings his stare to mine.

"Oh, I think you were quite clear." I hug myself. "I get it, don't worry. Just forget about it, really. No biggie." I fabricate an indifferent smile.

He shakes his head, folding his arms over his chest. "'Kay, I'm just going to say this straight up. There's no denying there's some major attraction between us . . . Or maybe more than just that."

To the small addition, my heart takes a little trip up north.

He clears his throat. "I don't believe that you're the type of person who'll just go with it, no expectations. Which is one of the things I really like about you."

My heart takes a few more steps higher. Anticipation prickles at my skin. *One of the things I really like about you . . . Tyler really likes . . . things*

. . . about me?

"With that said, I don't think that we should let what happened between us on Thanksgiving go any further. That's what I was trying to say earlier. And in no means insinuate anything else." His stare takes another slow, heated tour over me. "And that's why I tried to put some distance between us. When I said it isn't worth the trouble, I meant for *you*. It wasn't anything you did." His lips twitch at the corner. "It's about everything we didn't do."

I gaze at him, my blood rushing underneath my skin. My attraction to him leaves me strung with contradicting feelings. I feel like Eve looking at the irresistibly tempting fruit. Right in front of me — alluring, tangible — yet so sinfully forbidden and ominously distractive.

"You're quiet." His gaze, almost intimidating, burns into mine.

"I'm just." I swallow hard, Tyler's eyes tracing the motion. "Trying to fight what I'm feeling —" Abruptly, Tyler pushes himself off the wall. Snaking his hand around my waist, he tugs me forward. The tail end of my last soft words is swallowed by his mouth. When his lips meet mine, it's not a gentle brush or a hesitant request. Our lips meet agape, hurried. Mine surprised. His determined, demanding. Wide open against one another. Resolute tongues urgent for contact. It feels violently delicious.

Tyler pulls me against him into a tight hold. He kicks shut the door behind us, and together, we stumble through my room. His hard body against mine, directing us deeper into the space. He walks us farther, our bodies grazing with each step, heating up until the back of my thighs meet the high bed. We fall onto the bed in a haze of lips sloppily and possessively moving against lips, of feral sounds carried over breaths funneling into each other's mouth. We're in a blur of uncontrollable pull where the world doesn't exist anymore. Every time this man touches me, it's more perfect. Making me lose my hinges a little more. Bringing my sanity a little closer to the edge of a cliff. I don't want to think about what will happen if we take just one more step forward.

For what seems like an eternity, we kiss. Just eagerly and passionately kiss. We stay in the first base realm—clothes on, hands roaming and exploring. Lips never detaching. It's glorious.

When I ease back, feeling a little heady, I excuse myself to go to the bathroom. What's happening is intense and wonderful and a little scary. I need a moment to collect my thoughts. Tyler's hooded, lustful gaze follows me as I leave the bed.

Behind the bathroom's closed door, I wash my hands and study myself in the mirror for some long moments. Fighting to ignore everything that's screaming at me inside my head, I ask my reflection what the hell am I doing. Switching off the light together with my thoughts, I make my way back to the bed.

Under the moon's soft glimmer in the dim room, I find Tyler sleeping on my bed. My inner debate whether to wake him perishes as soon as my eyes rest on his serene, handsome face. Quietly, I climb back into bed, rest my head on his softly rising chest, and close my eyes. Warmness suffuses my belly when his arm moves to embrace me. Nothing ever felt so right and so terrifying at the same time.

———◆———

"Ivi, Ivi, you up?" Jeremy's yell brutally pierces into my heavy sleep. Only to be followed by my alarm going off with "Shiny Happy People" in a cacophony of loud assaults.

Dazed, I send my hand to stop the cheerful tune, while croaking out, "I'm up, Jeremy. I'll be downstairs in five."

Next to me, Tyler wakes with a start. Looking around in a haze, his brows crease. He lets out a grunt. Closing his eyes, he brings both hands to rub over his face. A murmur in the vain of a frustrated curse is whispered into his hands. He drops his hands and meets my eyes.

Before I'm able to say anything, his rough morning voice rumbles, "Jesus Christ, Jeremy is outside the damn door." He shakes his head, looking utterly frustrated. "It was a mistake. We shouldn't let it happen again."

And I was about to say that it was the best sleep I ever had. I bob my head and leave the bed. Entering the bathroom, I don't even give him a backward glance before shutting the door.

CHAPTER
Twenty

"Am I more than you bargained for yet..." Lyrics from a Fall Out Boy song,
playing repeatedly on Ivi's phone and in her head.

"Hey Ivi, smile." Jeremy grins, snapping yet another photo. I wouldn't be exaggerating if I said it's the hundredth photo the kid has taken today. As an assignment for a digital photography class at school, Jeremy has to try several different photographing techniques. Jeremy, being Jeremy, takes it as seriously as one can. And then some. "I'll try forced perspective now," he murmurs from behind the camera.

"What's that?" I ask, flipping through the old vinyl records box in Tyler's studio.

Aiming the camera at the control table Tyler is sitting by, Jeremy says, "Making an object appear further away than it actually is."

"Hmm, making something go away with a tiny click could come in handy in real life," I say under my breath, squinting Tyler's way. At that exact moment, he chooses to give me one of his dichotomic stares—part penetrating, part intimidating. The duality of my feelings for Tyler has slowly and gradually turned into a big fat question. One that came to life right after his rejection the morning after he'd kissed me silly and fell asleep in my bed. *Do actions truly speak louder than words?* A question that I promised myself to no longer dissect. Because I've decided to let it go. Because the reason I'm being paid is to mind the sweet kid and not to pine pathetically after someone who's the epitome of unattainable. Or maybe it was Jeremy almost finding out that his dad slept in my room a week ago that was the real wake-up call. That sobered me well enough to be able to be in close proximity to Tyler and . . . act, think, breathe normal after he'd slept in my bed. After he held me in his arms all night like it meant something.

The moment Tyler left my room that morning, an unspoken status quo had been forged between us entitled "clean slate." With "we have less than two months till we never see each other again" in fine print under Appendix A: Back to Business as Usual. An understanding we both have been following to a T.

Which brings me to now, to the look he just gave me which definitely violates the existing state of affairs and thus leaves me flustered. However, it's still not potent enough to even begin to scrape the thick Great Wall of Ivi I've built around myself against anything Tyler Lee Adams. Okay, maybe just a minuscule scrape.

Pushing on some buttons to turn down the music in the background, Tyler swivels in his chair to face us. A smile tugs at his lips as he eyes his son. "Hey bud, what do you want for Christmas? Anything you want."

Jeremy stills with the camera frozen before his face. He slowly lowers the device to his chest, revealing troubled eyes. Taking a deep breath, he casts his eyes down, fiddling with the camera for a few, long awkward beats.

Tyler and I exchange concerned glances.

Raising his face up, Jeremy doesn't look directly at either one of us. Honing his stare in on some indistinct point ahead, he says, "To spend it with my mom."

The immediate pain that surges into my heart goes out to them both. To Jeremy, who couldn't appear more discomfited and down, and to Tyler, who looks like he's been sucker punched.

Tyler's shoulders sink together with his features. "I see," comes out in a breath. He nods, eyes down to the floor. "I understand."

Willing to bring them both, or maybe the three of us, out of the tormenting silence that engulfs the room, I say, "Jer, what about your wish list?"

Tyler raises his hand my way, communicating *it's okay, I'm handling it*. He stands up and walks three silent steps toward Jeremy. Crouching, he holds Jeremy's shoulders. "You don't have to feel bad about expressing what you feel. I understand." Jeremy nods, still having a hard time meeting his dad's eyes. "But there's nothing much that I can do, Jer." Tyler bends lower, searching his son's eyes. "I'm sorry, bud."

Jeremy nods again. "Hmm, I'm just. I-I'm going to upload the photos to the laptop." He lifts the camera as if to take back his words. "It's for school, and I need it for tomorrow, and I need to do it now, and—" With the same ill-at-ease demeanor he's been wearing for the past few long depressing moments, he turns on his heel and scurries out of the room.

As soon as Jeremy leaves the room, Tyler's and my eyes slowly meet. My lips set in a supple, empathetic curve. Tyler heaves a sigh.

"I'll go check on him," I say on a soft chord.

Holding my gaze, Tyler subtly nods. He keeps watching me as I make my way to the door, naked pain furrowing his features. With every step I take, I fight the urge to turn around and hug him. Crossing the threshold, I turn back. "Tyler?" His eyes trail to mine from across the room. "You okay?"

He shrugs and says with a defeated breath, "Nothing I wasn't expecting."

———— ◆ ————

"Hey, why the broken spirit?" Jay shifts his attention from the oak shelves he's working on to me.

I return his stare from the floor, where I'm sitting crossed-legged and troubled, keeping him company in his studio, a steaming teacup cuddled in my hands. "I just feel bad for both of them." I run my finger around the rim of the cup, collecting condensation along the way. "It was going so well." I sigh again, taking some comfort in Jay's company. Staying at home after Jeremy went to sleep felt depressing and frustrating. No matter how much I tried, I wasn't able to bring back Jeremy's ever-present, joyful spirit. Not to mention how hard I had to hold myself back from climbing up to the third floor to comfort Tyler.

"Yeah. Though it's nothing Ty didn't see coming. It's still surprising how easy Jeremy has accepted him and bonded with him. Tyler anticipated some sort of whiplash all along. And voilà."

"That's exactly what Tyler said earlier," I murmur, still unable to shake off how wounded he looked. Both of them did. "I can't think of anything I can do to help." On a sigh, I add, "and it's so darn frustrating."

"I don't think you can do anything. It's one of those times in which you just need to let things calm down a little. The fact is Jeremy's mom is away, and he's with Ty till she comes back, period."

"I know. I just hate seeing them both like this."

———— ◆ ————

In bed, having a hard time falling asleep, I think about how the joyous, Christmassy feeling seemed to have passed over Tyler's mansion. Looks like holiday spirit is not something we'll be experiencing a la casa Adams anytime soon. The weighty feeling brings me back to a Christmas Eve when I was sixteen, which for me, held no less gloom and included a side dish of dread and self-contempt.

CHAPTER
Twenty-One

"I caught myself smiling without a reason then I realized I was thinking of you." #TylerLeeAdams #HesTheOne #HesPerfect. A tweet to @TylerLeeAdams by @TylerLeeIsTheOne. 653 likes.125 retweets.

"**L**et's get out of here. Do something wild!" I put on my most enthusiastic expression, nudging Jeremy's shoulder. We walk down the hall to his room after having cookies and milk with Adina in the kitchen.

Jeremy gives me a halfhearted smile. "I never understood why people use the word 'wild' as something positive. Wild is something uncontrolled, violent, or extreme."

I twist my lips, fighting an eye roll. "Then let's do something *fun*. We're good with fun? Do you want to go for a walk at the beach? The weather is nice. Play Frisbee?" Jeremy remains pensively quiet, prompting me to go on. "Hmm, go for a hike?" No response. "Get eaten by rabid honey badgers?" I grin, noticing the smile broadening his lips. I should have known that a computer game reference would do the job. "Well, kid, what do you say?"

"Nah, let's just stay in."

I send him a tentative, sidelong glance. "Maybe you can go hang a little with your dad. I saw him earlier by the pool."

"I still have some homework and . . . and there's this thing I need to do . . . maybe later." He accelerates his steps a little. "See you later," he mumbles and disappears inside his room.

Frustrated, I rack my brain trying to come up with something that will bring a stop to the rancid mood that descended on the house a few days ago with Jeremy's statement about his wish to spend Christmas with his mom. Melena is somewhere in Kenya, studying some isolated tribe or indigenous people or whatever it is anthropologists and human genetics professors do. The fact that it's two days before Christmas adds its share of foiling to my overall frustration.

As I let out an upset sigh, an idea pops into my mind. I quickly turn to my room with a spring in my step. Getting the paper I was looking for from my desk drawer, I go look for Tyler. Finding the deck empty, I climb up the stairs. His office is my next stop. I knock on the door.

"Come in."

Opening the door, I find Tyler engrossed in a call. His face is tense with concentration as he listens to the person on the other side. "Let me just write it down." He holds the phone between his shoulder and ear, reaching for a notepad on his desk. I watch him as he grabs a pen and bites the cap off; holding it between his teeth, he's ready to jot down whatever the person on the phone tells him. I gaze at him for the remaining moments until he finishes his call. Tyler looks nothing but scrumptious in ripped jeans and a black knit sweater pushed back to reveal his tattooed, veiny forearms. His hair is loosely knotted, and it appears his beard has been trimmed shorter.

"So, in five hours. Mmmhmm. The next day, okay. Jomo Kenyatta International. Got it. Eli, I don't care how much it costs, make sure it's the safest and fastest." Tyler clears his throat. "'Kay, I'll tell her." He concludes the call. Giving the piece of paper he jotted on another cursory glance, he turns to me. His gaze slowly crawls over me. He raises his brows in question.

"I thought." I bring forward the paper I'm holding. "The other day, Jeremy had put together a Christmas wish list, and I thought maybe you'd want it. Maybe it can help lighten his mood."

Tyler extends his hand for the list. He gives it a brief scan. A low chuckle rolls out of his lips. "Glad to see a trip to the moon has been crossed out."

I smile back. "I told him perhaps he could wait until his birthday for that one."

Tyler's eyes beam at me. I'd be lying if I said it had no effect on me.

"Thanks, I'll keep it for later." He folds the list and pockets it. "Where is he now?"

"His room."

Tyler stands up and walks over to me. Resting his hand on my lower back, he says, "Let's go see him."

We walk down the stairs in silence until Tyler breaks it. "What do *you* want for Christmas?" Amusement colors his voice as he adds, "I sure hope it's not to see the moon."

Not the moon, but I'm pretty sure you have it in you to make me see stars, sits on the tip of my tongue. "There's nothing I really need, to be honest."

A couple of steps further, just next to Jeremy's room, Tyler turns to face me. "I asked what you wanted, not what you needed."

The weight of his gaze makes me avert my stare. I cast my eyes down. *I want you.* "I'm still trying to figure that one out. Recently, my wishes have been changing." A thin smile curves my lips, and I raise my eyes to his. "I've always wanted a ferret." He gives me a puzzled grin. "What do *you* want from Santa?" I ask next.

Tyler nods at the door. "A happy kid." Opening Jeremy's door, Tyler gestures for me to go in first.

Jeremy swivels in his chair as we enter the room, trading glances between his dad and me. I lean on the wall, waiting. Tyler takes a couple of steps to sit on the edge of Jeremy's bed, facing his son. Bracing his elbows on his spread knees, he clears his throat. "So how quick can you pack a bag?"

Both Jeremy and my features set in query.

"Fast . . . I guess," Jeremy responds tentatively, slightly frowning.

"Good." Tyler nods twice "Good." He sends Jeremy the warmest glance. "Then start packing, bud. Your plane leaves in a few hours."

Jeremy tilts his head to the side, eyebrows pinched above plastic-framed glasses. "My plane?"

Tyler's eyes twitch at the corners, mellowing his expression into a grin. "Yeah, to take you to your mom."

Jeremy stares gaping at his dad.

"I told you, you could have anything you want, so . . . it's Christmas with your mom."

Jeremy perks up, swallowing hard, looking adorably baffled. "Really?"

Tyler nods.

Jeremy, beaming, jumps out of his chair. "Wow." His skinny arms embrace Tyler's wide shoulders. "Thank you so much, Tyler."

A dreamy, genuinely content smile lights up my face as I watch them.

"But there's one condition," Tyler says, bringing back the frown to his son's face. "When you're back, we'll do a little celebration here. I don't want to miss celebrating Christmas with you. Deal?" Tyler adds, and I swoon a little more.

Through a gigantic smile, Jeremy exclaims, "You betcha!"

Tyler and I stay in Jeremy's room, keeping him company while he piles up things he wants to take with him on the flight. Not more than five minutes later, I take control of the packing job. What with the little mountain of unnecessary, not to mention not plane worthy, items that have accumulated on the bed and the hyper-distraction of a kid having his Christmas wish granted, someone is going to miss their flight altogether if we don't get down to some serious packing.

"What are you doing? I need that!" comes an objection from the kid.

"Your telescope? Jer, you're going for four days. I think you can do just fine without a telescope." I set a couple of items more on the "staying" pile. "Or the binoculars or this funny looking helicopter."

"It's a Quadcopter." Jeremy rolls his eyes.

Tyler, sprawled on the bed, looking like something I'd like to be sprawled on, watches our little exchange, his eyes alight with amusement. And just like that, the lighthearted ambiance returns to the Adams' residence.

Jeremy is a fizzy fountain of blabber throughout the drive to LAX. Tyler and I, with undying grins, learn about planes in general and plane crashes in particular, about Kenya and the fact that corn is the top commodity there and that the dowry for marriage starts at ten cows.

Tyler lightly chuckles after that last tidbit. Glancing my way, he says, "I think Ivi is worth twenty cows, fifteen goats, and a tortoise, at the very least. What do you say, kid?"

I grin at the window.

"And a tablet!" Jeremy says elated, raising my value.

When I turn to look at Tyler, I meet his gleaming eyes. He winks at me, making my grin grow brighter.

Jeremy's excitement is hardly contained when he finds out his "ride" is his dad's private jet, complete with an entire crew just for him.

"Not too shabby, eh?" I nudge his arm with mine.

The kid is one gigantic toothy smile.

Tyler introduces Jeremy to the crew, letting Amanda, a middle-aged, soft-spoken flight attendant, lead Jeremy to the plane for a short briefing.

———— • ————

"So Melena will meet him at the airport?" I ask in an attempt to shake Tyler out of the pensive, glum mood he's been in since we waved Jeremy good-bye at the airport.

"Yeah."

Studying his concentrated, handsome face, I ask, "Will you be staying at home for the holidays?"

"Yeah." He glances my way. "You don't have to stay now that Jeremy is away. I heard Jay asked you to join him to visit his family."

My brows arch and a bewildered, "You talked to Jay about me?" jumps out of my mouth.

He gives me another look, this time a longer one, before turning back to the road. "Go ahead and join him." His expression doesn't back up his statement. If I didn't know any better, I'd say he looks irate by his own words.

"What's your plan for the holidays?" I ask softly.

"I'll just hang around the house and catch up on some projects I've neglected for far too long."

I bob my head, looking out the window. "How come Jeremy didn't go with his mom to Africa, to begin with?" To his silence, I quickly add, "I hope you don't mind me asking. It's okay. You don't have to answer." I swallow hard. "I shouldn't have asked," comes out on a discomfited murmur.

I inwardly gasp, feeling Tyler's hand cover mine. "It's okay," he says in a supple voice. Expecting him to retrieve his hand, I'm surprised when he doesn't. "The place where she's conducting her research is not the best environment for a kid, to say the least. Also, we—she didn't want Jeremy to miss so much school."

"So you agreed to have him stay with you?" I ask, my eyes roaming over his profile.

"Melena's parents are both older and not in good health. They can't take care of a child . . . And anyhow, we talked about telling him about me for a while now. So the timing and situation somehow led to him staying with me till Melena comes back."

"Why didn't he know about you till then?"

Tyler removes his hand from mine to scratch his bearded cheek. "Back when Melena told me she was pregnant, we agreed that the baby would be better off raised by her. I wasn't in a place in my life or a state of mind in which a child would fit. We had an agreement where I was to pay child support, and in return, she'd send me updates on Jeremy's well-being. About a year ago, we started talking about telling him about me. We felt like it was the right time, and when this opportunity came up, well, the rest is history."

"Are you two, um, friends?" I ask a question that comes from deep inside. From an inexplicable place that demands to know whether they are in some kind of a relationship.

Tyler's brows crease. "Not sure if friends would be the right term. We respect each other, and Melena knows that no matter what, she can always turn to me."

"How did you two meet?"

"You're full of questions today, aren't you?" Tyler asks, a ghost of a smile playing on his lips. Noting my discomfort, he squeezes my hand, leaving his hand on mine. "It's okay, ask away."

The sensation of our contact, skin on skin, raises little bumps over my entire body.

"She came to one of my concerts with a friend who had backstage passes. We had a few drinks together, one thing led to another, and —" He chuckles lightly. "We couldn't have been more different. She was this cute, geeky undergrad, a vision you'd rarely meet backstage. When she tracked me down a couple of months later to deliver the news, and we went through the process of validating that Jeremy was indeed mine, that's when we actually got to know each other. She's a cool person. I'm glad my son has such a great mother."

I open my mouth to further probe, but he cuts me off, saying, "Maybe you should call Jay; let him know you'll be joining him for the holidays after all."

Thinking about Tyler staying by himself during the holidays in that big house, especially with Jeremy being away, knowing just how much it affects him, I say, "I think I'll stay here."

Tyler doesn't answer, and his hand on mine becomes heavier. Wordlessly, he links his fingers with mine.

The rest of the drive is silent. Silence accompanied by stolen, loaded glances. And he never removes his hand from mine.

Twenty-Two

"Ho, ho, ho. Have you been a good girl this year?"
Mall Santa calling out to a sixteen-year-old Ivi, who wants to punch him in the nose.

Six years ago, Christmas Eve, Tallinn, Estonia

I shimmy my panties down my knees and bend to sit on the toilet, futilely trying to ease away the tight spring of apprehension building in my stomach. Burying my face in my hands, I murmur under my breath, "So here's my wishlist for this year: a leather jacket, a ferret, and for the little window on the stick to show only one pink line. Really, though, I want the one pink line on the stick thing more than anything."

I shake my head and snort in contempt at my nonsense. Another loud, anxious heave leaves my lips as I turn to remove the white stick from the packet and hold it under me. How did I let myself get here?

Christmas is my favorite time of year. The dinner, family, gifts, this amazing sense of belonging. And like every year, my family is crammed around the fireplace, drinking and enjoying each other's company. Only this year, I'm in the bathroom. By myself. Freaked to my bones. This year, I'm alone, waiting for the little window on the stick to tell me if two small pink stripes are about to dictate the rest of my life.

"Funny, I didn't know rock bottom has a basement," I whisper to the air. You know you've reached the bottom when at sixteen you don't even know who might be the father of the alleged human you might be growing inside you. In less than five minutes, I will find out whether my wild, rebellious year is about to come back and bite me in the ass.

As I wait for the results, the next three minutes are the longest three minutes of my life. So many "what-if" thoughts swirl through my mind I can hardly catch up.

115 seconds.

90 seconds.

One minute.

T-minus thirty dreaded seconds to my verdict.

I glance at the stick and let the breath I've been holding out.

I've never, ever before been so grateful. Never. One single bold pink line. My best Christmas present to date.

Standing up, I smooth my crimson, layered dress, wash my hands, and smile in relief at my reflection in the mirror. Pondering, I take a long, thorough look at my face and come up with an early New Year's resolution. I'm going to get my act together and get help for my growing "drinking matter of contention."

———◆———

Two and a half months later, during one of the toughest winters we've experienced in this arctic part of the world I call home, I found out that I'm not a certified alcoholic per se. Alas, I am on a very promising path to become one. And so I met Chris. My sponsor, sort of. An American volunteering in Northern Europe, helping youth get back on track among other blessed deeds. Chris became my mentor. He was also the one who introduced me to an organization that would change my life and me, as a person in particular, for the better. YWPO, Youth with Purpose Organization.

Less than six months after one of my lowest points, which I now like to call "Christmas on the john," I've fulfilled my New Year's resolution and so much more.

You could say I've found my calling.

Twenty-Three

CHAPTER
CHAPTER

"Follow your heart, but please, don't forget to take your brain with you."
Ivi's mom before Ivi's trip to L.A.

A lax smile takes over my lips as I blink my eyes open to the early morning illuminated room. Stretching, I inhale deeply. For some quiet moments, I lie still and savor the silence, enjoying the mellow ambiance but mostly the anticipation. I frigging love Christmas!

Humming a festive tune, I throw the blanket aside and get out of bed. Fueled by determination of turning this lonesome prone day, come hell or high water, into a flipping twenty-four hours of jolly good time, I turn to start my morning.

By the time the noon sun paints the day in a frosty glow, I've already helped at the Union Station with preparation for tonight's Dinner in the Park, I've run by Whole Foods for some special ingredients for the dinner I'm planning for tonight, I've decorated the first floor of the house with random, adorably corny holiday decorations, and I've washed my hair. A true accomplisher.

Which brings me to now, where I'm toiling over the wide kitchen island in an attempt to replicate my mother's traditional Estonian

Christmas recipes. Taking a sip of my mulled wine, I twist my lips from side to side, studying the pork roast I just took out of the oven. I poke it with a fork, frowning. I observe what's supposed to be a golden-brown, crispy roast glazed in mustard-honey-garlic-rosemary marinade and my frown deepens. I take another small sip of the richly spiced drink, not entirely complacent with the albino version of my mom's signature Christmas dish. Looks like some extra oven time would do the pale-ish hunk of meat swimming in the rather turbid water looking "gravy" a lot of good. Getting the pan back into the oven, I turn to work on the rest of the dishes.

Like a final whistle to a soccer match, the intercom buzz declares the end of my culinary expedition. At least the main and side dishes part. I wipe my hands on a dishtowel, making my way to check who's at the front gate.

"Wow, that's an impressive tree," I tell the delivery guy as he crouches with an excessive strain to move the gigantic tree that was apparently ordered by a one, Mr. Adams, earlier today. Infusing the air with fresh pine scent, the tree stands vigorous and tall in my favorite corner of the grandiose living room. Lofty and green, it seasons the space next to a plush faux fur rug and the wall-mounted stone fireplace.

As I'm about to tip the delivery guy, Eli marches in, followed by two bulky overall-donning gentlemen. Each of the Mario Brother look-alikes carts a prominent tower of perfectly wrapped presents in their hands. Like an oiled machine, both men place the first batch under the tree and march out of the main door, only to return with a new stock.

"That's . . ." I start telling Eli after he pays the gentlemen. "*A lot* of gifts."

Eli shrugs. "Tyler." As though that's enough to explain the plethora of professionally wrapped presents. He gives the tree another sharp glance, nodding to himself. "I'm going to talk to Tyler before leaving. Happy holidays, if I don't see you when I get back down."

"You too. Give Adina my love."

Eli tips his chin and starts for the stairs.

I send the living room an appreciative glance and head up to my room to change into something of the comfy-home-yet-festive variety. Fifteen minutes later, with a knitted red sweater, cute black shorts, and knee-high white wooly socks, I brush my hair and flip the light off. My next stop, Tyler's floor.

Finding Tyler's office vacant, I follow the muffled upbeat tune to the studio. I knock on the door and wait. Tyler opens the door, looking utterly handsome and casual in a white Henley and ripped jeans. Giving me a silent, extensive scan, he steps back and gestures for me to come in. Under his profound gaze, I step into the room. Tyler takes a couple of steps back to lean on the wall, his stare on me unwavering.

Passing by the mixing desk, I brush the dark surface with my fingers. Slowly, I lift my eyes to him. "Doesn't it get lonely up here sometimes?"

He folds his toned arms across his wide chest. For a stretched beat, his eyes penetrate every layer of me. "I was planning to spend the day with Jeremy," he says with a dejected bite. Tyler turns to look out the large window, his stare far-off. "Why did you stay here, Ivi?"

The tender quality of my own voice surprises me when I say, "I thought some company would do you good." A strange uncertainty enfolds me as I wait for his reaction.

He turns to me, his lips set in an easy smile. But he's still silent, as though gauging me, my intentions.

His smile dissipates my tension together with any inhibitions I might have had about inviting him to have Christmas dinner with me. "Mind helping me prepare the dessert for tonight?" I ask on an animated note.

His gleaming stare runs over me again, his lips tip higher. "We have dinner plans?"

I beam at him. "You betcha!"

He lightly shakes his head with a side smile. "Let me just wrap up something here." His lips tip higher. "I'll report to duty in five." He salutes me.

The grin curving my lips turns wholehearted. "I'll be in the kitchen." My grin remains unaltered when I walk down the stairs and as I assemble the ingredients next to the massive stove a few minutes later. Waiting for Tyler to join me, I pour milk, vanilla bean, and sugar into a pot. Though my lips have returned to their natural form, the smile resides within me. The anticipation of spending this evening with Tyler has my stomach in a sweetly tight knot.

"So what are we cooking?" Tyler asks, entering the kitchen, throwing a hair tie up in the air and catching it into a closed fist.

"Kaameli tatt!" I declare joyfully, whisking the slowly congealing mix. "Camel's snot."

His brows pull in. "Say again?"

I let out an easy chuckle. "The official name is Karamelli Kissell. In our house, we call it camel's snot. It's some sort of caramel pudding."

"Sounds better." Tyler ties his hair back in a bun and turns to the sink. Rinsing his hands, he sends me a glance of the flirty variety over his shoulder. "So how can I be of help, Miss Kert?"

Stirring the Kissell, I say, "Hmm, just . . ." I give him a sidelong glance, trying to disregard the cartwheels my insides make. "Here, grab the spoon and stir."

Tyler saunters my way with a glimmer of a smile. Deliberately or not, his fingers brush mine as he takes the wooden spoon from me. Ducking my head to hide the flush prompted by our brief contact, I say, "Keep stirring it slowly till it hardens."

He quirks a brow my way, and I roll my eyes, fighting the smile that's taking over my lips.

Busying myself, checking on the other dishes, I still manage to steal a peek or two at Tyler. The man even makes a simple task like cooking look like an opening scene to a promising porn movie. Of the award-winning kind. The flex of his muscles under the white shirt hugging his strong arms. The way the jeans hang low on his hips. His bare feet. The small tattoo peeping from the side of his neck. The loose knot holding his hair back. The little twitch of his lips amid his trimmed beard as he notices my "stealth" glances. The pudding is not the only thing Tyler is slowly bringing to a boil.

When the Kissell is well thickened, I take back control over the pot. Tyler watches me, hip leaning on the counter, as I pour the creamy substance into serving bowls and put it in the fridge to cool. I have half a mind to place my cheek against the cold surface of the fridge for some much-needed cooling.

"So what have we got here?" Tyler tips his chin at the steaming dishes assembled on the wide island. "What are we having?"

With a fork in hand, I point at the first plate in the row. "Boiled potatoes." Motioning with the raised utensil at the subsequent plates, I continue, "Sauerkraut, blood sausages and baked pork."

Tyler nods, trading glances back and forth between the food and me. "Can I have a taste?"

His question throws me into a brief, silent daze, given the way his eyes practically devoured my mouth while asking said question. I extend the fork his way in place of an answer, afraid my voice will give away the awakening he's just evoked in the pit of my stomach. Instead of standing there, gaping at him like a dork, I fetch a fork for myself and join the taste fest.

Tyler brings a forkful of sauerkraut to his mouth and frowns. I watch him as he chews somewhat tentatively. I bring a serving to my own mouth for a taste. We both grimace at the same time while munching.

Swallowing, Tyler briefly coughs. Pouring himself a glass of water, he takes a generous gulp. "What was that again?"

Still trying to figure out how I'd managed to screw up a store-bought product just by adding sugar and heating it up, I mutter, "Hmm, pickled cabbage. I might have added a tiny bit too much brown sugar."

Tyler grimaces and nods. "It's . . . interesting." He points at the mildly burned, thick sausages. "What's that?"

"Blood sausages but hold on a sec." I take a knife and scrape off some of the scorched, blackened parts under his amused gaze. "Here, better." I bring the plate forward. Let's just say the dish probably wouldn't make the cut for a glossy food magazine.

Having a hard time holding his smile back, Tyler takes a bite. I cringe at the crackling sound of overly fried, to put it mildly, meat.

As an act of solidarity, I dig in. "Wow, I really torched these poor suckers, didn't I?" I say while trying to chew on the hard chalky content in my mouth.

Nearly choking, Tyler croaks through a chuckle, "Singular texture."

This time, we both throw back a drink of water in urgency after swallowing the coal-ish delight.

"God, I hope it didn't scratch your vocal cords going down the pipes." I wince, biting on a smile. "I bet it's insured by a bazillion dollars. I'll have to give you my soul if you decide to sue me."

Tyler lets out an easy chuckle.

"So are we giving up?" I point at the last dish, the one I prepared from scratch. What should be *THE masterpiece,* thank you very much.

Tyler's eyes gleam at me as he shrugs. "Well, we got this far. Why stop now?"

Eyeing each other in amusement, we clink our forks and move on to the still somewhat pale-ish roast. I cut a piece that feels a bit rubbery and pass Tyler the knife.

"On three," Tyler says in an animated tone, holding his fork up. I mirror him, letting out a soft giggle. "One, two . . ." And we both bring the meat to our mouths.

Chewing on it once, appearing completely tortured, or better yet, nauseated, Tyler's eyes cut to mine. His look must be identical to the expression I'm wearing because whatever I've concocted tastes like a terminal disease. I dart my hand to my mouth, covering it. I swear I'm half a second away from retching all over the Tyler Lee Adams.

Tyler looks tormented as our eyes meet again, and in unison, we jump toward the sink. In complete harmony, we spit out the vile content of our mouths. I shiver at the hostile aftertaste, following Tyler with my stare as he yanks open the fridge's door and hastily pulls out a jug of apple juice. In no time, he pours two full glasses. Grinning, we clink our glasses and down it as if they were shots. At the same time, we set our glasses down on the counter with a little thud.

Tyler shakes his head from side to side in a subtle gesture. "Some larruping feast you've cooked us here."

"What's larping?"

He chuckles. "Well, *larping* is live-action role-playing." His chuckle grows to my o-shaped mouth and light flush. "Mind out of the gutter, Ivi. Not that kind of role-playing. I said *larruping*, which means exceedingly well. Unless you're into the other kind of role-playing, which I'm totally down with." He smirks at me, elevating my blush along the way. "What I was trying to say is do me a favor or, better yet, humanity a favor, and don't *ever* quit your day job." His smirk grows.

"Well, that sort of depends on my boss. You see, I'm not sure he'll need me for much longer." My turn to transmit a cheeky grin.

"Well, your boss would be a complete idiot to let someone like you go," Tyler says, bringing the room to a tense silence in an instant. "You're great at what you do." He sends me an easy smile in an obvious attempt to lighten the air. But after the words that have left his mouth, something shifts and I believe we're both more than aware of the sudden change. "I don't know about you, but I'm starving. Let's see what Adina left for us," he says next.

A little rummage through the fridge, some microwaving, and a trip to the pantry later, we're settled in the living room with our meals. Tyler, with a platter piled up with Christmassy goods that smells divine, sits cross-legged on the faux fur rug by the fire. Across from him, I lean my back on the sofa with a little bowl topped off with peanut butter filled pretzels on my crossed legs.

Tyler brings a forkful to his mouth, gazing at me. When I return his stare, he cocks his head. "Hey, come closer. Come close to the fire."

For a beat, I consider if getting physically close to him would be the right thing to do, knowing full well that the greater the distance I put between us, the greater the chance I'll survive this evening.

I'll survive . . . him.

Because something is happening between us. I can feel it in my bones, in the soft hum running over my skin. "I am." I stand up slowly and walk over . . . closer to the fire. *Maybe too close.* I'm about to get burned. I settle on the rug with my legs bent close to him, dropping my eyes to the bowl in my hand because his stare on me is just too much to handle. Too much from this distance. I take a sip of my champagne glass and slowly raise my eyes to meet his.

"You give new meaning to Christmas dinner." Tyler smiles, eyeing the bowl of pretzels on my lap.

I raise my glass. "Here's to fancy dining." I take another sip and bring a pretzel to my mouth. "These are so good; I can't believe I've lived over two decades without ever tasting them."

"I haven't had those in I don't know how long." Tyler tips his chin. "Let me try one." He slightly parts his lips, waiting.

Realization dawns on me that he's just asked me to feed him as I notice his full hands, one with a plate and a flute in the other. I inch up, holding the chunky, square pretzel between two fingers. Enthralled, I watch Tyler's lips wrap around the tips of my fingers. An action that makes my nerves fire on all cylinders. Overwhelmed by the heat wave that spreads under my skin and pools beneath my navel, I scatter back and hastily turn my head sideways while taking a very long drink from my flute.

"Tell me about your family," Tyler says, forcing me to face him again.

I set the bowl on the luxurious rug and bring my legs closer to my chest, hugging them. "My parents are what you'd call simple people." A supple smile plays on my lips. "Of the best kind. My father, and this is not out of snobbery or anything, isn't cut out to be a fisherman, which he is. He should have been a writer or an educator." Tyler's soft gaze encourages me to continue. "Growing up, he'd always tell me and my friends stories. Each somehow entwined with an important life lesson. He has this effortless gift to make people listen to him and teach you things in the most fascinating way. And my mom, she's a mother in every sense of the word. She's a secretary for the town's lawyer. Yeah, we have only one in my hometown." I return his smile. "She got the job right out of high school and has been there ever since. My parents never went to college, and they never left Estonia. They are hardworking people, with enough kindness and benevolence to fill a whole universe."

"I guess it's true what they say then. The apple doesn't fall far from the tree," Tyler says in a supple tone.

His words bring light heat to cover my cheeks. Being compared to my parents is the greatest compliment someone could give me.

"Why are you blushing? It's true. You're the kindest, sweetest person I've met."

"Tyler Lee Adams, is that your pick-up line?" I try to hide my unease with humor.

He shakes his head, his lips set in a cocky smile. "Ivi dear, I don't need a pick-up line." I roll my eyes with a thin smile. His expression melts into solemnity. His voice becomes softer and lower as my eyes trail up to his. "And the damn sexiest woman I've ever laid my eyes on."

I blink at him with a deer in a headlight daze. "You find me that . . . attractive?" My bewilderment morphs into a frown.

Tyler sets his plate aside and turns to face me. And like a slow-motion scene, he slowly leans in closer to me. And closer. My lips slightly part to the sensation of his hands cupping either side of my face. A tender bemused smile tilts his lips up, accompanied by a gentle frown as he returns my startled gaze. He dips closer, accelerating the rhythm of my heart as his face comes even closer. "Yes," he says, his lips mere inches from mine. "I find you incredibly attractive."

He eases toward me a little more. I can hardly hear his next words with the way my heart is hammering in my ears and the mayhem of feelings inside me. "And funny and sweet." His lips touch mine in a feathery brush. In a blissful electric current. "And sassy and beautiful." His lips move to leave a soft kiss on one corner of my mouth. "You're so beautiful; I have a hard time concentrating when you're around." He leaves a supple kiss on the other corner of my mouth. "That's how beautiful I find you."

My lips shiver with the desire to kiss him. Sweet, warm pain travels down my belly with how much I want him. With the effect of his words on me. With the effect of him on me.

Ever so slowly, Tyler brings his mouth to mine again, tenderly taking my lower lip between his. I inhale shakily as his lips move to kiss my upper lip. Slowly, in little, tender kisses, he traces my lips with his.

Tyler eases back to look at me for a charged beat. His heady breath travels into me as he dips his head toward me, his eyes absorbed in mine. Ever so gently, he slants his chin, leaning further down my way, slightly twisting his head. I part my lips with a throbbing heart. So does he, and his mouth meets mine again. This time, his tongue skims the tip of mine. The sensation is numbly electrifying. I gasp as my stomach twists, and my lungs turn void at the first touch. As our tongues unite, we lean deeper into each other. His fingers thread deeper into my hair. He tips my head to deepen the kiss. Our mouths dance in a delight of urgent, needy touches. It's perfect. And it feels like I'm making a huge mistake. One that I'm powerless to fight.

I squeeze my eyes shut, trying to take control over my spellbound mind. I bring my hand to Tyler's chest and inch back. Inhaling, I meet his questioning gaze. My voice comes out breathy, even slightly shaky, as I ask, "Tyler, what are we doing?"

The way he looks at me is a prelude to his next words. He brushes my cheek with his thumb. "I don't know." He swallows, eyes boring deeper into mine. "But I can't stop." His other hand brushes my skin, skimming my neck. "It never felt this amazing."

I know I'm about to give in. I feel it in my stomach. In my heart. In every fiber of my essence. I'm about to give myself to him. Completely. And just before I do, I ask, "What about Brooklyn?"

Tyler's jaw hardens; a deep frown settles between his brows. "Brooklyn is my friend. A very good friend. *Just* a friend." He inhales through his nose, his eyes a display of austerity. "This" — he motions his hand between us — "has nothing to do with Brooklyn or anyone besides you and me, Ivi."

"Then don't stop." My voice is both tender and raspy at the same time.

"Christ, you're . . ." He shakes his head just before his mouth collides with mine. This time, it's not just Tyler's mouth. This time, it's all of him. His hard chest presses against me, pushing me down. His hand moves to cradle my neck as he leans me down on the fuzzy rug.

I gasp as his mass spreads on me, heavy and warm and utterly glorious. I wrap my legs around his waist as he deepens our kiss. I slide my hands under his shirt. The sensation of my fingertips on his skin feels like I'm being shocked, whispering waves of desire along my skin.

Tyler's fingers trail to my waist, gliding over the exposed skin between my shorts and sweater, sending frissons of heat to my core. They continue up my ribcage, leaving raised bumps in their wake. I let out a breathy moan when they ghost over my bra. I lean into his hand when he cups me, his thumb teasing my pebbled peak. "You're so soft," Tyler murmurs to my lips as his other hand traces over my skin, slowly and perfectly from my knee up to my thigh.

Long, delicious moments later, I straddle his lap, kissing him profoundly, our torsos bare, brushing against each other. With Tyler sitting up, one arm wrapped around my waist, we're at eye level. Close and intimate. Tasting, exploring each other's bodies with great fervor.

"Tyler," I whisper to the spot in his wide neck where it connects to his ear and his trim, prickly beard.

Tyler eases back to look at me.

"In which universe does this work?" I burrow my face back in the nook of his neck.

His hands caress a sensual path down my bare back. "Where it feels this incredible."

I tip my face up to look at him. Tyler watches me attentively as I send my hand to the back of his head and release the tie from what's left of his knot after my unleashed hands' exploration. His dark strands fall to hang just shy of his shoulders, giving his natural bursting masculinity a delinquent air. With the feral look in his eyes and his hair framing his bearded, sharp features, and the tattoos covering his toned torso, he looks . . . sinful. Dangerous. As if possible, the flames kindling beneath my navel grow wilder. A low groan rolls up his throat as I pull him into a scorching kiss. Releasing the uncontainable desire in me to taste him. My body is humming. My head is swimming. My need for him almost unbearable. I've never, in my entire life, felt this attracted to anyone. It feels like I am on the verge of losing control. Of sweet insanity.

A sensation that only intensifies with Tyler's hands curling around my shoulders, arching me back, allowing himself better access to leave hot, hungry kisses down the valley between my breasts. The fire in me builds up when his mouth moves slowly to my hardened crests.

He takes his sweet time alternating between each breast. Savoring me, teasing me, he makes me burn for him until his name leaves my lips on a breathy plea. Painstakingly and thoroughly, Tyler attends to every part of my ignited body until he finally leans back on the sofa and helps me straddle him again.

We're completely bare, our breaths labored, our stares locked and leveled as he says, "I want to watch you when I'm in you." And he lightly lifts me with his arm around my waist while the other directs him to me. We hold our breaths, lost in each other's stares as Tyler sinks into me. I close my eyes, relishing the contact, and the raw growl channeling from his mouth into mine. His hands drop to my waist, working my body to glide over him in slow, rhythmic bliss.

Unbreakable, lustful, scorching eye lock, drunken sounds of desire, sweat slowly trailing down glistening skin—sensations so exhilarating at the verge of sheer aching bliss they take us to an incredible, euphoric climax. A moment when our names coming from each other's mouths mingle into a recognition. An admission that nothing had ever before felt as perfect.

My mind is still Tyler-addled as I try to comprehend what I'm feeling. Lying on Tyler's inked bare chest, with his fingers trailing leisurely up my spine, my mind keeps telling my heart to take a step back. That as amazing as this evening has been, whatever we are doing, Tyler and I, is transitory.

Right as it may feel, it has an irrefutable, bound expression date.

CHAPTER
Twenty-Four

CHAPTER

"Love is a battlefield, a war never ending. Wounded souls, wounded egos, wounded hearts. You want me, you say. You need me, you claim. Wounded souls, wounded egos, wounded hearts." Lyrics to a song by Tyler Lee Adams that never saw the light of day.

"Hey," Tyler whispers into my hair, nuzzling it with his lips.

I slowly raise my head to look at him.

"You're quiet."

I gaze at him for a silent beat, taking in all the beauty that is him. Head rested on his bent arm, hair strewn around his strong, sharp features. Flames dancing in the fireplace reflect in his rich brown eyes. Pouty lips amid dark beard set in a pensive line. The question leaves my mouth before I have enough time to consider it. "What's next for us?"

"Presents." Tyler's lips quirk up at the side.

Though it's more than obvious to us both that he's avoiding my real question, I play along. Maybe this conversation is meant to be had fully clothed and where the air is not still heavy with remnants of lust. "Aren't we supposed to wait for tomorrow morning?"

In place of an answer, Tyler sends his hand to the nape of my neck and brings our mouths to mesh. Long moments later, as we catch our breaths, he gives the grandfather clock a glance. "Tomorrow's here. Time to open your presents."

Warily, I peek at the medium-size, beautifully wrapped box and envelope Tyler places in front of me. I take the box and lightly shake it under his amused stare. Twisting my lips, I murmur, "Hmm, not a ferret, uh?" He shakes his head. "Dang, I really wanted a ferret."

Tyler lightly chuckles. "Wait, you were serious about a ferret?"

"They are the goofiest, sweetest animals." I steal a glance at his absurdly attractive, toned chest.

His lips tip higher. "Next year . . ."

Avoiding an insta-analyzing session of the casual statement, I busy myself unwrapping the box. "Oh wow. That's- that's." I clear my throat. "That's quite a unique gift. Much different from the one I got from my last employer."

Tyler scratches his bristled cheek, a smile playing on his lips. "What did he get you?"

"You know, the traditional pound cake, a tea mug, and a handshake."

He nods, holding back a grin. "Thoughtful."

"Well, this- " I put the garment in my hand back with the others in the fancy velvet box, sensing light heat sneaking up my cheeks. "This is also quite thoughtful, I'd say."

He nods again, his fight to subordinate a grin much palpable.

"Did you, hmm . . ." I attempt to muster a frown, which turns into an awkward smile-frown hybrid. "Did you buy it yourself? Did you, uh, handpick them?"

That wicked, sinfully wicked grin of his lets loose as he bobs his head in confirmation. "See, I can do thoughtful too." The grin morphs into a smirk. "Just like your previous employer."

Tyler Lee Adams handpicked what looks like twenty gorgeous bras for me. I guess my boss is trying to bestow me with a heart attack for Christmas. That . . . and a mind-blowing orgasm.

"Oh, believe me, nothing is remotely similar about the two of you." I send him a cheeky grin. "So tell me, what's the story with your Get Ivi's Bosom Covered crusade?"

Tyler let's out a light chuckle. Pulling me to straddle his lap, he kisses my lips. "At first, it was distracting. Not sure if you've checked yourself out, but you have an impressive rack."

Playing along, I crook a finger into my shirt and look down. Lifting my eyes, I say, "Yeah, pretty notable."

"Fucking perfect." Tyler steals another kiss. "Back when you just arrived here, it was about all the dickheads around enjoying the view way too much." He sends his hands to my temples, threading his fingers into my hair. He fists it into a ponytail, holding it with his hand. "Now." His eyes capture mine as he slightly tugs my hair back. "Now I don't want anyone even thinking about them. Or you, in general, for that matter."

Or you, in general, for that matter. My body is flooded with sweet warmth as my pulse quickens. The coarseness lacing his voice kindles my satiated desire. Still holding my head slightly tilted back, he leans in to draw soft bites along my jawline. "Open the other present," he says to my neck.

I blink my eyes open, yanked out of his delicious spell. Leaning back, Tyler's eyes hold mine as he sends his hand to the envelope on the rug next to us. Fishing it with two fingers, he hands it to me. Still straddling him, I push my finger through the crevice and gently slit it open.

Frowning, I pull out a thin, rectangular piece of paper. It takes me a moment to realize that the piece of paper in my hands is a check. My heart squeezes as I notice the endorsee: Youth with Purpose Organization. I blink a couple of times, glancing at the amount. My lips part and my eyes widen as I slowly trail them up to Tyler. My hand comes up to my parted lips, and through my daze, I whisper, "Tyler, that's . . ." Swallowing my emotions, I feel unexpectedly vulnerable. "I- I don't know what to say. This is beyond incredible and generous. It's . . ."

Tyler's eyes cast down in the sweetest, humble way. When his stare re-meets mine, it's followed by a tender smile. "Thought it'd make you happy." Something seeds deep inside me. Something I can't name. Something overpowering and jarring and sensational, but I know well enough it's because of the man holding me in his arms. "And it is for a good cause," he adds with a coy shrug.

"I can't thank you enough. That's just — wow, wonderful. It's enough to do everything on our wish list for the village I'm going to soon and . . . then some." With the tail end of my sentence, my excitement takes a little nosedive because "going to soon" also means leaving Tyler soon. Not to ruin the moment with unbidden glum, I slide my hands up Tyler's bare chest, inching to brush his lips against mine.

Reciprocating, Tyler's tongue dominates mine. In harmony, his hand cups the nape of my neck, pulling me deeper into him.

Sinking into the feeling, I close my eyes and murmur, "I got you something, too."

"What did you get me?" Tyler says to my earlobe just before wrapping his lips around it.

Shaking myself out of the Tyler Lee Adams pleasure trance, I gently push his chest and hop off his lap.

"Hey, where do you think you're going?" He pouts.

I raise a finger in the universal "hold that thought; please continue doing that to me in a few" sign and sashay up the stairs.

"Have I told you just how much I like the knee-socks-bare-ass look on you?" He calls after me. I send him a cheeky smile over my shoulder. "Scratch like. Love. *Love* the look. I never loved anything as much in my life." His voice holds sweet joy and teases as it follows me to the second floor.

My heart does a little jitter. "I'll keep that in mind," I call back. The ginormous smile on my face is not something I'm controlling anymore.

I worry my lip, handing Tyler the simply wrapped gift about a minute later. It looks a bit lame in comparison to the extravagantly, sophisticatedly wrapped gifts sitting under the tree. I wince at the thought.

Tyler glances at me, holding my present in his hand. "One shouldn't look so stressed when giving someone a present." His lips quirk.

I return his smile, relaxing an iota.

His brows bunch as he observes the wooly black material in his hands. A smile mellows his features as he unfolds the pair of socks I've knitted him. His grin turns into a wholehearted smile when he notices the gray skulls mid-sock.

I shrug. "A little something for the badass vibe."

"Fucking love it!" Tyler mutters while shrugging the socks on. Standing up, Tyler motions at his feet with his hands, modeling my creation for me. On any other guy on the entire planet, the boxers and wooly socks stretched up to the shins look would be a completely dorky, ridiculous turn-off. Now, on Tyler Lee Adams, it's a completely different story. Tyler with a post heavy-rendezvous-between-the-sheets look, black boxer briefs, impeccably toned body, alluring tattoos, and wool socks is an unbeatable aphrodisiac.

"Looks good on you." I beam his way.

Grinning at me, he offers me his hand. Helping me up, he kisses me silly. Still nibbling at my lips, he murmurs, "Dessert time."

A thin smile hovers my lips as I let Tyler lead me to the kitchen. "Maybe I'd better put my panties on." Not waiting for a response, I turn to shimmy into my underwear.

Tyler turns to give me a bothered glance. He shakes his head. "You're way too dressed." And to my surprise, he grabs the hem of my shirt from both sides and yanks it up over my head. He nods approval and takes my hand.

Half-jokingly, I say under my breath, "We're going to eat. I should have a shirt on."

He turns to give me a "don't be ridiculous" look over his shoulder. "No such thing will happen." And pulls me after him. My eyes crinkle at his grinning profile.

Perched on the counter, I follow Tyler with my gaze as he gets a bowl of Kissell from the fridge then returns and sets himself between my thighs.

I drop my eyes to the bowl he holds between us and look up. "Are you a masochist? Sure you want to have some more fruits of my labor?"

His lips twitch wickedly. He shakes his head, his eyes gleaming mischievously. "You'll go first."

I murmur, "What a gentleman."

"Never said I was one." Dipping a finger in the crème, he brings it to my mouth. "Bet it's delicious. After all, I was in charge of this one. Saved it from your cooking 'skills.'"

Before I'm able to retaliate, his finger lands between my lips, painting sweet pudding along my bottom one. In one slow stroke, he renders me quiet. I dart my tongue out for a taste. A wave of sweet, home, and everything good washes over me as the flavor melts over my tongue. Just like my mom's, just as sweet, or even better right here with Tyler between my thighs, served on his finger. "Perfect," I say licking my lips.

"It's the Tyler Lee magic touch." He wiggles his brows and leans in to press his lips against mine in a luscious kiss. Drawing back, he says in a breath, "Yeah, perfect."

"Your touch does work magic." My murmur earns me a thankful yet amused head tip.

An easy smile adorns Tyler's lips as he dips two tattooed fingers into the dish. I follow his cream-coated fingers with my gaze, swallowing hard as they end up on my upper lip. A frisson of desire overwhelms my insides as he ever so slowly drags his fingers downward. Over the mound of my mouth to my chin, he paints a trail of cold cream down my throat. My lips part as his mouth hovers over my skin, and his tongue sluggishly traces the sweet trail. Heat pools in anticipation in the pit of my belly as he turns to dip his fingers into the bowl once more. This time, he brings them to my exposed breast, stealing my breath as they come in contact with my nipple. I lick my lips, watching his finger erotically draw circles of cream around my nipple. A strangled moan escapes me when his tongue, spread wide, slowly laps it off me. His eyes on me are pools of fire while he drags his tongue along my skin, following his fingers as they paint trails of sweet cream on my skin. My other breast is next. Painstakingly torturous, he plays my nerve endings to shudder.

"Delicious," Tyler whispers to my skin. Resting his hand between my breasts, he gently pushes me back to lie on the counter. Holding the bowl in one hand, he piles cream on his fingers. I arch a little when they meet my heated skin. Sensually, he circles them around my belly button, drawing a path to the hem of my panties. By the time he discards my panties and kisses me where I'm literally burning for him, I'm at a total loss of control. His to do with as he pleases. And he does, right there in the kitchen amid my abandoned, rancid holiday dishes and the bright florescent light.

"I'll never look at Kissell the same way," I say to Tyler's pecks, where he embraces me under a soft throw blanket on the rug next to the fire, post "dessert."

"It just became my favorite dessert." His voice reverberates under his warm skin, eliciting a smile on my face.

The smile remains unbroken as I let my heavy eyelids rest. A thrill-laced concern runs through me as this moment registers. How this day ends. A day that started with one clear goal—to make it a happy one—

had turned into something I wouldn't even allow myself to entertain, not in a million years. Falling asleep in Tyler's arms. As sweet and perfect as it feels, I can't help but think about what tomorrow will bring. Despite being the optimistic person that I am, I'm still as realistic as the next gal. I genuinely believe we can make this world a better one. But even I am not gullible enough to think that anything beyond what happened between Tyler Lee Adams and me tonight has any kind of future.

But hey, I'm lying in this amazing man's arms, and no one can take that away from me. Malignant thoughts, please take a hike and let me immerse at this moment to the fullest. It's not every day I am able to kiss Tyler on a whim. So why not take advantage of the lovely gift Santa endorsed me with this year.

A Christmas card, sent by a Canadian relative ages ago, pops into my head as I think of this night. *May all the sweet magic of Christmas conspire to gladden your heart and fill every desire.*

Grinning to myself, I raise my head and inch a little higher up Tyler's body, surprising him with one hell of a happy Ivi kiss.

Merry Christmas to me!

CHAPTER

Twenty-Five

CHAPTER

"So many faces. So much makeup and scanty dresses. I can hardly keep up. Lordy me. Life is too precious to spend it on strumpets! It's not all about big bosom and red lips, my darling Ty. Find a good girl, make Nana happy, why don't you? And good grief boy, shave. You look dirty."
Tyler Lee's beloved grandma, Dottie, to twenty-year-old Tyler Lee about his dynamic 'dating life' making the front page of every possible tabloid around.

The smell of pine and smoky burned wood assaults me as I flicker my eyes open to the pale morning. The crackling sound of the last few logs burning away follows me as I look around, searching for Tyler. I'm not one to jump to conclusions, but the twinge of concern that poked at me before falling asleep about the night being a one-time thing comes back, this time with a raised brow and a sneery smile. Just like the ebbing fire, my mood drops. "Tyler?"

Nothing.

Cinching the throw blanket around my scantily covered body, I can't help but notice there are no remains, no evidence of Tyler sleeping beside me. *Me*, the naïve girl with the slightly scathed ego and the wild bed-hair. Brushing, or at least opting to brush away the self-deprecating thoughts, I square my shoulders and tip my chin up, making my way to the kitchen. For tea, of course. Not to look for Tyler because I don't really care that he left me to wake up by myself, and I really don't care that he didn't bother to leave a small note. None of that. Tea is the only thing on my mind.

I take the first sip of the aromatic beverage and slump in the chair, contemplating the last few good minutes. What's wrong with me? This insecure creature fretting about waking alone after a night of shenanigans is not me. I don't operate this way. Such ridiculous behavior. A bit pathetic, if not pitiful. I had sex with the man last night, so what? That doesn't grant me an immediate pledge for a start of a relationship of any sort. I need to own my actions and deal with the ramifications, unpleasant as they may be.

I swirl the cup in circles, about twenty minutes later, whirling the little remnants of tea leaves at the bottom of the cup. Determined to make myself scarce and avoid an awkward "morning after" moment, which is undeniably coming, I take my cup to the sink. Try as I might, I can't keep at bay the memory of the first time Tyler saw me in this very kitchen. *"Fun is over, babe, you have to leave now."* Which now feels like an omen. In my head, a loud, wicked laugh follows.

Still caught up in my thoughts, I set the cup to dry and turn around. I do a double take when I see the person entering the kitchen because, for the first few, slow moments, he looks familiar but doesn't really register. My lower back meets the hard counter when I take a startled step back.

"Good morning, sleepy," Tyler's animated voice greets me.

"Um, g-good morning." I push myself forward, studying him curiously. I take a few hesitant steps his way.

He closes the gap between us with three languid steps. Before I'm able to say a word, he touches his lips to mine, banishing my insecurities back to the depths of my self-conscious closet. I must say, usually insecurity is not my thing, but for reasons, even unclear to me, I feel especially vulnerable this morning.

Drawing back, I give Tyler a closer look. Reaching my hand to his chin, I lightly touch it with the pads of my fingers. "What happened to your beard?"

He shrugs, trailing his hand downward to roam over my lower back and south. "Shaved it." Nibbling on my exposed collarbone, he says to my skin, "The lady we're going to visit doesn't like it." His chuckle is an afterthought. He gives my skin another soft kiss and straightens to look at me. "Says I look like a hobo."

So much to address in these two short sentences, but all I can do is be drawn by the magnificent sight that is a smiling, freshly shaven, Tyler. My heart does a little flutter to the dimple sinking into his cheek. A perfect duet with his smile. Tyler with a beard is pure masculinity. But a shaven Tyler, with a dimple thrown into the mix—that's a whole new level of swooning.

When the gorgeous male spell lightly fades, I ask, "Where did you say we were going?"

He gives his watch a glance. "I'll fill you in on the way. We should get going."

"What should I wear?" Reluctantly, I detach myself from his intoxicating freshly showered scent. Sweet and spicy and uniquely Tyler.

"Casual." He gives me another dimpled smile, a sweet one that turns my eyes dreamy.

I turn around and yelp in surprise to the stinging slap on my butt. Looking at him over my shoulder, I'm rewarded with yet another dimpled smile, this one straight out of the sinful realm. Climbing the stairs, I feel like I'm floating, high on whatever is happening between Tyler and me.

———— • ————

"You're taking me to visit your grandma?" My question conveys the extent of surprise the notion brings.

Tyler mutters a flat, "Yeah," turning the wheel and rolling the car into a small, tattered diner parking lot.

His utter nonchalance leaves me all the more confounded. Okay then, meeting Tyler Lee's grandma it is.

Idling the massive SUV, Tyler turns to me. He scratches his cheek, smiling somewhat coyly. "So you mind getting us breakfast?"

My brows wrinkle. "Sure," I answer tentatively.

He points at the tinted window in a way of explanation. "Um, I don't think that me walking out there would be the best idea."

"Oh, right," I say softly, bobbing my head, pleasantly surprised to find out how easily his casual, sweet behavior makes me forget who he is. "Right," I repeat, shaking off my mind's sudden detour. I guess Tyler Lee Adams sauntering into a diner could cause some commotion, to put it mildly. Taking his order, I shake my head at the money he extends my way.

"Ivi." It's a warning.

"Tyler." I mockingly imitate his voice.

His features set into a scowl. "Ivi, take the — "

Jumping out of the car, I leave him with the bills hanging in his hand and a scolding expression. I give him a cheeky smile, looking at him through the gap in the open door. My smile only broadens to his glare. "Sucks being you sometimes, huh?" I tease and shut the door behind me. Beaming, I add some extra twerk to my walk, not looking back.

"Black coffee and two danishes." I hand Tyler his coffee and place the pastries on the armrest between us.

Tyler takes a long drink of his cup and leans in to take a bite of the muffin in my hand. The one I'm about to bite into. Chewing on *my* breakfast, his lips tip up as a counter to my glare. Swallowing, he pecks my lips, sets his coffee in the cup holder, and cranks the car. I can't get over how casual and natural it feels with him. Us hanging out as a . . . whatever we are. An inner smile lights up my inside as I give him a quick peep, vanishing as soon as my mind starts analyzing the situation. The more wonderful it feels right now, the harder it'll be to say good-bye soon. Winnie the Pooh once said, "How lucky am I to have something that makes saying good-bye so hard." Taking the wise bear's advice, I let this something take over me in full force. Consequences, broken hearts, and scathed egos will be dealt with when my private "crushing (hard) on a rock star" bubble bursts in my face. In about a week and a few hours, to be precise. I can't believe over six months have fled so fast.

Holding a sophisticatedly wrapped box with "Teuscher" emblazoned on the top in elegant black letters, Tyler knocks on the door to room 10A, in what can only be described as an ultra-fancy village. Complete with tennis courts, swimming pools, Spanish style villas, and golf carts with silver hair (or what's left of it) slicked sideways, donning diamond sweater gentlemen.

"This is a retirement home?" I ask quietly.

Tyler nods.

"For reals?"

He gives me a side smile, saying in a low voice, "Don't repeat that in front of her. She gave me enough crap about this place being posh before finally agreeing to stay here."

My lips tip up. "I like her already."

His response is a silent one, yet it speaks louder than words. His eyes soften as he caresses my cheek and leans in to leave a tender kiss on my lips. It feels like I mean something to him at this very moment. And the feeling is beyond wonderful.

An adenoidal, "Coming!" followed by, "Patience, these legs aren't young anymore," comes from behind the azure Spanish style door.

Tyler snorts a laugh and to my utter surprise takes my hand in his, leading us in as the door opens wide.

"Oh, honey." The petite lady with a short, white bob wraps her arms around Tyler's waist. She rests her cheek just below his chest, her eyes closed and her features shining with delight.

Tyler almost bends in half to reciprocate the hug and kiss her on the cheek. "How you doing?"

"Good, good." When Tyler hands her the expensive looking chocolate box, her eyes light up. "You always spoil me, honey." She squeezes his forearm. "Come on in." She takes a step back, gesturing for us to follow.

Reaching the living room, she turns to us with a smile. Her eyes rest on me. The cursory gaze feels like she already knows everything there is to know about me. The look takes a mischievous shade, followed by a quaint smile. "So who have we got here, Tyler Lee? Your sweetheart?" Just as Tyler parts his lips to answer, she carries on, "Oh, my darling, she's so pretty. Like an angel. Look at those eyes." She opens her arms, looking at me encouragingly. "Come here, sweetheart, give an old lady a hug."

Tyler's grandma takes me into a warm, bony embrace, which I return with no less sincerity. "What's your name, sweetheart?" She draws back, keeping her hold on me. With her hands on my forearms and a gentle smile, she waits for my answer.

"It's Ivi. Nice to meet you. You have such a lovely place." I mirror her kind expression.

"Oh, and what's the origin of this sweet accent?"

"I'm Estonian."

Her thinly, drawn-on eyebrows raise in question.

"A little country in Europe, neighboring Finland," I elaborate.

"How exciting!" She claps her hands, finally letting me go. "I have a visitor from Europe."

Tyler follows our exchange with slightly quirked lips. His smile stretches wider when his grandmother takes my hand and squeezes it. "I'm Dorothy, but you can call me Dottie."

"Sure, Dottie. It's a delight meeting you."

"Take a seat, please." She motions a lean, veiny hand at the exaggeratedly floral living room. Her soft gaze trails over us as we walk to the sofa. "What are you drinking, Ivi? Tyler, would you like some of that cider you like so well?"

When Tyler nods, she turns to me.

"Um, how about I get the drinks, if you don't mind, Dottie," I suggest. "Stay here with Tyler; I bet you have a lot of catching up to do."

Dottie's brief surprise quickly morphs into a complacent smile. She trades a flit stare with Tyler before telling me, "That would be lovely, actually, if you don't mind. These ancient bones could use some rest." I nod with an easy smile of my own. "There's cider in the clear pitcher, and some freshly baked cookies on the table."

"Cider and cookies coming up." I turn on my heel.

A grip on my hand stops me mid-turn. I bounce back to face them, my eyes falling on Tyler's hand holding mine. Wordlessly, he brings my hand to his lips and presses a kiss to my skin. The stare he has on me while doing so is unfathomable, yet potent enough to make my belly twist sweetly. "Thank you," he mouths, letting my hand go.

A tray with a plate of cookies, two glasses, and flowery napkins await me as I enter the small, homey kitchen. My focus remains on the duet of glasses—just two—telling me Tyler didn't give Dottie a heads-up about bringing a guest. Tagging me along to visit with his grandma wasn't a premeditated idea, but he still did it after the night we shared together. The notion, together with his little gestures of affection throughout this morning, has my heart doing a little impromptu cha-cha, complete with the final hand raise. Adding another glass to the tray, I make my way back to the living room.

"Where's Athena?" Tyler asks Dottie as I take a seat next to her on the sofa.

Dottie rolls her eyes. A gesture that doesn't seem to bode well with Tyler. "I told her to take a couple of hours off." Dottie stops whatever was about to leave Tyler's mouth with, "I can still take care of myself, Tyler Lee. I don't need someone fussing over me twenty-four hours a day."

Tyler jaw flexes. "When is she due back?"

"Soon." Dottie dismisses him, waving her hand and turning to me. "So how long have you two been courting?"

I almost spray out my next sip when I hear her question. My eyes slice to Tyler with alarm.

"Six months," Tyler replies over a smile, appearing to be about to burst up in fits of laughter at my distress.

Dottie's hand covers mine. "I sure hope he's been treating you well."

"I wouldn't let him treat me any other way." I try to tone down my cheeky smile as I squint Tyler's way.

Dottie's features light up. "Good for you."

The next few good minutes are carried away by easy conversation, where Dottie reminisces about Tyler's childhood with a nostalgic beam. That is until something alternates in her demeanor. Her stare turns far-off, as though she's not with us anymore. I shoot Tyler, whose easy air has tensed drastically, a concerned glance.

Dottie looks around the room confused, as though seeing it for the first time. She blinks a few times and brings her eyes back to us. When her stare lands on me, she frowns and perks up. "Eva, I won't let you send him off at this young age." Her gaze on me hardens. "Whose best interests do you have in mind exactly?" she snaps, anger tinting her thin voice.

At a loss, I turn to Tyler again. Tyler raises his hand a little and nods, gesturing I shouldn't worry.

"Dottie," he says in an imposing tone, drawing his grandma's attention. "Do you recognize me?"

Her expression mellows on cue, but just a little. She still looks riled up. "Of course Ty-Ty, darling. Don't worry, honey. I'm here for you. I won't let them send you away. You're too young."

"No one is sending me away. I'm right here." Tyler's eyes focus in on hers.

"Of course, you are. I won't let them," she repeats, fisting her shaky hands on her lap.

Abruptly, she shifts back to me. "Who are you?" Startled, her stare returns to Tyler. "Ty-Ty who is this lady, and what is she doing in my house?"

"Ah, I-I'm Ivi." My voice clearly conveys my confusion.

"Ivi. She's my friend," Tyler assures in a gentle chord.

"Nice to meet you, Ivi. Have you heard my grandson sing yet? So talented yet so young. Can you believe that they want to send him away at this young age? Thirteen!"

The notion that Dottie must suffer from some sort of dementia strikes a sad chord in my heart. "He has a beautiful voice, Dottie," I say softly.

The emotions in me grow as Tyler walks over to sit by his grandma. He takes her hand in his, caressing it with his other.

"Sing something for me, Ty-Ty. How about my favorite song?"

Holding his grandma's hand, Tyler licks his lips and starts singing. Unconsciously, I take one of the floral throw pillows and hug it to my chest. Enthralled, I watch Tyler singing a quiet, raw version of "Halleluiah" to Dottie. She's watching him affectionately, gradually calming down. Slowly, Dottie snuggles closer to Tyler's side. He slides his arm around her shoulder, prompting her features to mellow with contentment.

Not long after, my own stare mimics hers and so does what I'm feeling for Tyler.

The squeaking sound of a door opening draws our attention.

"I'm sorry it took me so long." A thick waist blonde with rosy cheeks says through labored breath. "Oh, hi Mr. Adams." She throws her purse on the table and rolls up her sleeves. "It's time for a little rest, Dottie."

Tyler nods.

"Who are you?" Dottie clips.

"Athena, Dottie." Athena and Tyler have an unspoken conversation, where it seems like Athena assures him that she's taking over. "Let's say good-bye to your guests." She extends her hand to Dottie.

The walk back to Tyler's car is a silent one. A pregnant silence.

CHAPTER
Twenty-Six

CHAPTER

"WHERE IS TYLER LEE ADAMS? LIKE IF HE'S NOT IN BED WITH ME, WHERE HE AT?" A post on Tyler Lee Adams Facebook Fan page by @ HeisMine
"Probably IN Brooklyn Mars" comment #1 out of 200 and counting

"Where are we?" I ask Tyler as he brings the car to a stop, ten minutes into a quietly meditative drive.

Pocketing the key fob, he turns to me. "Just a place I come to from time to time to think, write music." Sending his hand to the door handle, he adds, "After seeing Dottie."

"It's beautiful." I glance at the windshield. "A perfect setting for one of those 80's cult horror movies where the silly girl gets lured into a trap and gets murdered by a handsome psychopath."

Tyler snorts, shaking his head. A shadow of a smile plays at his lips as he lets himself out of the car and circles it to open the door for me. He offers me his hand and leads me to the front of the car. I'm in awe of the picturesque view of magnificent mountains, stunning coastline, and greenery. A backdrop of all shades of vibrant green.

I let out a startled yelp when he lifts me up to perch on the cooling hood. I follow him with a quizzical gaze as he hops on the hood next to me and rests his back on the windshield. His thin smile returns as he winds his long arm around my waist and tugs me over to sit closer to him. Keeping his arm around me, he lets me comfortably mold into his side. "Dottie's Alzheimer's is at a moderate stage. Been that way for a couple of years now." Tyler stares ahead. "So hard to see someone you care about slowly lose herself. She used to be so independent and opinionated, in her own unique way." Tyler sighs. "And now, now she needs someone to take care of her." I look up at him, cataloging the frustration in his eyes and the tension in his set jaw. "When I tried to persuade her to move in with me, she wouldn't hear of it. I caved when I realized we spent most of her sober moments arguing about it."

"I can only imagine how agonizing it must be to see someone you care about that much wither before your eyes," I say in a quiet voice.

Tyler nods, his gaze far-off. "And there's nothing you can do about it."

"What about your parents?" My question is unanswered. And remains so as the sky above us opens up, pouring down rain.

We both jump off the car and run to the door.

"Let's stay here a bit longer." Tyler takes my hand in his and helps me to the backseat. Getting in, Tyler settles with his back to the door. He opens his arms, beckoning me to lie on him in the back of the car. I settle between Tyler's legs, my chin propped on my hands on his chest. "There's something about rain and a wet, pretty girl." He grins at me, droplets still hanging at his long lashes.

I mirror that smile with a little heart flutter. Tyler's hand moves a strand of damp hair from my forehead. The cadence in his eyes makes my heart miss a beat. I'm equally nervous and thrilled to have him look at me this way. I'm afraid to read too much into it, yet I can't ignore the way it makes me feel.

"You know, sometimes I have these 'I wish moments,'" I say, easing my way off from the impending confrontation between my heart and mind. Tyler nods, encouraging me to go on. "Where I wish for things that I know are almost impossible."

"Like?" Tyler asks tenderly. His hands gently roam over the nape of my neck to the hem of my dress and up again. A touch that's warm and slow and absolutely wonderful.

"Like, I wish something could help your grandmother." I swallow hard. "Or I wish I could really know what you're thinking right now."

His expression turns profound. "You want to know what's on my mind, Ivi?" In tandem to his question, his hand crawls under my dress, gently caressing the back of my thighs. His eyes lock with mine. "That I'm not sure what I want more—to kiss you or keep listening to you talk."

Our kiss next is so tender and warm, full of something that makes me wish it'll never stop. Tyler must feel the same way because the way he looks at me when we slowly ease back can't mean any other thing.

"Tell me more about you." My voice comes out slightly husky, still harboring the effect of kissing this man. "Your past."

Tyler pecks my lips and leans back to rest his head on his bent arm on the door. Playing with a strand of my hair with his other hand, he tips to square our stares and tells me about the beginning of his career. About joining a boy band at a relatively young age. "At thirteen, I fast-tracked into a world I had jack shit ammo in my arsenal to attempt to tread by myself; better yet, I have pushed off the plank. I experienced things kids three years my senior or older could only fantasize about. Women, alcohol . . . the addictive limelight." The tail end of his words comes out in a flat tone. "This lifestyle both amps you and brings you down at the same time. I was too young, way too young to know what I was doing. And really, what do you even know when you're thirteen? That tits are your kryptonite, and that life begins and ends in your dick. One day, you're playing soccer, adding fresh scratches to your knees, and the next, you're shacked in hotels fit for kings, having cameras on you everywhere you go, and girls . . . girls. Beautiful girls of all ages, shapes, and colors swoon at your feet, offering themselves up like you're some kind of god."

"What about your parents?" I clear my throat. "Is that what Dottie was talking about when she, when she was muddled?"

He nods, wrinkles appearing between his brows. "In retrospect, I can say that my parents got a little blinded by everything that was happening, what with me signing with a label and being in a band known worldwide. Fame, money. A lot of money, a very comfortable life."

"Did you want all of that at the time?" I thread my fingers with him, waiting for him to answer.

"Now, I can say that I was scared and not yet ready to leave home. Signing the contract meant going on a six-month tour the very next month." His hand moves to draw little circles on my collarbone. "My parents played off my nervousness as thrill and excitement. Dottie fought them at every turn, arguing that I was too young. That if I got such an offer at thirteen, others would come along when I was older, when I was ready."

"How was it, though? It sounds both exciting and, to be honest, scary as hell."

Tyler chuckles, leaning in to give me a quick kiss. "It was indeed exciting and scary, but as I was the youngest, the other members quickly took me under their wing. They instantly became my family. And for a while, I really needed them."

"Did your parents travel with you?"

He lets out a chuckle laced with bitterness. Lightly shaking his head, he said, "Never. They were too busy cashing in on my success." For a stretch, he seems to consider his words. "I felt abandoned by them."

His words tug at my heart, surprising me with the quality of candor they carry. He looks no less surprised by his own openness. At the same time, the fact that he's sharing this with me makes whatever I feel for him stronger, much stronger.

"It's one thing to push your child to succeed. It's a completely different thing to let him go at such an early stage in his life. Let him go in every sense of the word. Abandonment is a tough cross to bear." His eyes deeply connect with mine as he says, "Fast forward a decade later, and that's why I sort of agreed not to be a part of Jeremy's life. I didn't think, at the time, that I'd be able to be there for him. That I would even know how to. I was touring the world for a few good months at a time. I wasn't available physically or emotionally to be a father. At the time, it felt like the best thing to do for him. Let him have a healthy, normal childhood. I thought I was doing the right thing. The unselfish thing." Tyler's eyes focus in on a freckle on my collarbone. His voice takes a graver shade when he adds, "Which was completely selfish. That, I know now."

I nod, swallowing over the little lump in my throat. Leaning in, I tenderly kiss his lips. "Why did you decide to leave the band?"

"It took me a few good years to do that. When I turned eighteen, I decided to take my life into my own hands and cut the umbilical cord. But I didn't have a clue how to even begin the process. Then Eli, who was the band's rookie assistant manager, came along. He was the one person who listened. He was the one person who understood when I said I was jaded, that I wanted to write my own music and do my own thing. He was everything both my parents weren't.

"With Eli's help, I fired my father as my manager and also finally separated my finances from my parents. Felt like a pyrrhic victory." He grimaces. "I had my freedom but in a sense lost my family." He sighs. "Right after, I quit my contract with the label."

"Are you still in touch with your parents?"

He nods. "Not as family should be. It's impossible to love someone when you've lost all respect for them."

"Tyler." His name on my lips is saturated with emotions. "It means so much to me that you shared all of this with me."

He nods. Sending his hand to my waist, he brings me to lay higher on his chest, so our mouths hover next to each other. "I'm having an 'I wish moment' right now," he says to my lips.

"Tell me," I whisper, swallowed into the heat his look transmits to me

"I wish you didn't have to leave so soon."

Twenty-Seven

CHAPTER
CHAPTER

"Music? I'm like a monk when it comes to music; it's everything to me. It cleanses my mind. Makes me see better. Makes sense of things. You know what I mean? It gives me peace and lucidity. Transcendence. I don't think I've encountered anything that makes me feel more alive than music."
Tyler Lee Adams, interview for Rolling Stones *magazine.*

One day. Twenty-four hours before my little Tyler Lee Adams fairy tale turns back into a pumpkin, or to the "what the heck are we doing" state of affairs it was before our magical Christmas Eve. Tomorrow morning at seven thirty (probably sharp,) Adina is due back.

I'll take a wild guess and say that a few hours later, Eli's severe expression will haunt every corner of the house. And not to mention, Jeremy's return in the late afternoon. As optimistic of a person as I may be, even I don't see Tyler and me kissing under every tree in the garden with a house full of people to witness. I can't help but think it's not too soon before a heartbreak will come a-knocking. But you know what they say. Life's short and dance like no one's looking and all that. And that's exactly what I have been doing these last glorious twenty-four hours. Stupid I may be—no one can blame me for not living life to the fullest.

"You up?" Tyler's raspy morning voice hovers above my ear before his lips nuzzle mere inches below. His arm finds its way around my waist.

Shuffling in his embrace, I turn to face him. A dreamy smile loosens my lips to the sight of a drowsy Tyler. "Good morning." I press a chaste kiss on his lips.

Pulling me up to lie on top of him, he asks, "Sleep well?" Tyler's hands roam over the back of my thighs, casually making their way up.

"Perfect." I can't help the contentment in my voice. "This bed. I gotta get me one just like this one." I give him a tiny, feisty smile. Tyler's bed is by far the most comfortable piece of furniture I've ever rested my weary head on. But even this luxurious bed has nothing on how good it felt sleeping in Tyler's arms with his chest as the most comfortable pillow.

Tyler feigns a frown. "So it's just the bed?"

I put a finger on my lips in pretense of contemplating his question. "Um, yep, just the bed. Wait, why? Was there anything else?" Yelping, I rub my spanked bum. "That was unnecessary."

"Oh, it was." Tyler pushes my hand away and rubs the uber-corny-play area. Quickly, his hands take the liberty of exploring territories under my lacy boy shorts. I tense a little when his playful air morphs into a brooding one. His brows pull in as he retrieves his hands to more chaste ground and searches my eyes. "Jeremy is back tomorrow." A causal statement with such a loaded undercurrent.

"Yeah," I say in a small voice coated with mild concern. Guess it's time to acknowledge the impending "fairy tale's about to end" elephant in the room.

His gentle strokes along my skin turn from luring to soothing in a heartbeat. As though pacifying the blow that's about to come. "We'd better not let him get his hopes up about . . . us." He clears his throat, watching for my reaction. "You know, get the wrong impression."

Reading the message loud and clear, I wish I could school my falling features to remain poised. But it's mission impossible. I've never been a great actress. In a way, it feels like the end of a (one-sided) terrific one-night stand. *How'd you manage to stick around? Fun is over, babe. You have to leave now.*

When I nod, trying to stealthily roll off him, Tyler's hold on me tightens, keeping me close. "I'm really fucking this up, aren't I?" he says with a sigh, looking no less muddled than I must appear.

"Think you might be onto something there," I confirm flatly.

Only to be reward with a boyish, repentant smile. "Listen, Ivi—"

"Stop, Tyler. Please—you don't have to." I manage to clear disappointment off my face. A nearly impossible task. "I get it, really. No need to expose Jeremy to something provisional. Confuse him. I'm with you on that. It's what? Less than a week before I leave?" As certain as I feel saying that, there's nothing I can really do about the way each word leaving my mouth twists the spring in my stomach a little tighter.

"Ivi." Tyler holds my face, appearing discomfited. "Ivi, I never meant it to—"

I couldn't be more relieved by the interruption coming from my phone in the form of an incoming message. The last thing I want is to listen to any repentance coming from Tyler about the last few days. Repentance about me.

"I'm expecting that," I lie, wriggling out of his hold to dart for my phone. I fake a content sigh at my mom's message, though its effect at this very moment is entirely different.

Tyler frowns. "Who's texting you so early in the morning?"

"Tyler Lee, do I detect jealousy in your tone?" Teasing, I bat our previous conversation out of tense field.

"Maybe," he drawls. Flabbergasted, I process Tyler's casual reply, giving him enough time to nimbly snatch the phone from my hand. "Ma armastan sind ka, Kiisu?" e He reads with a comical accent, prompting my lips to curve into a smile.

"Ma armastan sind ka, Kiisu!" I repeat in a way that actually sounds Estonian.

"What does it mean?" Tyler asks, his eyes profoundly on me.

"I love you too, kitten," I say, my lips tipping higher.

He grimaces, his brows scrunching closer together.

"It's from my mom. An answer to a message I sent her last night." My smile brightens at his mellowing expression. He looks . . . relived?

Tyler's lip arches at the side. "Kitten?"

I shake my head, tossing my phone to the nightstand. Feigning indifference to his growing grin, I drop my legs off the bed. Tyler's quick hand around my waist stops my attempt to stand up.

"Where do you think you're going, Kiisu?" I let out a light giggle at the endearment coming from him. Tyler brings me to straddle him. "Darling Ivi, care to explain the origin of the loveliest nickname?"

I fold my arms over my chest. "You have to promise never to make fun of me if I tell you."

Tyler's grin grows. And grows. Melting his dimple into his cheek. Along the way, making my own lips stretch wider. What can a girl do? That Tyler Lee Adams smile . . .

"I swear," he says in a way that transpires absolutely nil sincerity. To top it up, he offers me his pinky.

I let out a giggle at the offered finger. "You couldn't look more untrustworthy even if you tried."

"I'm heartbroken by your mistrust, Kiisu." I throw my eyes to the skylight ceiling. Tyler shakes his head with feign exasperation. "That's how you want to play, eh?" In a sneaky, swift move, he drops me to my back and looms above me. Trapping me below his mass, he holds my hands tight above my head with one of his. Sealing my giggles with his mouth, he kisses me senseless. Drawing back with a devilish grin, he says, "Now, spill it, Kiisu."

I roll my eyes again, more than enjoying playful Tyler. "Oh God, you're going to have a field day with this one. I just know it."

"Kiis . . ." Tyler warns with utter mischief.

I lightly chuckle, raising my head to steal a kiss. One that Tyler returns with a smile. "So my mom says that when I was young and would drink my warm milk before bed, I used to lick my lips with so much gusto, it reminded her of a little kitten. Ergo . . . Kiisu." I frown at Tyler's wholehearted chuckle, murmuring, "Shocking."

Tyler's eyes morph tender as he trades glances between mine, a supple grin on his lips. "Pure gold." He leans in closer, bringing his lips to mine. "Kiisu, I like the name. I think I'll borrow it." In a husky voice that holds no amusement he repeats, "Kiisu."

I like it no less when he whispers it to my mouth, my neck, my breastbone, before undressing me and ravishing me till *his* name falls from my lips in breathy incantation.

———•———

"Have you ever played 'In Your Smile' in an acoustic version?" I ask Tyler, biting on a piece of toast now that we've finally managed to peel ourselves off each other in favor of breakfast. Straddled on his thighs in the kitchen, feeding him our joined breakfast, I add, "I'd love to hear that. I think it would sound amazing raw."

Taking another bite of the toast in my hand, Tyler says, "Anything for you, Kiisu."

I'd be lying if I said I didn't like him calling me that. "What? You have it stashed somewhere around here?"

Tyler stares at me with such flustering undercurrent. A look he doesn't break even when he takes a sip of his coffee. He licks his lips. "Let's go."

I follow him up the stairs in anticipation, which only grows as he takes my hand and leads me to his studio. "Here." He pulls a chair out for me at the control table. Tyler types something on a keyboard, looking up at the wall-mounted, large screen. Finding what he was looking for, he tells me, "When I signal you, press enter." Without further ado, he plants a succulent kiss on my lips and jogs to the foam lined isolation booth.

I watch him in fascination from behind the glass as he adjusts a set of headphones. Stepping closer to the standing chrome microphone, Tyler nods at me.

As told, I press enter and wait. The first line of "In Your Smile" funnels into the room, the melody trickling into my belly. Tyler's stare captures mine as he grabs the mic with two hands. His eyes don't waver as he leans forward for his mouth to hover next to the microphone. "I could search the whole world over."

Goose bumps cascade down my arms when his smoky voice fills the ample room.

"I would never find another you."

Entranced, I drink him in through the misty glass. Slightly bowed, tattoo-covered arms bent, hands grasping the mic, toned chest lightly gleaming from the small overhead light, snug white boxer briefs and narrowed dark eyes blazing into mine. "In all the ways you showed me what love is all about."

A clan of butterflies erupts from the center of my belly, wildly fluttering their wings around. Like a weightless marionette, I'm being lifted, helpless to the power his voice and gaze has over me. Effortlessly, he tosses me into a whirlwind of emotions by the cadence of his voice alone. Easily taking control over my heart and mind.

"In your smile, in your smile," Tyler sings the chorus one last time, lyrics that tamely bring me back down from the spell he put on me.

I tear a page out from a notebook I find on the desk and grab a sharpie from a pencil cup. I write the number ten in thick digits on the white paper, lifting it up above my head. Tyler's lips twitch at the sides before he bows in gratitude.

Straightening, he looks at me with eyes that could burn my skin with the amount of heat they send. He dips his chin to speak into the mic, "I'm having an 'I wish moment' right now, Kiisu." His voice echoes through the ample room.

I nod, signaling for him to go on.

"I wish I could see you with that toolbox of yours again."

Frowning, I grab the sharpie again and write a question mark on the back of the page. Raising it up again, I bend my other hand in question.

"I just had a déjà vu moment of that day when I saw you under the sink." He licks his lips. "You looked so damn sexy that day, you nearly drove me insane."

The flush that covers my cheeks comes in tandem with the smile I'm futilely trying to control. Slowly inching up from the chair, I make my way to the booth. Sending my hand to the handle, I give Tyler a thin, promising smile.

He mirrors me, drinking me in.

I take a step inside the softly lit space. "Well, you just made my wish come true. Having you sing that to me. Let's just say I might just return the favor someday."

"You just might, huh?" he murmurs, watching me with tapered eyes as I close the distance between us. A sinful glee brightens his eyes when I bring my hands to his chest, lightly pushing him backward. He raises an eyebrow, his lip faintly curved. Tyler follows my lead until his back meets the foam wall.

Desire courses my veins, heating up my skin as I trail my hands over his bare chest, down the defined muscles of his abdomen. Slowly bending to my knees, I steal a glance at Tyler who's watching me with heated eyes and slightly gaped lips. He swallows hard as I hook my fingers in the waistband of his boxers and slowly tug them down.

"Ivi." My name is a raspy groan as I take him in my mouth.

The sounds he makes. The way he grabs my hair. The shudders going through his body. His reactions to me set my own need for him on fire, encouraging me to make him lose control *over me*. I'm swimming in waves of sensual burn when Tyler eases back and lifts me to straddle him. His next moves are hurried and rough. He pushes me against the wall, pinning me with his pelvis. He kisses me next, nibbles on my skin, his hands roaming all over me as though he wants to touch every part of me at once. Tyler's unrestrained desire to have me brings my own craving to levels I never knew I was capable of feeling. I'm literally shaking with want, begging him with my body. "This is . . ." He growls as he pushes my panties aside. "You drive me fucking insane." He pushes himself into me. "Insane."

I'm lost. I'm completely lost in him.

Pushing hard into me, Tyler stills and murmurs something in my ear. Something that sounds like, "I'm not letting you go."

My mind, in a mush of ecstasy and Tyler, has a hard time interpreting the hushed, hoarse words.

———◆———

Between naps, light dinner, and long, laid-back conversations, the rest of the day lazily rolls into the evening. Late evening dusk envelops us as we slouch on the leather armchair in Tyler's office. I'm cradled in Tyler's lap with my legs tucked under me, wrapped by his toned arms that hold his guitar. I close my eyes, listening to the soft melody. I blink them open to yet another kiss that Tyler presses to my hair. In Tyler's arms, looking at his long, tattooed fingers strumming the guitar with the heat of his skin warming my back, I know nothing can feel as perfect. At the same time, I know that this bliss is slowly coming to an end.

His lips nuzzle my ear. "Want to go to bed?"

"Let's stay here a little more. I love listening to you play."

It's past midnight when we finally decide to go to sleep. Tyler presses a white button on the wall, and a soft buzz is followed by the curtains slowly drifting apart. I watch him from the bed as he stares at the starry-night unveiling from the master bedroom panoramic windows. A realization unravels in me as I watch Tyler stare at the night. Right now, I want nothing more than for him to turn around and tell me he doesn't want to let me go. Tell me that he wants us to explore the feelings we seemed to have developed for one another over the past six months and especially the last few blissful days. I want him to ask me to be his. More than anything. Confusion startles me with the understanding that the desire to be with him, to be his, suppresses my longtime dream. I want to stay here with him more than I want to go on my mission trip. A sensation that confounds me and makes me dislike myself more than a little.

Twenty-Eight

"I'm yours now. Forever, baby, is too long a time."
Tyler Lee Adams first solo single.

losing my eyes, I tip my head back, letting the warm water cascade over me. Even the rooster hasn't crowed yet, and I'm already up and about. Less than ten minutes ago, I tiptoed out of Tyler's bed with my restless thoughts in tow. My perfectly sliced pie chart of unyielding thoughts. One-third allocated to Tyler Lee and everything he makes me feel, and the remaining two parts are equally split between what I opted for my future and what I want now. The dichotomy of my feelings about my approaching mission trip leaves me troubled and confused. To sum it up, everything that I wanted, or thought I wanted before, has shuffled and jumbled, leaving me uncertain of what I want anymore. Or better yet, I clearly comprehend what it is that I want, but in the same breath, I know just how impossible it is to have. How foolish it is to even entertain the idea.

Even if I tried, I know I'm unable to control my feelings for Tyler at this point. It's not just a few days of casual lust and fun. It's a person I've gradually developed respect, a deep connection, and feelings for.

It's a person I've grown to like more than I ever thought I would. The real Tyler caught me off guard and seeded himself little by little in my heart. I don't think I will ever be able to erase his presence there.

Leaving the bathroom, I let out a scornful snort. The music playing from my phone couldn't fit the moment better. Mick Jagger's singular voice admonishing, telling me how I can't always get what I want.

"Ain't that right, Mick?" I murmur, shimmying into denim cutoffs and a button-down flannel.

———◆———

"Good morning, darling." Adina's gentle voice is like a balm to my edginess.

"Good morning." I give her a wholehearted smile, walking right into her warm embrace. "Did you have a nice holiday?" I say, inhaling her clean, lavender scent. For some nostalgic beats with Adina's scent and the sense of tranquility she diffuses, I'm teleported home. Right into Mom's embrace.

Easing off, Adina flicks on the kettle. "It was quite lovely. Seeing all the family together and my grandchildren, it's always a blessing." Inching up, Adina gets a white mug from the upper shelf. "But it's always good to be back at work. How was your holiday?"

I drop two pieces of bread into the toaster. "It was nice. Quiet." Avoiding her eyes, I turn to the fridge for butter.

"Nice."

Turning back, I meet Adina's attentive eyes. I murmur, "Mmmhmm."

Holding out a steaming cup of tea for me, Adina asks, "Did you go somewhere special?"

"Um, no" —I clear my throat—"just hung out around here."

Adina's lips draw into a faint, satisfied smile. She nods. "I'd better start on lunch. I'm making all of Jeremy's favorite dishes."

Easily, we move on to a light conversation about Jeremy's return and how Amelie made Adina promise her to bring her over for a visit before Jeremy moves back home.

Though my plate has nothing but crumbs and a few drops of honey left on it and my teacup is two sips away from empty, I stay in the kitchen with Adina. Keeping her company as she shaves off zucchini with a swivel peeler, telling me about the guy her youngest daughter brought home for the holidays. I smile when she raises her concern about people permanently marking their skin with "senseless tattoos," as she puts it. You'd think she'd be accustomed to that, what with working for such a long time in a house where unmarked skin is a rarity.

When Adina disappears in the pantry, I collect my cup and empty plate. Tyler's distinct footsteps entering the kitchen stop me from standing up and walking over to the dishwasher. For the span of a few short beats as he closes the distance between us, I watch him absorbed. His recently shaved jaw, now dusted with a few days' worth of stubble, his hair still damp from a shower, knotted at the back of his head. His chest bare, tattooed and nothing but utterly tempting.

Before I'm able to signal that we're not alone, Tyler leans toward me. His fingers thread into my hair while his lips, near mine, whisper, "Sleep well, Kiisu?"

"Ty—" The rest of his name remains in my mouth as his lips close over mine.

A shuffling sound and the pantry door closing mere steps away makes Tyler draw back. A little smirk adorns his lips when he spins to face Adina.

"Morning, Adina," he greets her in complete carefree nonchalance.

Adina's thin, clandestine smile returns for an encore. "Tyler, hope you managed to rest a little. Holidays were good?"

"Very good. Minus when Ivi here tried to bump me off with

poisoned food, that is." Tyler's smirk broadens when I give him the stink eye.

"You didn't just say that, did you?" I glare at him and turn to Adina. "I tried to make my mom's Christmas dishes, and it didn't exactly turn out as planned."

"You totally butchered those harmless recipes, Kiis-Ivi." Tyler chuckles, squeezing my shoulder amicably. The casual banter, light atmosphere, especially after Adina had clearly seen Tyler and me bump tongues, jar me more than a little. So much for laying low.

I make myself another cup of tea and hang with Tyler while he has breakfast. It feels so pleasant, the three of us carrying a light conversation. Feels like I belong.

Refilling Tyler's coffee mug, Adina excuses herself, murmuring something about tidying up the second floor. Her faint, enigmatic smile ever-present.

Before Adina's back is even out the door, Tyler's lips, tasting of coffee and him, are on mine. He's inched a little over the table, framing my face as he kisses me like we haven't spent half of the night doing exactly that, and then some, glorious, some. Easing off, he looks at me with a happy glee. "Wake me up the next time you leave my bed."

I blink at him. "Jeremy is back today!" Really meaning, aren't we keeping it low? Aren't we taking a few steps back?

"Right. I'm going to pick him up in twenty."

I watch him, incredulous for a stretch of seconds. "Tyler . . . didn't we say we're going to stop?" I swing my finger from him to me. "This."

Standing up, Tyler cups my cheek and kisses me silly. "Did you really think that that would include cutting this off?" Mirroring me, he points his finger from me to him. He slowly shakes his head from side to side. "Not happening. I have a hard enough time thinking about letting you go soon."

The contradiction of what his simple sentence conveys both lifts me up and tosses me down in the same breath. *Tyler having a hard time thinking about letting me go,* but at the same time, *he is* going to *let me go.*

Giving me another kiss that I feel all the way to my toes, Tyler leaves me to go get Jeremy.

———◆———

I'm deeply absorbed in reading blogs posted by missionaries who've been to the village I'll be traveling to in less than a week when my phone vibrates next to me. Glancing at the message, my mood climbs higher.

Chris: Can you talk, kiddo?

Ivi: Always!

"How's my favorite girl doing?" Chris asks a moment later.

I hold the phone between my shoulder and ear. "Doing just fine. Been missing you."

"That so? In that case, how about seeing me today?"

"Sounds wonderful. Wait a minute . . . you're in L.A.?"

He chuckles. "Visiting with my beautiful granddaughter."

"How long? When can I see you?"

"Tomorrow morning. I can meet you downtown any time after two."

"I'll have to check with Ty- with my boss first. Is it okay if I let you know in thirty?"

"Sure thing, kid."

———◆———

"Ivi!"

My smile comes as a reflex to Jeremy's voice. "Jer?" I lean over the banister on the second floor. Crooked smile and eyes shining from under blue-rimmed glasses look up at me. Taking the stairs at a hurried pace, I reach the ground floor in no time. Right into the most adorable hug.

"I missed you, kid!" I say to the center of Jeremy's head.

"I've got so much to tell you."

Jeremy's grin is so wide; I can't help but mirror it.

"Tell me everything."

"Maybe later," Tyler says, watching Jeremy and me. His eyes crinkled at the sides.

"Yeah, later, Tyler is taking me out for the best burger I've ever tasted. But really, they have the coolest things in Kenya. And it was so awesome. And I told my mom all about you."

"Later then." I can't seem to ease my grinning. It's possible that I'm hopelessly in love with the kid. "So if you guys are going to be away." I look to Tyler. "Would it be okay if I went out for a couple of hours?"

Tyler's jaw hardens. He folds his arms across his wide chest. "Where to?"

I raise my eyebrows in surprise. "Um, somewhere downtown to meet up with my friend Chris." To Tyler's glare, I add, "I think I told you about him. Chris, my friend from YWPO." I bite on my smile. "The kind grandpa . . ."

I can't resist smirking when Tyler finally drops the "pissed sergeant" stance. "We're actually heading over to Joey's; we can give you a ride."

"That would be great. Be back in a sec. I'll just go change." Climbing up the stairs, I need to hold the giggle threatening to escape my mouth. Tyler's little jealousy act being the fertilizer of my amusement. And also, it may or may not serve as a little wind beneath my ego's wings.

———— • ————

Tyler and I trade entertained glances in the rearview mirror as a reaction to a Jeremy Nathan Brown blabber torrent.

"Did you know that Kenyans celebrate birthdays by hiding around corners and dumping buckets of water on the birthday person? Oh, and that there are more than five ways to say cool in Swahili? My favorite's bomba!"

"I wonder how you say kitten in Swahili," Tyler murmurs under his breath.

I send him a grin, which he counters with a devilish one.

"Oh, and Ivi, I told my mom all about you, and she really wants to meet you when she's back. You need to meet her."

I stiffen a little. "Um, Jer, I'm not sure we'll be able to make it happen this time. I'm leaving in a few days." I must say that I'm showing a stupendous effort of will by not searching for Tyler's reaction.

"That means you're coming back!" The hope in Jeremy's question is another blow to my gut. And all the more is Tyler's silence.

I clear my throat, looking out the window. "I'll probably visit the States sometime in the future so maybe then."

Less than twenty minutes later, in a small, full of character coffee shop, Chris's wide grin turns solemn as he contemplates something for a span of a long moment. He unfolds the rectangular paper, glances at it once again and raises his eyes to me. "Ivi, that's a lot of money."

I nod in contentment that fades when Chris scrubs a hand over his gray stubble, looking uncomfortable and almost apologetic. "I hope this doesn't come out the wrong way." He heaves an exhale through his nose. He squares our stares. "What's the nature of your relationship with Mr. Adams, Ivi?"

Once realization sinks in, my features coil with horror. I grimace. "What are you asking me exactly?"

Chris eyes me gravely. "You know I think of you as one of my daughters, right?"

I nod, feeling a little sick to my stomach.

"One of the world's most famous singers donates over five hundred thousand dollars to a small, hardly known organization as a Christmas gift to his young, very attractive employee. Now, think about it . . . say a reporter gets ahold of this story. How do you think it'd be perceived? It could help a great deal to have someone like Tyler Lee Adams show interest and endorse our organization. But it's you I'm worried about."

I look around, focusing my spinning mind on the few colorful chairs and benches on the street where we're having our drinks. Inhaling, I center my attention back on Chris. "Whatever goes on between him and me happened after he gave me that check." I never intended to tell anyone about Tyler and me, but the pressure of how it could be perceived, as Chris suggested, and everything reeling inside me with no one to talk to, I just can't hold it in.

Chris's white eyebrows pull in under the visor of his Cowboys cap. "I have no doubt. I trust you more than you know." He sighs. "I just hope you know what you're doing, kid."

I take a sip of my drink. "I thought I knew, but I think I'm way too deep now." I bite on my cheek, looking away. "All of a sudden my mission trip is not my first priority." Hesitantly, my eyes come back to Chris.

I couldn't appreciate more the fact his stare holds no judgment. "You could always return after the trip."

I give him a dejected smile. "I'm not sure I'd be welcomed."

Covering my hand with his, Chris' expression becomes fatherly. "His complete loss. And if he chooses not to ask you to come back, then it's better for you to go away in a few days and leave it all behind you as a nice memory."

I nod, swallowing over the rock in my throat.

"And I'm here for you, always. Family and friends keep you grounded. Love keeps you blissfully silly and frighteningly afloat. Even when you fall in love, it's better to have your family and friends around. Have someone to catch you when you dive back from the emotional high."

"I guess I should re-examine my goals," I say in thought.

"Speaking of goals, one of the reasons I wanted to see you is because I may have a job offer for you. For when you're back from Nepal, I mean. If you're interested."

I perk up, my curiosity lighting my face. Chris's lips twitch. "We're looking at adding a new project coordinator to the organization's headquarters. It's not yet decided, but I assume we'll have the full scale of the position figured out in a couple of months."

"I'll have to move to Texas." I more than dislike that the first thing that jumps to my mind is that at least I'll be in the same country as Tyler. Sad, really.

"You'll be based out of Texas, but the job will require a lot of traveling."

"I think my parents would be happy for me." I think out loud. "Their hope has always been for me to find some sort of permanency with a job and town to call home. Sounds great. I'd definitely be delighted to be interviewed for the job when the time comes."

Just before hugging Chris good-bye, I give him Tyler's more than generous donation check. "Can you please be the one to hand it in?"

Chris nods and hugs me again, this time a little firmer. "Take care, kid."

——————— • ———————

Unsure of what the new rules are now that everyone's back in the house, I go to my room after hanging out with Jeremy just before he goes to sleep. The last time I saw Tyler, he was talking to Max, Killer, and Eli in the living room. Passing by them, en route to the indoor pool, the fragments of their conversation sounded of the work variety. The look Tyler gave me while deep in conversation still plays before my eyes and tickles at my heart. In one little glance, he managed to tell me that, just like him, I've also been on his mind for the greater part of the day.

Were we still alone, I'd be in his arms in a heartbeat. But risk running into Eli with my inability to hide my deepening feelings for Tyler? No, thank you, I'll pass.

I take a quick shower instead. Applying lotion on my damp skin, I notice a missed call on my phone that's next to the basin. Cleaning my hands on the towel I wrapped around me, I check who called. I dial Jay's number next, beaming.

"Seriously missed your face," he says in the way of greeting.

"That would be a mutual feeling."

When Jay asks me about the holidays, I quickly steer the topic to anything other than the last four days. A lump in my throat hitches my answer when he asks me if I'll hang out with him tomorrow at the intimate birthday party Tyler is throwing Killer. A party Tyler never asked me to join. Guess these are the new rules.

A knock on my door stops me from answering. "Hold up," I tell Jay.

With the phone pressed to my chest, I check who's at the door. Tyler's side smile greets me from the narrow gap as I step back to let him in. Before I'm even able to utter a word, Tyler wraps me in an embrace. His lips meet my neck when I tell him I'm on the phone with Jay.

"Can I call you back later?" I ask Jay, my eyes locked with Tyler's mildly irritated ones.

As soon as I end the call, Tyler's tongue trails up my neck. "I've been starving for your taste." His lips find my jaw next, delightfully advancing with gentle nibbles toward my mouth. "I'm throwing Killer a party tomorrow evening," he says to my skin. "His girlfriend asked me to have it here so it'll be a surprise. Just a couple dozen people." His mouth presses against mine. "And you." Relief warms my skin knowing he wants me there. Less than a heartbeat later, I'm spread on my bed with Tyler hovering above me.

"Tyler, Jeremy is only two rooms away. Maybe we should take it somewhere else?"

"Let's go to my room." He deepens his kiss.

I lightly press on his chest. Frowning from above, Tyler cocks his head. "Why don't you go first. I'll be there soon."

Reluctantly, Tyler pushes himself off me. "Do it quickly."

Smiling, I give him a little wave. With his hand on the door handle, Tyler glances at me over his shoulder, his lips twitched into a sinful grin.

To the little click sound of the door closing behind Tyler, I hastily pull my shirt off over my head. At the same time, I stumble, shimmying off my panties. Making my way to the closet, I almost crash into the wall. Rampaging through my lingerie drawer, I fish out a lacy pink bra and thong set.

I go through my belts next, choosing a simple, wide leather one that I buckle low around my hips. With a crafty smile, I walk to the wide chest of drawers where I keep my very pink and very handy toolbox. Biting on a smile, I stand in front of a full-length mirror, hooking my pink hammer through the belt to hang over my left hip. My pink wrench goes on the right hip. Twitching my lips from side to side, I give myself another scan that ends with untying my hair tie and letting my hair fall down to my waist. White, crochet knee-high socks are the last article of clothing I put on before hiding it all under a white, fuzzy robe.

I don't even get to properly knock on Tyler's door before he swings it open. I barely make it into the room when Tyler's lips find mine. Over a grin and a mouth covered by his, I try to get his attention. "Tyler."

"Shh," he says to my mouth.

I quickly draw back when his hands find their way to my thighs. Tyler cocks his head, his brows raised in question, not seeming the least bit content with my withdrawal. I bring my hands up to his chest and lightly push him back. "Sit on the bed," I order.

Tyler's eyes are locked on mine as he slowly walks back until his calves meet the wide, round bed. He drops to the bed with a predatory gaze on me. Slouching back, he rests on his elbows and watches me raptly.

Keeping our stares locked, I untie my robe, letting it fall to either side of me.

Tyler's growl is clearly heard all the way to where I'm standing by the door.

My lips curve up. "I'm a woman of my word. Told you I'd return the favor."

Tyler brings his hand to scrub over his stubble and parted lips. He drops his hand to his chest, huskily commanding, "Turn around . . . slowly."

I do as requested, giving him a little glance over my shoulder with my back to him.

"Get over here, Kiisu," he says in a raspy voice as his blazing eyes rake over me.

I take slow steps, halting between his parted thighs. Wordlessly, Tyler hooks his pointer finger in my belt and tugs me forward. Eyeing me with enough heat to set the room on fire, he presses his lips just above my belly button, murmuring, "Are you even real?"

Ever so slowly, he licks a path toward the valley between my breasts. Inching back, he looks at me with wicked glee. His lips twitch at the side. Tapping his finger on the hammer, he says, "Creative."

I shrug with a small smile of my own. "I try."

Eyes back on mine, he pulls the hammer from the belt. Unwavering in his gaze on me, he unceremoniously tosses the tool to the floor. His other hand finds its way to my ribcage, grazing slowly down my side, to my waist, to the wrench. In the same fashion, the pink tool finds itself on the floor. Next goes the belt. Tyler's hands wind around my waist. He lowers his lips to kiss a trail from my left hip bone to my right one, mere inches above the hem of my thong. He lifts lustful eyes to me. "Do you even know what you do to me?"

A cloud of heat settles in my belly. I cup his face, leaning down, and I bring my lips to his. A soft whimper escapes my mouth to the explosive sensation the connection of our tongues brings. Long moments into our kissing, Tyler leans back, taking my hand. "Come here, lie on the bed."

Propped on his elbow, Tyler gazes at me as I lie next to him. His fingers brush across my chest, down my belly, to the hem of my panties and up. Leaning in, his mouth follows the same route with sensual kisses. He worships my body with slow strokes, scorching kisses, and soft bites until my skin feels on fire. And that's when he discards his clothes and sets the fire in me.

My body's reaction to Tyler's scent, Tyler's rough beauty, and Tyler's body overwhelms me each time anew. I'm shivering with want. I'm uncontrollably adhered to him when he touches me like that. I want to cry. I want to beg him to never stop.

When we reach our release together in tangled bodies and hurried heart paces, a little tear escapes my eye. Because it's too much. A tear I stealthily brush away before he notices. Just as I've been trying to conceal how I feel about him. How the thought of leaving in a few days tears me up inside.

"Good night, Tyler," I whisper to the darkened room, a little after midnight. Lying on my side, spooned by the man I've slowly fallen hard for.

"I've been waiting to tell you something all day." His low voice reverberates between us.

My heart hammers down my ribcage as I wait for his next words. Hope for something suffuses me. I'm not even sure what I'm hoping to hear; nevertheless, the suspension is almost agonizing.

"Jeremy called me dad for the first time today. When I met him at the airport. And I don't even know why." He lets out a chuckle that holds more surprise than humor. "But you were the one person I wanted to share this with."

Though it's not what I wished to hear, the delight it fills me with couldn't be more candid. I lace my fingers with his, bringing our joined hands to my mouth. I press a slow kiss to Tyler's skin. "I'm so happy for you, both of you. That's wonderful, Tyler."

Tyler lifts our joined hands to my cheek, gently turning my head so our mouths can meet. Something about the way he kisses me this time has my heart flying to my throat. I wish he'd put into words what he just expressed with his kiss.

CHAPTER
Twenty-Nine
CHAPTER

"False advertising. Use of false or misleading statements when promoting a product." The topic for today's social sciences lesson, written on the blackboard in Jeremy's classroom. A matter he'll discuss with Ivi after school.

It's a bit jarring how almost seemingly life can fall back into a routine. For a few days, you're rolling in and out of bed with one of *GQ* magazine's attested sexiest men on the planet, and two days later, life goes on as if you're not still absorbing the impact of all the canoodling.

"Oh, I got you something from Kenya. I forgot to give it to you yesterday. I have it . . . Hold up, it's somewhere in my backpack, I think . . ." Jeremy tells me just as I'm about to leave his room. Just as Tyler gets in.

I train my focus on Jeremy. Not too inclined to test my ability to act indifferently around the dad person in front of the kid. "Ooh, what did you get me?"

Jeremy retrieves a crumpled brown paper bag out of his backpack. I watch his attempt at smoothing it with a lingering smile. "Here." He hands me the puffed bag.

The item in the bag feels soft and plush as I squeeze it through the paper. "Um," I hum in anticipation.

"Just open it." Jeremy rolls his eyes and smirks.

"Oh my god, you got me a ferret!" I declare with excitement. Trading joyful stares between Jeremy and the plush toy, I add, "You're the best!"

Jeremy shrugs, grinning with satisfaction. "I like you. You're the coolest girl I know."

I lean in to squeeze the kid into an embrace. "That's the nicest thing anyone has ever told me." Tyler's raised brow doesn't escape me. "And the best gift!" I give him another squeeze. "Thank you! Good night, Jer."

Nodding at Tyler because honestly, I'm having a hard time being normal when all I want to do is jump him, kid or not around, I hurry out of the room.

"Do you think you'll have more kids?" Jeremy asks Tyler when my shoe hits the threshold. I stop in place and wait. Don't judge, even a saint would be tempted to hear the answer.

Since my back is to the room, I don't get to see Tyler's expression, but I can distinctively hear the hitch in his voice when he says, "Um, don't think so. Where's that coming from?"

"We learned the word 'semelparous' today in class. It means someone who reproduces only once in a lifetime, and it made me think of you."

I'm glad Tyler's chuckle is loud enough to swallow my snort. Stifling a giggle, I scurry away.

Tyler is out of Jeremy's room by the time I reach mine. I turn around with a hint of a smile to the sound of his footsteps.

Closing the gap between us, he dips his head and whispers in my ear, "I like you. You're the coolest girl I know, Kiisu."

I tsk a couple of times, lightly shaking my head. "For shame! THE Tyler Lee Adams needs to rip-off the words of a young boy to get lucky. What has the world come to?"

Tyler grins. A belly-flipping grin; dimple at full force. "What?" he asks over a chuckle. "Kid's got game."

I nod. "Certainly does." Feigning contemplation, I say, "He'll forever be my true love. He gave me a ferret."

Tyler's turn to shake his head, a lingering smile on his lips. "Damn, I need to up my game with little Romeo around."

My lips curve into a flirtatious smile. "Fight for the title of my true love?"

"Maybe." He shrugs. I'm still absorbing the casual yet startling answer when he surprises me with a succulent kiss on my mouth, in the hall for everyone to witness, and leaves. "Later, Kiisu," Tyler says over his shoulder, a teasing hue to his voice.

The easy, Tyler-induced smile on my face remains while I get ready for the party that began over half an hour ago and stays unbroken until I'm ready to leave my room. In a black halter-top, leather shorts, red Mary Janes, and an antique gift from my grandma—a silver cross pendant that reaches just shy of my belly button—I'm ready to meet and mingle.

"Bless up, Mary P!" Max is the first one to notice me. Surprised, I try to wiggle myself out of his muscled arms and unglue my lips from his beer glazed ones at the same time.

"Glad to see you too, Max," I murmur, contemplating if wiping my lips would be taken as a rude gesture.

"Every day we were apart felt like an eternity. Every twenty-four hours I was dying a little more," he says with enough theatrical flair to draw some curious glances our way. Probably from people who aren't familiar with the phenomenon that is Max. At first, one should be exposed to him in small doses. There's no other possible way, as I see it.

"How morbidly poetic of you. I'm flattered," I beam, noticing Jay making his way toward us.

"As so you should be, Mary P. You're the chosen one. The Neo of our generation. One out of thousands upon thousands of willing women who want a piece of this." He runs his hands over his red tartan plaid suit. "Just say the word, and I'm yours."

"The word." I grin at him.

"Have you checked out the bartender, dude?" Jay intercepts another one of Max's not so covert cop a feel maneuvers. "It's the redhead from the last party."

Slicking his unruly hair back, Max turns to me. "Sorry, M.P., but you'll need to learn to share."

"Of course," I say with all the sincerity I can muster, which is absolutely zilch. "Get us drinks while you're at it, tiger."

Jay, and I give Max our orders.

At Max's exuberant swagger, Jay and I chuckle in unison before meeting for a warm embrace.

With a bottle of beer in our hands, Max, Jay, Killer, and I fall into easy conversation. Sophia, Killer's girlfriend, joins our group, lightening the atmosphere and making us laugh by retelling the story of the time she introduced Killer to her parents. A tale of late night skinny-dipping, a broken toe, a parsley bush, and an NDA, which leaves us all breathless from laughter and on the verge of tears.

I'm more than enjoying myself and have been giving the group my almost full attention. The many flit glances I throw the ample room come out of the part of my brain that has been forever etched with a certain boss.

Although the place is a bedlam of music, drinks, laughter, loud conversations, and beautiful people, the only thing my mind can focus on at this very moment, while transmitting pain to the center of my belly, is a tongue. Spread wide and slowly licking its way down a trail of salt over a tanned, glittered cleavage.

A giggle, followed by a high-pitched, "Oh, Tyler Lee, feel free to explore," bursts my transfixion. And apparently, also calls for the attention of the rest of my group. Besides Jay, everyone just shrugs or shakes their heads with an "as if that's anything new" gesture and carries on.

"You okay?" Jay's eyes ask mine.

I shrug with indifference, or at least, that's what I'm trying to communicate as I take a sip of my drink, which only makes my stomach feel a little sicker. In an act of self-flagellation, I squint my eyes Tyler's way. Straightening up from his tasting tour, he throws back a shot, and his stare collides with mine. The hands of the lady he's just licked still hold his forearms. He's still leaning toward her. And me? Simply put. Aching.

He winces, his features twist with something that looks half confusion, half repentance. I bounce my eyes back to the people around me, avoiding any voiceless confrontation . . . or further regret. Evading causing a scene or letting anyone know my mood has taken a downward spiral, I plaster on an easy smile and count the moments until I can excuse myself without raising any suspicion. Jay's wary look at me doesn't help me in keeping it cool.

A whole of five long minutes more is all I can take before I excuse myself, discard the bottle in my hand, and sneakily climb up to the second floor. When my foot leaves the last step, I let my features drop and my anger and disappointment take precedence over my composure.

Three steps before my room, I sense him before I realize he'd followed me. I close my eyes tight when his arms wrap around me, bringing my "escape" to a pause.

His embrace tightens, pressing my back against his chest. I feel his body curling around me; his mouth dips to the center of my head. I choke with frustration, swallowing over the swelling in my throat, hating how I mellow into his enveloping touch. My body's Pavlovian reaction to Tyler: surrender, utter submission. Our closeness is like the force between two magnets. Something almost impossible to fight, unless you keep a certain distance.

"Ivi." His voice is deep with sentiments.

I squeeze my eyes shut tighter. My own voice is low and raw. "Why did you do that? Couldn't you at least wait a couple of days more until I left? Out of respect for me, Tyler. Nothing else. You're free to do as you wish, but don't disrespect me. I'm worth so much more than this behavior."

His lips in my hair repeatedly plant soft kisses. "You're right. I'm sorry." His embrace tightens. "I'm sorry. I don't know what . . . I'm not used to—"

I stiffen under his hold. "What, Tyler? You're not used to what? Caring about other people's feelings?"

I feel his warm breath on my scalp when his face burrows in my hair. "To feeling like—" He sighs. "You throw me off balance." He gently turns me to face him, his hands never leaving their hold on me. Locking our eyes, he rasps, "To feeling what I'm feeling." His brows wrinkle. "I don't know how to do this." He points his finger back and forth between us. "Whatever we're doing."

Countering him with no less soberness in my stare, I say, "Keeping your tongue off other people's cleavage or skin, for that matter, would be a good place to start."

He hangs his head. "I deserved that."

When he brings his eyes back to mine, I say, "Yes, you did. And just for the record, so far you've been doing just fine. So I think you do know how to do this." It's my turn to point my finger back and forth between us.

He nods, utter sincerity softening his expression, and I decide to be me, let it all out, lay it all on the table.

With a supple tone to my voice, I start, "Tyler, I've developed all these feelings for you. And it's hard enough to say good-bye in two days. Please don't tarnish it in the time we have left."

Tyler's lips part, about to comment, but the sound of someone climbing up the stairs stops him. We both turn to Jay.

"All okay?" Jay asks, his gaze directed to me.

Not wavering his stare from mine, Tyler growls, "Get lost, Jay. I'm trying to grovel over here, made my girl upset."

My girl . . .

"Sure thing, Tootsie Roll, you better treat my Ivi well, otherwise—"

"*My Ivi*, asshole," Tyler cuts him off.

Jay chuckles and turns on his heels.

Sparks of hope fill me when the last few moments register. *To feeling what I'm feeling. My girl. My Ivi.* Sparks of a maybe there's hope for more. Maybe my impending departure will not be the cut-off date of this. Of Tyler and me.

Silence falls between us as we stare at one another for a pregnant stretch. *What now?*

Tyler is the first to break it. Clearing his throat, he laces our fingers together, his focus split between my mouth and my eyes. "I just want to wrap myself around you. Let's not waste the time we have left together."

And with one sentence, he extinguishes any hope of maybe.

CHAPTER
Thirty

CHAPTER

"Christmas was nice, though we missed you, Kiisu. Hope you had a special one. Can't wait to hear all about it. Ready for the real fun to begin?" An email from Ivi's parents.

"**H**ey, where did you go? Earth to Jeremy." I wave a hand in front of the kid who seems to have taken a journey down the valley of contemplation.

Brown, smart eyes focus, zooming in on me. He frowns, about to speak. His frown deepens, and he snaps his mouth shut. Jeremy scratches his unruly mane. "Do you think . . ." His brows bunch closer. "I was just thinking, er, maybe—maybe I should get my mom and Tyler to hang out together when my mom is back."

I take a sip of my mint lemonade; bless Adina and her culinary gift. "Hmm," I hum non-committedly, enjoying the nice, rare January sun and the backyard serenity-inducing backdrop. The black, reflective infinity pool will *never* get old. Especially when thin rays of sun pepper it with shiny diamonds. Though my "never" around here has an unyielding expiration date. Not much longer to enjoy the view. To be precise, it's exactly seventy-two hours that are ticking away too fast for my liking.

Jeremy takes a generous drink of his glass. Wiping his mouth with the back of his hand, his eyes sway to me. "Do you know the movie *All I Want for Christmas*?"

"Sounds familiar. Remind me what it's about."

"These two kids try to make their divorced parents get back together. I saw it on the flight back."

I nod with a placid smile that wavers as Jeremy's last comment about having his parents spend time together and the current topic piece together in my mind. My attempt to remain smiling only twists my lips into something of the sour grin assortment. "Yeah, I remember that one," I say in a breath.

Jeremy pushes his glasses up his nose. "Maybe if Tyler and my mom hung out, they would, you know, decide to be together in the end."

I feel like the wicked witch of the west, what with the unpleasant thoughts that barge into my head. My lips part as I mull over a response that won't convey my true feelings on the matter. "I think your mom and dad are good friends, Jeremy." I study his big, clever eyes. "Sometimes, that's even better than actually being together — married, I mean. Sometimes adults — "

"Hey."

Startled by Tyler's husky voice, I lurch up in my chair. His eyes run from Jeremy's solemn expression to my bashfully perplexed one. Unease tingles at my belly. The answer I just gave Jeremy doesn't sit well. Knowing full well that it was born out of my growing feelings for his dad makes me feel somewhat ashamed.

Tyler gives us an amused look. "Looks like I'm interrupting some serious talk."

I drop my eyes to my drink while Jeremy says, "How about you come for dinner when I'm back home. Mom makes the most delicious grilled cheese sandwich."

I keep my eyes on the fascinating woodwork of the deck's floor. By his voice alone, I can sense Tyler's surprise. "Hmm, yeah. Maybe. Why not?"

I lift my eyes to Jeremy's wide, satisfied grin and wince.

"How about this weekend?" the kid asks enthusiastically.

"I'll be on tour all of next month starting this Friday, but—"

Tyler doesn't get to finish his sentence. "So when you're back!" Too excited to keep his surreptitious masterplan a secret, Jeremy blurts, "You and Mom can hang out after I go to sleep. She can tell you everything about Africa. You guys can do things together . . . drink wine, watch a movie or whatever adults do."

I send Tyler a tentative glance. He stares at Jeremy, a brief grimace marring his handsome features. Tyler rubs a hand over his stubble. "Bud," he starts. "I'd love to spend more time with you, as much as I can. Always. Now, Malena and I are friends. I couldn't be more grateful for the great job she's done raising you, but . . ." Jeremy listens, his grin slowly dropping into a flat line. "But that's what we are; good friends who share the best kid in the universe."

I feel like I've been privy to something I shouldn't have. Uncomfortable with the situation, I straighten in my seat. About to stand up and excuse myself, I'm stopped by Jeremy's question that both makes me freeze and tightens my stomach.

"Do you have a girlfriend?"

Tyler's "no" comes out like a flying bullet, plowing right through my heart. When his eyes slice to mine, a flinch hurdles his face. He clears his throat, his troubled stare bouncing between Jeremy and me.

"I need to . . ." I murmur, pointing at the house, heading to the Victorian doors. Two and a half minutes later, when I close the door behind me and fall to my bed with a huff, I'm more than exasperated . . . with myself. What did I really expect Tyler to say? Declare his undying love for me? Tell Jeremy that we're going steady?

Just like Tyler clearly implied many times before, I'm leaving soon, and that's that. No hidden meanings. I shouldn't be reading into something that's not there. Just a forthcoming end to a superb, consensual dalliance. It's time I got that into my thick head, and the sooner, the better. Any other way, I will just make a fool of myself when the actual time to say good-bye comes.

Trying to utilize all this surplus restless energy I'm harboring for a good cause, I pull out my laptop and browse the hell out of the place I'll be heading to in three days, reading every available piece of information posted by other volunteers. In a way, I'm starting the process of bringing closure to the past six months and mentally shifting my hopes and desires toward my next venture.

————— ♦ —————

"Did you know that a human heart can actually be broken?" Jeremy asks Jay and me, slurping a long noodle into his mouth. Along the way, a splattering smatter of red sauce mottles around his lips. "It's true." Nodding, he wipes his mouth with a napkin. Jay and I trade an animated glance. Though mine, if I'm being frank, is not of the sincere realm. In my defense, the broken heart fact strikes a little too close to home at the moment.

Jay grins at Adina who places a plate of spaghetti aglio e oili in front of him. Yep, that's Adina for you; everyone gets his favorite dish. One pot of spaghetti, three different sauces. I'm going to miss these people so much. Another thought that squeezes my heart a little tighter.

Jay inches to plant a kiss on Adina's cheek, an action that she rewards him with a warm smile. Digging a fork in a heap of shiny noodles, he nods at Jeremy. "Tell me everything."

"Tell you what, Snugglemuffins?" Tyler says, entering the kitchen.

My body comes alive when he chooses to stand by my chair, casually placing his hand on the back where his fingers covertly thread through my hair. He leaves goose bumps on my skin with the slow brush of the pads of his fingers against my skin.

Jay sends Tyler an evil grin. "Young Jeremy here was just about to educate us with some cardiovascular facts, Bonbon. Smart spawn you got. Seems like sometimes the apple falls miles upon miles away from the tree."

Tyler snorts a chuckle and turns his attention to Jeremy.

Swallowing another mouthful of noodles, Jeremy perks up. "So a heart can be broken, for real. It's even got a name, Broken Heart Syndrome."

Jay's brow arches with animation. Tyler hums, and I want to applaud Mr. Smarty-pants for his little felicitous anecdote. Young Jeremy preaching about broken hearts while Tyler silently caresses my skin. *Oh Irony, you have such a wicked sense of humor.*

"It's when you experience a sudden chest pain as a reaction to something that's emotionally stressful." Jeremy takes a rapid guzzle of his drink and continues. "It can even happen after a good experience. And it's more likely to happen to women."

I roll my eyes and let out an unconscious, derisive snort.

When three sets of eyes turn my way, I dart for my glass, throwing back a generous gulp. *Bless your kind heart, whoever you are,* I inwardly praise the person who just buzzed the intercom, innocently liberating me from an awkward moment.

Like a nimble ninja, Eli appears out of thin air, reaching the intercom before any of us can even make a move in its direction. "Right, send him in," he curtly tells the guard at the main gate. "Max is on his way." He turns to Tyler. "Can we have a few words?"

Tyler nods, wordlessly following Eli out of the kitchen. Both Jeremy and I snicker when Jay stands at attention and salutes Eli's back.

"What up, people of the commoners' kingdom?" Max's toothy, bright smile illuminates the kitchen with joy a beat later.

Jay frowns at Max. "Dude, what happened to the rest of your clothes?"

Max makes a whole production of swiping his eyes down his body. He smooths his red tie over his white tank top. Pocketing his hands in his gray board shorts dotted with little pink flamingos, Max frowns back at Jay, communicating *what's your problem, dude?*

Jay just shakes his head from side to side. He tips his chin at Max. "Didn't you say you're bringing Alyssa?"

"She'll drop by later. The shooting's running late."

"Who's Alyssa?" I ask, putting our glasses in the dishwasher.

"My cousin from Australia," Max says, checking out whatever Jeremy is doing on his tablet. "She's been wanting to slow bone Tyler for ages."

An unbidden frisson of irritation shoots through me. "Hey," I bite out, gesturing with my hand at Jeremy, though the irritation is a smaller part inappropriate language in front of Jeremy and a much greater part the fact that someone wants to slow. . . someone's lusting Tyler. Assuredly, there must be many more people, gender irrelevant, who would be more than happy to do that to Tyler Lee Adams. But hearing it firsthand, knowing that the lady in question will shortly make an appearance, doesn't bode well with me, to say the least.

Soon, I learn that apparently, there's a little soiree in the making. Killer and another friend of Max's are on the way, plus the concupiscent cousin. A tidbit that gravitates my mood to half-mast. Three days before I hit the road and it's definitely not how I hoped to spend my evenings. Behind a locked door, alone with Tyler, is more like it.

"Be back soon," I tell Jay and Max before joining Jeremy upstairs as he gets ready for bed.

When I return to the living room area less than twenty minutes later, it's to an animated conversation. More than half a dozen people occupy most of the sitting space in the smaller sitting area. The cozier one, next to the fireplace. The same spot that became my favorite corner of the house on Christmas Eve. I swear, each time the faux fur carpet crosses my periphery, an image of Tyler above me, sweaty and impassioned, flashes before my eyes.

Spotting me, Jay pats a hand on the cushion next to him, motioning for me to join. If a stare actually held weight, I'd say that the one Tyler has on me as I make my way to join Jay would be at least a ton. I feel him, his presence, his attention, his aura in every bit of me. It throws me off a little, how of all the voices in the room, his is the only one I'm actually hearing.

"Listen, Ivi, you can't not come back after Nepal. You're family now," Jay says as soon as I take my place next to him. "Been thinking about it. You can work at the studio." His stare hovers on my expression.

"You're way too sweet." I give him a side hug. "Feels so odd, it feels like I'm leaving another home. You guys have really gotten under my skin."

"So come back after Nepal, simple." He shrugs.

I squint at Tyler who seems to split his attention between whatever Killer is telling him and my conversation with Jay. "It's not that simple. There's the visa issue for one." I huff. "And as cool as your shop is, I'm not sure that that's what I want to do." What I don't tell him is that I want Tyler to ask me to come back. I want Tyler to want me to return. Also, after all, it's Tyler's turf. I won't come back uninvited. If he'd rather end our thing when I leave, I won't come back to be in his face. I'm not that kind of person. I won't change my ways, not even for someone as worthy as him. I believe that there's power in letting go. Pining for someone who doesn't want you is not how I operate.

"Yo people, we should have a toast," Jay says to the room. All eyes turn to us. "Ivi is leaving us in three days to save the world!"

Killer frowns. "But you'd be coming back after your trip, right?"

I bite my lip, slightly shaking my head. "I'm not sure what will happen after Nepal."

"You can't do that to me, Mary P. I'm in love with you. You just made my heart bleed," Max hollers from two seats away.

I give him a thin smile. When my eyes accidentally meet Tyler's, I move them away because what they transpire has me on edge. "C'mon," I tell Max with a smile. "With all those beautiful ladies flocking around you, you'd forget all about me even before my foot hits the airstair." Why does it feel like what I'm saying to Max is essentially directed at Tyler?

"I can't see that happening." Silence falls over the room. A prolonged silence. Because the murmur, a morosely sounding one, didn't come from Max. My eyes cut to Tyler who seems not to care that a room full of people are watching, and gives me a look that matches his sullen-ish tone.

Max, oblivious to what's going on or not, says, "Nah, you've got the bestest rack, babe. Unforgettable."

Tyler, still holding my stare, raises his brows, his eyes dancing, communicating, "He has a point."

My constant savior, Jay, coughs. "I'm getting drinks." He tugs on my hand to follow him as he rises to stand.

When Jay hands me a frozen bottle and asks if whatever's going on between Tyler and me is serious, I ask him to drop it. Not something I'm inclined to get into right now, especially with a room full of people and a few more on the way.

Walking back to the living room, Jay manages to liven up my mood, teasing me about Max's and my undeniable attraction and how beautiful, yet weird, our spawned offspring will be.

Huddling the drinks close to my chest, I bump his hip with mine. "You're such a dork."

Entering the room, we both grin widely at each other. About to place the drinks and glasses on the low table, Jay's smile widens while mine rounds in awe.

"Alyssa!" Jay says before stepping over to wrap an utterly stunning lady into a hug.

"Hey handsome," she says in a lighthearted Australian accent. Hugging him back, she seems more than delighted to see him.

I can't help but give her a thorough scan. The silky, long black hair, the clear green eyes, the delicate features, the unbelievably perfect, slim body. She's tall and lithe and beautiful. Utterly beautiful.

"This is Alex," Alyssa motions at another pretty woman who stands next to her. Jay shakes Alex's hand, who, with a cheeky smile, pulls him into a kiss-hug greeting.

Jay introduces me next. Both ladies smile, giving off carefree vibes and sincere affability. Seems like the ladies were introduced to the rest of the gang while Jay and I were in the kitchen. In no time, Max practically glues himself to Alex's thigh, giving her his usual spiel, which seems to do the trick this time. She appears more than interested.

The rest of us fall into a humored conversation where Max is the center of attention. Try as I might, I'm unable to ignore how openly Alyssa is coming on to Tyler. Albeit tactful, it's still confidently *strong*. She is a lady on a mission; she knows what she wants, and she has no reservations to openly show it. Tyler gives her the same attention he rewards the rest of the people in the room. Maybe all the people in the room besides me. I get an extra dose of loaded stares. Stretched, loaded stares.

When Alyssa's hand travels up to curl around Tyler's bicep as she garners his attention once again, telling him about the photo shoot for some renowned brand the ladies just came from, I look away. Regardless of some beautiful times together and a sense of something special developing between us, he's not mine. *Not mine.* Not mine to have any claim on.

Maybe the limited access to the cyber world in my next destination, where access to any sort of Wi-Fi is nearly impossible, is not a bad thing. Tidbits about Tyler's life are, true in nature or not, a constant on all gossip outlets. Especially the speculation about the women he's been seen with. Typically, I'm not a jealous person, but when it comes to Tyler . . . let's just say that right now, I'd be more than glad to see Alyssa swim in the pool with a nice chunky boulder tied around her flawless throat.

Oh lord, what's wrong with me?

I don't even recognize myself anymore. Enough is enough. As of this moment, I'm going to un-spell myself from the Tyler Lee voodoo. I have half a mind to take this person I've become, which is completely new to me, to see a therapist. The moment you begin to dislike yourself or the way you act is when it's time to extract whatever influences have brought you to said recognition, or at least get them under control.

"So what do you say, guys?" Alyssa asks ten minutes later, drawing my attention back to her. She pats Tyler's chest in a friendly fashion. "Everyone's raving about this place."

"I'm game," Jay says to whatever Alyssa just suggested. "Shmoopy?" He tips his chin Tyler's way.

Tyler tries to catch my eyes, but I feign interest in Killer's frown. Squinting, I catch Tyler giving Jay a one-shoulder indifferent shrug.

The jury is still out on going to a party Alyssa's agency is holding at a new it place for humans of the celebrity and pretties cosmos until Max adds his two cents. "A scene full of fine-looking babes, ah, what's the question? Gather your possessions humans and let's get a move on."

A few chuckles and a light bustle of purses thrown over shoulders, wallets tucked into pockets and vehicle keys fisted, and a quick pit stop later, everyone is at the door.

Alyssa has her hand on the handle when Tyler narrows his eyes at me. "Ivi, you coming?"

All eyes turn to where I'm still seated on the couch.

Ignoring the disappointment poking at my stomach, I manage a smile. "It's Wednesday, Adina's half day off . . . someone needs to mind the kid snoring upstairs."

"Oh, what a bummer." Alyssa opens the door wider. "Hooroo, see ya later." She waves at me and tugs on Tyler's hand, pulling him after her.

My cringe is involuntary.

Tyler tilts his head, his hand stretched ahead by Alyssa's hold.

I plaster on a lame smile and nod. "Have fun."

When the door closes behind the jolly lot, I swallow all the bitterness threatening to inflame my immediate glum and unclasp my bra. I throw it on the low table, grab an extra fluffy throw blanket, and nestle back on the sofa. Not letting myself dwell on . . . *anything,* I flip the TV on and snuggle deeper under the comfort of the blanket. The opening scene is a teary breakup, which makes me send my eyes to the ceiling. Not sure if it's due to the corniness or the fact that I'd rather have the misty screen now veiling my sight remain unshed. A comfort session by the best friend begins when the sound of the front door opening yanks me out of my concentration on the screen. My lips slightly part and my brows draw in when Tyler enters the grand foyer and throws his keys on the table. I follow him with my eyes and my head cocked in question as he makes his way to the living room followed by a pouting Max and the rest of the group.

Tyler's lips twitch as he closes the distance between us. The curve of his lips tips higher when he notices my abandoned bra strewn on the table.

I clear my throat. "Aren't you guys going?"

"Tyler changed his mind," Max bites out, folding his arms over his chest like a petulant child.

"Told you to go without me," Tyler says over his shoulder, eyes adhered to mine.

"Naw, that's cool, Tyler Lee," Alyssa says. "Get you something to drink?"

Tyler shakes his head while ever so nonchalantly grabbing my bra from the table and pocketing it. He flops on the sofa by my side, stretches his long legs on the table in front of him, and turns to me with a smile. He tips his chin in the direction of the TV. "So what did I miss, Kiisu?"

I glance at the room around us. Besides Tyler and me, everyone has taken a seat somewhere across the sitting area. However, no one is even remotely interested in what's playing on the TV. Most hold a drink in hand and chat. I return my stare to Tyler, who's still watching me expectedly. I give him an awkward, brows twitched, lips askew smile, assessing his sincerity.

"Well?" he asks with an easy smile.

I point at the buffy blonde guy exiting a red sports car. "That one," I say, amused by Tyler's complete attentiveness. He shifts sideways, sending his hand to rest on the back of the couch just behind my head, smiling at me encouragingly. "He just broke the cute brunette's heart, and now, the groveling commences."

Tyler nods, his mouth still in a gentle smile, his eyes traveling over my face. I go on, adding my own interpretation as I mockingly tell him more about the plot. Tyler chuckles, his fingers, as though having a mind of their own, play with my loose hair.

Our conversation gradually moves to other topics. Our voices take softer, mellower tones. Our eyes, lambent with joy, lock as we're transferred into our own little bubble in a room buzzing with energy and people.

We've talked about Jeremy, and a song Tyler has been working on, and my excitement about my upcoming trip when Tyler's fingers leave my hair and casually trail up to the nape of my neck. I lose track of what we're talking about. Tyler's eyes gently caress my features, docking on my lips for a stretched beat. His eyes lift to mine, hooded with intent. Time stops when he leans closer and gently brushes my lips with his. Everything around us fades when he presses them harder and kisses me as though we're the only people in the room. The kiss is gentle, warm, profound, and languid. Carrying equal part lust and emotions. Carrying my heart up to my throat.

Like waking from a deep, sweet dream, we slowly ease back. Tyler's eyes as they drift open into mine are hooded, light flush tinting his prickled cheeks. By the heat warming up my own cheeks, I can only assume we might be wearing the same expression. The very picture of desire waiting to be further explored.

A cough breaks the steely silence in the room, viciously spiraling me out of our moment and back into cold reality. I chance a tentative glance behind Tyler's wide shoulder and the heat on my face fires up. Each and every person in the room is gazing at us, frozen in their places. Following my line of sight, Tyler looks over his shoulder. I can only see Tyler's profile, but when Max opens his mouth to speak, Tyler gives him a look that prompts him to pretend to lock his mouth and toss the key far, far away.

"Darling people, why don't we go check out that party, after all?" Jay says, motioning to the main entrance in a let's-make-ourselves-scarce gesture. He trades a glance with Tyler that ends with Jay's lips stretching into an approving smirk.

Some amused and some less entertained good-byes follow the groups as they shuffle out the door. Alyssa gives me an unfathomable look, appearing to be reassessing me in an entirely new light.

The door hardly closes behind them when Tyler has me pinned back on the sofa and his lips hungrily claiming the skin of my neck. "Your taste," he growls. "It's the only thing I could think about today."

CHAPTER
Thirty-One
CHAPTER

"Taste the Explosion." A phrase boasted on the Rock Pop candy packet idling on Ivi's desk.

"What are you humming?" Tyler asks as I gather my stuff before heading to his room for the night.

Though caught in the middle of a lawbreaking act, reflexively, I force my lips into a flat line.

Sitting by my desk, legs propped up, rhythmically tapping his fingers on my desk, he cocks his head. "Why did you stop?"

Bent over my lingerie drawer, I murmur to the lacy pair of boy shorts in my hand, "Oh, it's for your own good, believe me."

"What did you say?" is half a question, half a chuckle.

"I never sing next to other people." I give him a look over my shoulder. "Or any living organism for that matter." This part is a murmur.

Amused eyes counter my frown. "Why's that?"

"Singing out of key would be a compliment to what I do to innocent songs."

Tyler chuckles as if he finds me adorable.

"Let's just say that when I tried out for choir in school, the teacher suggested, after miserably cringing for the entire minute and a half of my audition, that I help out with decorations for the shows."

"C'mon, it can't be that bad," he says with a chuckle.

"Oh, it can." I end the conversation, entering the bathroom to get my toothbrush. Coming out, I salute Tyler with one hand while the other holds my stuff huddled to my chest. "Reporting for duty."

Tyler grins, pushing himself off the chair. Standing up, his eyes catch a sight of something on my desk that has him stop in his tracks. He fishes the little packet with two fingers and brings it forward for a closer look. His brows pull in with amusement. "Rock candy?"

"Another gift from Jeremy."

Utterly animated, Tyler says, "Kid's really laying it on thick, eh?"

I nod with a grin.

"I really need to put more effort in, huh."

I shake my head, pursing my lips. "Nah, I wouldn't bother. You'd never stand a chance."

"That so?" Tyler narrows his eyes, tilting his head to the side. Before I know it, I'm swept into the mother of all foreplay kisses. *God, this man can kiss.*

I'm still a little lightheaded from the kiss when Tyler's phone chimes; he gives me a soft peck on the forehead and answers the call. "Eli," he says, starting for the door. I follow him, taking the stairs to his room.

Pointing at the en suite, I let Tyler know that I'm going to take a shower. He nods at me, his features furrowed in concentration as he listens to Eli on the other line.

With the feel of Tyler's lips still pulsing on mine, I close my eyes and let the water warmly caress my skin. Anticipation laced delight spreads through me with the thought of spending yet another night with Tyler. I don't let the niggling notion that it's one more night out of two infiltrate and extinguish my happy. I've come to realize just how much more than lust, passion, and fun it is for me. It's so much more. More emotions. More new and exciting feelings. More than listening to him sing. Listening to him talk. Learning about the real Tyler. Have him look at me with so much attentiveness and fondness. Have him hold me close like I mean so much. Like he feels just the same as I do. Like he is also . . . falling.

Relishing the feel of warm rivulets coursing over me with everything Tyler in mind, I start singing one of Tyler's songs. "You will always be the answer for everything I need," I croon. I push my voice higher, singing the next riff, "You'll forever be my always." With my eyes still closed, I futilely tap my way on the tiles, looking for the shampoo. Wiping water away with my palms, I open my eyes to look for the right bottle. Having a sense of being watched, I crane my head sideways and let out a startled yelp. It doesn't take long to recognize Tyler through the water drops trailing over the foggy shower door. Slightly opening the door, I scold, "God, you scared the living soul out of me."

"Sorry." Tyler grins, looking as far away from repentant as possible.

I glare at him as he leans on the tiled wall, arms folded across his chest and a big smirk. Dimple full on.

"What?" I ask, my scowl slowly collapsing into a grin with his contagious smile directed at me.

Tyler takes two steps forward and cups my cheeks with both hands, leaning forward under the spray. "You've just savagely slaughtered my song, and I find it completely charming." He holds my gaze with his gleeful brown eyes. He dips closer to press a sweet kiss on my slightly parted lips. Drawing back just a little, he leaves a sliver of air between our mouths. "I think you put a spell on me, Kiisu." His voice becomes raspier when he adds, "And I like it. A lot."

"I think this magic works both ways, Tyler," I whisper, lifting on the balls of my feet to meet his mouth.

He doesn't kiss me next; he conquers my mouth with his—frantically, zealously, keenly. I counter him as eagerly, my fingers lace into his wet strands and tug him to me. My heart is racing, that warmness in my lower body expanding, leaving me drunk on him. He sucks my bottom lip between his, still holding my face near. Pants entwined with carnal hums waft through our searing connection. Gradually, he leans back, breaking our mutual trance. The grasp of his teeth slightly pulls my lip back. He releases my lip, inclines back to brush my mouth with his again, and drops to his knees. My eyes follow him. Water flows over his face, enhancing his masculine, hard features. Droplets cling to the long dark lashes fencing his raw-brown stare that's holding mine with irresistible intent. Slowly, he lowers his mouth to meet the spot between my thighs. I shiver, watching him with my breath held in anticipation. When he tastes me, gently at first, I close my eyes and give into the feeling. For an eternity of achingly sensual bliss, he brings me to levels of desire that are on the verge of irrationality. I'm completely at his mercy.

Spiraling in ecstasy, I lose my ability to stand on my own two feet, letting Tyler hold me to him. I let the waves of my after bliss wash over me, resting my head on his hammering chest as warm water strokes us both, steadily dropping from above.

Tyler lifts me up to straddle him, pulling me closer. My breasts graze against the light hair on his chest. I seek his mouth, desperate to connect once more. Our bodies unite anxiously. Ecstatically, wildly moving against each other. Fitting perfectly as pleasure diffuses to every part of us. We consume each other, hands touching frantically, mouths savoring hurried and sloppy, tongues tasting in electrifying need.

I let my head fall as Tyler grabs my waist, positioning me to arch back from where we're joined. Taking me deeper. I moan his name, nearly losing my mind. His thrusts are fervent, as is the chant of my name on his lips. Our moans of pleasure come out stuttered as we fall into a shuddering release in unison.

For languid, still moments, only our heavy breaths and the running water color the silence as we come down from our high. My head rests on his shoulder while our heartbeats slow.

———— • ————

I kiss Tyler's chest as he lifts the blanket higher to cover my back. His fingers slowly stroke my skin under the cover, a perfect pairing to the reverberation of his voice as he tells me about the first time he saw a photo of Jeremy. I can hardly contain the happiness that's saturating me to the brim, lying in his arms and just listening to his voice. Just being with him. We talk in soft voices and easy laughs, opening up further and deeper to one another. About the little village in one of Estonia's national parks; my favorite place on the entire planet. About when Tyler met Dante for the first time, joining the boy band when he was nearly thirteen. About how Dante took him under his delinquent wing and opened the door to everything that till then was forbidden and fascinatingly tempting. About how much I loved my grandma and how broken I was when she passed away. About how ambivalent he feels about his parents meeting Jeremy. About how fulfilled and blissful I feel after each mission. About a new track, he'll be recording for a much-anticipated movie.

When a loud, meow-ish sounding yawn flits my mouth, Tyler chuckles and suggests he'll let me go to sleep.

"Where are you going?" I ask sleepily, running my finger up his arm, over colorful tattoos and a coiling vein.

"There's this tune looping in my head that I want to try." He flings his thumb in the direction of his studio. Gazing at me snuggled on the bed, he smiles and tucks his hand in his pocket.

"Mind having company?" I ask.

He sends me an easy smile and shakes his head from side to side. "Stay naked, though . . . for inspiration." Fumbling with something in his pocket, his grin broadens. I watch him as he pulls out a small packet.

"Hey, that's mine." I pout.

With a mischievous, naughty grin, Tyler rips open the packet and lifts it up to his lips. Little popping sounds come from his mouth as the Rock Candy chunks of sugar meets his tongue. I yelp when he jumps on the bed, hovering above me. He wiggles his eyebrows, slowly leaning closer. I giggle at the blurry popping sounds coming from Tyler's closed mouth. His intent is clear, and I lift my head a little to meet him for a kiss. An explosion of sweetness and sizzle washes my mouth when his tongue touches mine. A tingle of tiny blasts tickles at our tongues as we slide against each other through the syrupy, bubbly taste. Popping sounds and chuckles fill the room as we enjoy each other and the ride.

I lick Tyler's lips as we pull back. He smiles at me, dropping his legs off the bed. He shrugs his deserted jeans on and extends his hand for me. Standing naked on the bed, towering over him, I relish the way his eyes admire the sight of me. Tyler bends to grab the blanket from behind me and yanks it over. With the blanket in one hand, he bows a little to leave a quick kiss on my bellybutton. He shawls the fabric around me next and pulls me up to straddle him. I rest my head on his shoulder, alternately nuzzling his warm neck with my lips and nose as he walks us to his office.

Hours roll into pitch-dark with me sitting on Tyler's lap as he strums on his guitar, stopping from time to time to jot down a few keys or cross through others. We hardly talk. It's just a kiss here and there. A stolen caress. His lulling music. My soundless sighs of contentment.

A socket of forthcoming bittersweet longing forms in my stomach. There's nothing monumental about this evening, yet I don't want it to end.

CHAPTER
Thirty-Two

CHAPTER

"How did I let it go so far?" A comment repeatedly traced next to a flight booking reference number in Ivi's organizer.

Most of the morning passes on autopilot with indie chill tunes in the background as my only distraction. I'm in my room, halfheartedly packing the stuff I'm taking with me in one ginormous, tattered backpack. The rest of my valuables go into small size cardboard boxes with my home's address on them. Gear for a godforsaken village in Nepal and gear for L.A., besides toiletries, has no kinship, whatsoever. Kitten heels, everything glittery, tight, or remotely fancy goes back home. Cargos, jeans, thermals, wool sweaters, boots, and a couple of saris (procured on my previous mission trips) continue with me to my next destination.

Thoughts of Tyler, who's hollowed somewhere in a recording studio in Burbank with none other than the Dante and the ridiculously gorgeous Brooklyn Mars, are exiled to a provisional "emotions aside" space in my mind that I'll have to visit eventually, whether I want to or not. I banish thoughts about saying good-bye to Jeremy in a few hours to the same location.

Dusting my hands off, I glance at the window. The sky is gray, contemplating rain, aptly reflecting the glum clogging my throat. I left pieces of my heart in so many places around the globe, in each mission trip with the people I met, the places I fell in love with, but it's the first time that the leaving part is so hard. This is a good-bye I know my heart will never fully recover from.

———— • ————

"Hey." I give Adina and Eli a little wave, probably a product of my edginess. Why else would I be waving at people I had breakfast with earlier this morning. Adina lifts her eyes to me. Eli takes a drink of his cup of coffee. "Am I interrupting anything?"

Adina shakes her head in response before I complete my question. Eli sets his cup aside, craning his neck my way. "Pie?" Adina gestures at the mouth-watering apple pie cooling on the table.

It's my turn to shake my head. I worry my lips. "Um, I have a couple of boxes to send back home. Any chance you could help with that?"

My question is directed at Adina, but the answer comes from Eli. "I'll take care of them."

I reach for my pocket to retrieve some money. Taking a step forward, I offer it to Eli.

He shakes his head. "Don't worry about it." Eli takes the cup in his hand. Focusing his eyes on the coffee while twirling the remaining sediments around, he says, "Will you be coming back, Miss Kert?"

Taken aback by the question, especially coming from him, I mumble, "Ah, um, I-I don't. I'm not sure." I feel my insides sag. My next words sound more like a defeat. "I don't believe I will be."

He raises his austere gaze to me. "We'd love to have you visit again." I gape at him. He would be the last person I'd expect to want me back here. I blink at him, not missing Adina's supple smile and her futile attempt to hide it with a sip of her tea. Under my startled gaze, Eli rises to stand. Depositing his drink in the sink, he turns to me. Motioning with one hand at the door, he says, "Show me those boxes."

The span of moments it takes us to reach my room is packed with an uncertain sense of oddity. At least on my side. Eli, on the other hand, is his usual poised self. Entering my room, Eli gives the few boxes lined against the wall a cursory glance. Feels like the boxes were the last thing on his mind coming into my room.

With his legs slightly parted, he folds his blazer-clad arms over his chest and sniffs. "If you decide to come back, Miss Kert . . ." His unnerving stare holds mine captive. Uncomfortable as I may be, fidgeting with my hands, I can't seem to cast my stare away. "You need to understand that you'll be signing up for much more than what you've been accustomed to so far."

Confusion creases my face, asking him to elaborate.

"When you are with Tyler, you get the full package. Everything he comes with. You'll have time to think about it when you're gone. Think if you are up to sharing your life with millions of people. Anonymity is not something you can keep when you become a part of his life. Nor can you avoid being subjected to irrational hatred just because someone cares about you." He sniffs again.

Someone cares about you . . .

"We'd all be glad to have you return, Ivi, but think about it long and hard before you make your decision."

Still gaping, I murmur, "I'm not sure what you're talking about." *Tyler never asked me to come back . . .*

Eli gives me a fatherly look as if he forgives me for being naïve. "Think about it before you make any decisions; that's what I'm saying." He unfolds his hands and nods. "You can always call me if you have any questions." Another nod and he turns on his heels.

"Why are you telling me all of this?" There's a hitch in my voice, a product of the whirlwind of confusion spiraling in my head.

Eli pivots his head back and frowns. "My job is to always have Tyler's best interests in mind. You coming back and then running away is not in his best interest."

Not waiting for my reaction, he gives me another firm gaze and walks out the door.

What. In. The. Heavens. Was. That?

As if I needed any additional stress to the already tension-bound day, my little talk with Eli literally throws me off-kilter.

Somewhat shaken, I walk over to sit on my bed. Looking out the window, I can't shake off what I'm feeling. As though I've been stealthily attacked. All of a sudden, I feel like I don't belong anymore — like I'm an outsider. It's clear as day that Eli's little speech wasn't really about looking out for me. It's Tyler's best interests he was after. His words taste like a warning. *"Don't play around with Tyler; he has important things to focus on, and you can't get in the way unless you are serious."* When, in fact, deep in my heart, I feel like Tyler is the one playing around with me.

At this moment, as vulnerability seeps deeper, I'd give anything for some sort of security in knowing Tyler wants me to stay or come back.

———◆———

"You got everything you need?" I ask Jeremy after helping him pack his stuff to go back home.

Looking around, he checks the books and games he decided to leave at Tyler's again, and then he nods. "Yeah." Cocking his head, his mussed hair falls to the side, and he studies me for a beat. "Do you know what Anatidaephobia is?"

"Nope, don't think I've heard the word before. Some sort of fear, I'm guessing?"

His face lights up, announcing the arrival of his boyish, crooked smile. "Anatidaephobia is a fear that somewhere in the world there's a duck watching you." Jeremy snickers.

My voice shudders over a giggle. "For reals?"

Snickering louder, Jeremy bobs his head in confirmation. Still grinning widely, he says, "Can you imagine this duck with black sunglasses, a hat, and a fake mustache, lurking behind an open newspaper, constantly watching you."

"Stop it." I push his arm, laughing. Deep inside, I am thanking Jeremy for making me laugh, for helping me climb up from the dumpster dive my mood has taken early today.

We goof around, taking the whole sleuth-duck theory to the extreme. By the time our duck has a secret worldwide espionage operation, working for wealthy, corrupted governments and Russian oligarchs, I beg Jeremy to stop so I can breathe.

We're still reeling back from excessive laughter when Tyler materializes at the door. Tyler's eyes crinkle at the sides watching Jeremy and I tittering while wiping our eyes. Tyler's expression softens as his gaze bounces back and forth between us. When our stares hook, an expression crosses his face, one that has my smile flatten and my heart climb up a few good steps toward my throat.

"Bud, Victor's here to take you home."

Jeremy's lingered grin dissolves when he looks my way.

"I adore you. I seriously adore you, and I'm so bad at good-byes," I tell him taking a couple of edgy steps to reach him. "So I won't embarrass myself by turning into a blubbering mess —" I envelop him in a bear hug. "Let's do this as quickly as possible. Okay?" The hitch in my voice is a preface to forthcoming tears.

Jeremy hugs me back tighter than I'm expecting, his head bowed. A notion that strums at my already wounded emotions. There's a light shudder to his voice when he says, "I'm going to miss you, Ivi."

And that's as far as I can hold myself. On cue, little tears escape my eyes. The lump in my throat expands as I bite on my quivering lips.

"Me too, Jer. So much."

"Let's go, bud," Tyler says softly, reaching for Jeremy's backpack.

"Okay now, go. Go!" I give Jeremy a watery smile, playfully pushing him away.

Watching him follow Tyler tears my heart a little. A little piece of my heart will forever belong to this uniquely sweet boy.

Crossing the threshold of Jeremy's room, Tyler sends me a thin, empathic smile over his shoulder. And the lump swells.

The moment they exit my periphery, I scuttle to my room. Landing on my bed with a huff, I wipe my eyes and take some long, deep breaths. I close my eyes, swallow over the lump, and stretch to grab my laptop from the nightstand. Three shaky, heavy breaths later, I go on to Craigslist and skim through the latest "missed connections" because nothing can chase funk away like little gems such as promiscuous bunnies or convenient store pat downs.

Yes, saying good-bye to Jeremy has definitely left its mark on me. An immense one. Five minutes later, I set the laptop next to me on the bed and drop my head back to the mattress. Covering my face with my hands, I squeeze my eyes shut. I can't fool myself. Try as I might to distract myself, whatever I'm feeling won't go away. Doesn't look like the rock in my throat or the smarting twinge in my chest are going anywhere soon. If this is how I feel after saying good-bye to Jeremy, how will I ever survive letting his father go?

There's a light knock on my door, but whoever it is doesn't wait for any confirmation. Tyler enters the room, wordlessly closing the door behind him. He watches me attentively as he closes the distance between us. Tipping my head up a little so the moist screen in my eyes won't fall down as tears, I wait for Tyler to reach the bed.

Eli's words still resonate in my head, making me feel a little distant. Not sure how to act. I take a deep breath, opting to calm my inner battle. With my next exhale, I decide to let it go. What harm can it do?

We only have a few hours left anyway. Why not enjoy it.

Sitting next to me, Tyler leans down to press a gentle kiss next to my mouth and takes my hand in his. "Busy?" He tips his chin at the open laptop.

Taking an inward composing breath, I inch up, leaning on my elbows. "I read the Missed Connections on Craigslist sometimes; it's ridiculously fascinating, disturbing, and amusing at the same time."

He furrows his brows, light amusement sparking in his deep brown eyes.

Sitting up, I set the laptop on my thighs. Refraining from sinking deeper into the glum bubble that's floating above me, I clear my throat. "Take this one for example: I want to feed you all night."

Tyler snorts and makes himself comfortable, lying on his side, his elbow supporting his head. Focusing on me, he listens attentively.

"I served you water and bread. You smiled at me each time you took a bite. Then I was behind the bar. You were in some pink shirt and a skirt. I'm married, but I can't stop thinking about you. Maybe we could meet up, just for a chat. Or I could feed you things." I shake my head. "Then he adds—do not contact me with unsolicited services or offers."

"Sounds promising," Tyler murmurs. "So little faith in true love, Kiisu. That's just depressing," he mocks me. "Too bad I didn't know these existed before, might have used it that one time."

To my dismayed expression, when I'm trying to figure out if he is serious or not, Tyler nods in reassurance. He makes a production of clearing his throat. "You killed me with your pink toolbox." His eyes dance to the stretch of my lips, and he carries on, "You were lying on the floor under a sink. Your sexy thighs exposed, pliers on your stomach."

"A wrench, it was a wrench," I say with a grin.

He shushes me, feigning concentration. "It's my ad, don't disturb."

When I giggle, he turns to lie on his back and tugs me to lie on him.

I fold my arms on his chest and rest my chin on top, staring at him with an adoring smile.

"You looked so incredibly sexy. I couldn't control myself," he continues, the corner of his mouth twitching. "Maybe we could meet up, just for you to play with my tool."

I snort, and he shushes me again.

"Do not contact me with unsolicited services or offers."

"What if I have some very interesting unsolicited offers, Mr. Adams?" I cock my head.

Tyler's hands dock on my bum. "Signed, Big Tool." And he pulls me against him, showing me that the name does fit the bill. Innuendos and playfulness give way to kisses and rushed hands peeling off clothes when he half whispers, half growls in my ear, "I can't get enough of you."'

Long and delicious moments later, with waves of pleasure still washing over me, I nuzzle my cheek on Tyler's chest.

Drawing his fingers softly up and down my spine, Tyler hums a soft tune.

"I like the sound of it," I whisper to his skin.

"Something new I'm working on." His voice comes out equally lazy. "I'm famished, want to grab something to eat?"

"Mmmhmm." I make no attempt to move. This moment, here on Tyler's chest—really, does a girl need more? Food is overrated anyhow.

"What are your plans for tonight?" Tyler asks next.

"My plans are whatever you're doing."

Abruptly, unceremoniously, and very much unwelcomed, Tyler kisses my hair and inches to sit. "Be back soon." He drops another airy kiss on my hair and leaves.

Watching the door to my room close behind him, a thought bubble pops up above my head with a crass question and a few good exclamation points. Much more than necessary. Five minutes later, I glare at the door. Ten minutes after, I give it the stink eye and drop my head back to my pillow, pulling the blanket over my head with frustration.

I jump with surprise a beat later when in lieu of a knock, Tyler opens the door. "Hey, where did you go, Kiisu?" The question is still fresh on his lips as he peels the blanket off me. My scowl is returned by an amused stare. A scowl that turns into a perplexed question when my eyes run over him. Wherever he went, he'd changed into a white pinstripe, elbow patched button-down and fit blue denim with thick white stitching. One of those hanging chains looped between his belt and pocket. His hair is held back with a leather string, and he looks nothing but heart-stopping handsome. Tattooed fingers with silver rings scratch at the hem of his bristled square jaw. The other hand reaches me, helping me out of bed.

"You dressed up," I dumbly state the obvious. My mind works in half capacity, fighting the other half that's been beauty-stricken to function again.

A slow grin followed by a low chuckle snaps me out of The Tyler Lee Adams Effect. "That I am." He pulls me to his chest and presses a gentle kiss to the center of my head. "I just realized I've never taken you out on a date. No better time like the present to rectify that, Kiisu."

The little frothing puddle on the floor would be my heart.

Rather than yelling, "I'm head over heels for you, Tyler," I mumble, "All my nice clothes are packed."

Another easy chuckle leaves his mouth as he takes my hand and leads me to my closet. "Mind if I pick something for you?" He looks at me over his shoulder.

"Be my guest." I motion at the few items still folded on the shelves, inwardly asking, *could you be any sweeter?*

"I'm just going to grab a quick shower," I say with the pile of clothes Tyler picked for me huddled to my chest.

"No makeup besides that glossy thing you put on sometimes," I hear him say behind the bathroom door. A request that paints a little, silly smile on my lips.

While I have a quick wash, butterflies go to town in my stomach. Like jet fighters on a mission, fierce and aggressive. I'm going on a date with Tyler. I've done *so much more* with Tyler, but this, especially coming from him, feels like we've moved to another level. Making me feel like there's hope for more again.

With this heady sensation where I feel like I'm floating a little above ground, I don the attire Tyler chose for me. I dab a touch of pink gloss on my lips like my . . . like Tyler asked, and give myself a slow scan in the mirror. A black V-neck Henley, skinny jeans, light-blue Chucks, and pink-ish lips—that's how he wants me. I look as natural and casual as I could possibly look. Another notion that makes everything inside me stir in a very good way.

I open the door to Tyler lying on my bed, his legs on the floor, arms crossed under his head, looking at the ceiling. He rises to sit as I near him.

His lips twitch with pleasure, appraising me. "You're so beautiful, Kiisu." Standing up, he whispers on an exhale, "So beautiful to me." Taking my hand, he leans in closer and gently presses his lips on the bridge of my nose. And another kiss on my cheek. Then the other cheek. When his mouth finds my lips, his fingers thread with mine, our palms become one. The next kiss is the most delicate, sweetest kiss.

———◆———

"You always get this kind of royal treatment?" I ask Tyler, still taking in the loveliness of this restaurant where we're having dinner.

Tyler, sitting across from me, in this cozy and intimate sunroom, sets his wine glass on the table. "Rivka, the owner, is Adina's sister." A simple statement that should explain why we were ushered into a separate part of a very busy restaurant where it's more than obvious that the place has been arranged especially for us. A single table set up for two with a crisp white tablecloth and a few tea lights in the middle of the otherwise vast sunroom where plants entwined with tiny string lights attest to my assumption. Though I still believe he gets special treatment everywhere he goes, close relation or not. But I can't deny that the fact he won't admit to having some special privilege doesn't warm my heart just a little more.

When a waiter comes in with a tray full of little plates and a basket of heavenly smelling fresh bread, even though we haven't placed our orders yet, I look at Tyler in question.

"We're having the tasting menu," Tyler begins to explain when the chef himself enters the room, following our waiter with a warm grin.

"David." Tyler stands up to shake the chef's hand.

"Always great to have you here." The older gentleman pats Tyler's back.

"David, this is m—" For a stretch, Tyler seems undecided, searching his mind for a way to introduce me. "Ivi."

When Tyler finally closes his mouth and turns my way, David breaks the awkward moment by extending his hand to me. "Nice to meet you," he says, holding my hand with both of his. "I have some special dishes for you tonight. How's the wine?"

"Lovely," I say, returning his gentle smile. I listen next as David tells us about each dish the server places on our table.

"I hope you enjoy your dinner." David turns to me after a reassuring nod from Tyler. "Any special requests for dessert, Ivi?"

"As long as it's sweet and delicious, I'm fine." I return his smile.

We share the delectable starters and the chilled wine, engaged in easy conversation and teasing flirtations that come naturally to us both. It may be the wine, the cozy sunroom surrounded by plants in all sizes and shades of green, or maybe, it's the rain rhythmically drumming on the windows, our conversation, or plainly, the man sitting across from me, but everything besides us is forgotten. I'm dreamily smiling at Tyler, feeling like Cinderella, having one of the best nights of my life. But just like the damsel in the subject, as the evening progresses, I seem to forget the impending part of the night when the clock will strike midnight, and I'll be left wondering if there's any future for my prince and me. And just like the damsel, I know that yearning for the prince is futile and that the prince will return to his castle and kingdom, and *my life* will return to . . . ordinary.

"Tell me something that no one knows," I tell Tyler, studying him above the rim of my wine glass as he brings a piece of bread to his full lips. When his brows bunch together, and a hint of a questioning smile adorns his mouth, I elaborate. "Something that will make your devoted fans renegade from the Tyler Lee Adams legion."

His initial response is an amused chuckle. He shakes his head, a thin smile hovering his lips. "I once bribed an innocent kid for Sour Patch Kids." He finishes with an easy chuckle.

I frown at him and admonish. "Tell me you did not corrupt a child, Tyler Lee."

Tyler chuckles again, this time his dimple comes out to play, peeking from under his five o'clock shadow. "It was on the longest tour ever, and I couldn't wait to get home. I passed by this kid in the airport who was gobbling down the candy like there was no tomorrow. I don't know what possessed me at that moment, but I just had to have some too. I could feel their tangy taste on my tongue."

"So what did you do?" I ask through a giggle. "Promised him backstage passes?"

"If it were that easy." Tyler feigns a frown. "Paid the little brat twenty bucks for half a pack."

"You have got to be kidding me."

Tyler shakes his head. "True story."

Noticing his attempt to hold a grin, my own lips twitch.

"True story, Kiisu."

"Darling Tyler Lee, I'm sorry to disappoint, but that doesn't constitute bribing. That's what we call getting ripped off . . . by a tot."

"Here I am, baring my soul, and you're making fun of me. Not cool." Tyler grabs my hand, making me flinch with surprise as he lightly bites my knuckles. Chuckling to himself, Tyler soothes the place with small, heated kisses. Lifting his eyes to mine, Tyler's smile alters into a pensive line. He opens his mouth, as though contemplating his next words, and then closes it. At this moment and many more that occur during the course of this evening, it seems like something is on the tip of his tongue that he is struggling to let free, yet time after time, whatever it is, it's kept padlocked behind his glorious lips.

Sensing my confounded, curious state, Tyler's gives me one of his reassuring grins. The one that helps him dissipate any resentment coming his way. Hell, this specific smile can serve as a tranquilizer gun. It has no less power in sending me into a googly-eyed, sedative state.

Tyler stands up under my dreamy gaze and circles our table. He offers me his hand. When I sink my palm into his, he gently tugs me toward him. When I'm flush against him, he engulfs me in a tight embrace full of warmth, hard planes, and heady perfect scent that's part fresh linen and greater part Tyler.

Tyler keeps holding me tight against him even when the waiter comes in, croaking with mild embarrassment something about clearing the table. Everything around me melts away, from the greenery with its vines and stems climbing up the windows, to the light music in the background, to the waiter coming back again with a cart of desserts, as Tyler's lips unite with mine.

His supple lips part, tasting mine and encouraging me to let his tongue in. Gentle, with the tartness of red, sweet wine and warm flesh, Tyler's tongue makes love to mine. Emitting an intoxicating wave of perfect within me. Like warm liquor, sweet and burning, it enters my body, urging my mouth to open wider, seek a deeper connection. Making my eyes drift close. Flowing down, squeezing my chest in its wake. Trickling lower to my stomach only to release powdery warmth flooded with emotions. Branching lower, the sensations travel to my navel, warm and enticing, then swim even lower, making my knees weak. I let out a moan. Tyler's taste, scent, and feel have spread to every part of me. I'm floating. My soul is melting into him. I'm his. I'm undoubtedly, wholeheartedly, and concededly his. A feeling that defies all laws of logic.

Walking out of the restaurant after dessert and a short chat with David, I feel Tyler's arm snake around my waist and pull me to his chest. His arms swallow me into a warm embrace. Resting his cheek against mine, he whispers, "You looked so incredibly gorgeous tonight. Thank you for the date."

"Thank you," I say back. "It was perfect." *You are perfect.*

The drive home, walking up to Tyler's room, seems like a blur when Tyler, bent above me with hungry eyes, slowly and reverently peels my clothes off me.

Sweet pain needles my heart when he sinks into me because what his eyes transpire, what his touch conveys, the way his kisses feel, makes me believe that this time, he isn't just going to touch me. This time, he is going to make love to me. That the heavy feeling of letting go of what we have has the same effect on him. That I'm not the only one finding the thought of tomorrow almost impossible to bear.

CHAPTER
Thirty-Three

"We wake up every day to a blank page. We're the composers of our present and future. It's in our hands and our hands only. We decide if it's going to be an upbeat, optimistic song or a complicated, depressing melody. We compose the tunes that will lead us to our future."

Tyler Lee Adams during a visit to an underprivileged youth center.

I'm not under any illusion of a happily ever after, but when I wake up in Tyler's arms with less than twenty-four hours to the grand good-bye, my mind is wandering to places where our farewell will be in the vein of a predictably fabricated cinematic moment. Boy runs after girl to the airport and promises her forever, rewarding the audience with their happy end worth of nine bucks and two hours of their lives. Last night's date and the hours that followed in his bed have planted a seed of something with a side dish of hope in me.

I decide to leave my hidden wishes on the pillow and face this day as it is, my final day here. Because even if it's not what I want, I'll be leaving it all behind in less than twenty-four hours. The man, the boy, complete with the glimmering sparkle of la la land.

Tyler's phone hollers from the nightstand, causing him to rub his stubble and murmur, "Someone had better be dying." He blinks one eye open, squinting at Eli's name across the phone's screen. "Eli," Tyler answers in a graveled morning tone. The angry cadence of Eli's voice on the other end funnels the room. I'm not able to decipher what's being said, but the tone of voice is unmistakable. Eli is not pleased.

"What time is it?" Tyler asks, scratching his abs. A few more curt words coming from the other end makes Tyler sit up with a start. "Oh, fuck." He looks around him, seeming troubled. When his eyes land on me snuggled under the covers, the hills of my breasts slightly showing, Tyler sends me a temerarious smile. He says to the phone, "It's been a long night." Tyler bends to give me a luscious kiss then tells Eli, "I'm on my way. Tell them I'm stuck in traffic."

Between shrugging on a pair of dark jeans and grabbing a white button-down, Tyler explains, "I have a meeting with the label in five . . . in West Hollywood."

"You'll never make it on time."

"You worried about me, Kiisu?" he asks before stealing another kiss and leaving the room.

"Have a great day," I say to the empty room. I know full well that this is what I should have expected. I shouldn't and can't expect Tyler to spend the day with me. Yet after our amazing night, I can't help but feel a little hurt. Our final moments together feel so precious to me, yet he dashes off with barely a good-bye. I know I should face reality — *this* is reality. Me . . . without Tyler.

————— • —————

As late evening rolls in, I can officially declare this day as a not great one. My last day in L.A. has been just another day. Lacking anything monumental. And greatly, glaringly lacking a one Tyler Lee Adams. Let's just say that the highlights of my day were a long stroll along the Abalone Cove shoreline *by myself* and a lobster taco from Nelson's. A rather sad way to depart from the most wonderful six months of my life, I admit.

With a ridiculously early morning transatlantic flight looming over my head, I make sure everything I need for tomorrow is packed and prepare for an early night. Luckily, the final good-byes from Adina, Eli, and Jay are behind me, and there's only one last person on my list to part with. The bitter feeling Tyler's absence has caused today only intensifies as I make my way to check whether he's back home.

To the muffled sound of music coming from his room, the bitter feeling grows. He's home, and he didn't bother looking for me. With each step forward, I feel it deep inside that I'm in for a disappointment, at the very least.

I knock on the door and wait.

My stomach tightens to the sound of Tyler's steps nearing from behind the closed door. Anxiety takes over me as he opens the door for me. He's in worn jeans and a black sweater, his hair loosely knotted. Everything about him radiates casualness. Everything besides the deep frown knitting his brows and the graveness in his eyes as they run over me. Wordlessly, Tyler takes a step back, opening the door wider for me. The radio silence on his part throughout the day intensifies the apprehension in me as I wait to see how our good-bye will play out. Because this could possibly be it — the last time we see each other. Ever.

Taking a deep breath, while plastering on a thin smile that I'm not buying, Tyler takes a step forward.

"All packed?" he asks, rubbing my arms from both sides. "Ready for your big adventure?"

Really? This is how it's going to be? A disappointment prone frown ruffles my features.

Tyler takes another inhale. "I need you to take care of yourself for me." He squeezes my shoulders in a brotherly manner.

I guess, yes. That's how it's going to be. Playing along, I say, "Puff, you don't have to worry about me. I'm a total badass . . . deep, deep inside. I'm a tough cookie, as tough as they come." My voice of its own volition wavers, just when my traitorous eyes cast down, which immediately discredits the cool act I'm trying to pull off. "Only I've done an outstanding job for the last twenty-three years of persistently failing to bring all the badass-ness out."

A light chuckle comes back as a response in tandem to Tyler's large hands cupping my cheeks. He slightly tilts my head up to look at him. His easy smile morphs into a flat line just before he dips in to brush his lips against mine. Just before his arms band around me and squeeze me into the center of his chest where his heart drums distinctively.

A rock lodges in my throat when his lips drop to my hair and his hold on me tightens. On the one hand, it feels so incredibly good and safe to be held by him. On the other, it feels so much like a good-bye that my heart cracks a little more.

I want you to want me. I want you to want me to stay, Tyler. My heart speaks from the confines of my aching ribcage. But different words leave my lips. "So I guess this is good-bye," I say to his sweater, buried deep in his hold.

"In which universe does this work?" Tyler whispers as though to himself, his lips still nuzzling my hair.

I squeeze my eyes shut, caging the tears that threaten to break free. I whisper the words he said to me on Christmas Eve back to him. "Where it feels this incredible." But my voice is so soft, broken, that I'm not even sure he hears me.

Tyler slowly releases his hold on me, tipping back to look at me. "You're going to have a great time doing what you should be doing."

I nod, begging him with my eyes to say something more, to ask me to come back to him. To his stretched silence, I gather the last bits of strength. "I will."

Tyler's eyes search mine for a tense beat. "What is it that you want, Kiisu?"

I bite my quivering lip, hesitating. "This . . ." My eyes drop to his arms around me. "You," is a tender, raw breath.

Looking to the side, Tyler's jaw clenches. A silent, loaded answer.

A bitter smile takes over my lips. I nod. "Yeah, I get it. This is not a fantasy world where my kind ends up with yours." I try to make my voice sound light.

Tyler's stare slices into me. His features harden. "Don't you ever say that. I'm the one who should be grateful for you to be with me. Maybe I'm good at singing, but you, you're the sweetest, kindest, most genuine person I've ever met. You have so much to offer. I can only strive to be half the person you are."

"Tyler, you are so much more than your image," I counter, shaking my head in disagreement. "You are beautiful and generous and incredibly talented. And this image you are selling, I can understand the draw, you literally shine like the star that you are. I like it too. But you know what? It's the unplugged version of you that I've been falling for."

Tyler closes his eyes, brings his forehead to mine. "Ivi."

Empowered by my words and by how much I care about him, I go on. "You know what, Tyler, I'll take the risk of sounding naïve and even immature, but since my cards are all here laid on the table, I'll go ahead and say it. I want you, so much. I want the infinity kind of thing with you. And I'm well aware that you're both the only one who can give it to me and you're also the only one who can take it away."

"You got it all wrong, Ivi. You're not naïve or immature. You know what you want." Tyler sighs, pulling back to look at me. "There's so much more for you out there. You're young. You haven't accomplished or tasted even half of what's waiting for you. Ivi, my life is here. I have a child. You're just spreading your wings. I can't see how this can work without you compromising everything that's ahead for you. I can't do that to you."

"Tyler." My voice comes out shaky, but at this point, I don't care.

I have nothing to lose. I realized I just lost the one thing I wanted the most. If there's enough will, everything can be worked out. If he wanted me as much as I want him, he'd make it happen. I stretch up on my tiptoes and kiss his lips softly. "Good-bye, Tyler."

Slowly, Tyler's hand falls from mine as I take another silent step back.

"Ivi, stay with me tonight," Tyler rasps.

I take another step back, my eyes trained on his. I slightly shake my head. It's too hard. I feel like every step is hammered down by some unexplainable force that I need to fight.

Tyler rubs his hand over his stubble. "Stay."

Stay and what? Prolong the painful moment. Why should I stay the night and make it even harder for myself? I shake my head again and take another step back. My heart squeezes in an unbearable ache when I realize I just lost the one thing I wanted more than anything.

"Stay with me tonight." His voice is raw. Begging now.

I know the way Tyler looks at me right now will haunt me. I shake my head and slowly walk backward, giving him one last chance to really make me stop.

But he doesn't. He remains silent as I cover the final space to reach the door, and the little hope I had breaks, together with our intent, locked stare, as I cast my eyes away. Silence is an answer too, and at this very moment, it's the worst kind.

As I finally lay my head on my pillow, I feel claustrophobic, as if my thoughts are closing in on me and the pain is absorbing all of the oxygen in the room. I force my eyes shut, opting for oblivion to come and take it all away.

CHAPTER
Thirty-Four

"The experience opened my eyes and changed my mindset for the better, I believe. I've learned that we should all embrace what we go through because even though sometimes it bruises our souls, it also teaches us that we can survive whatever life brings. And that we were lucky enough to experience it. Have faith in ourselves and others."

An entry from Ivi's blog during her second volunteer mission.

I wake up with a start to the sound of my alarm and yelp a moment later when my hand meets another hand on its way to kill the noise. With my hand pressed against my chest, I flip to my side. I gasp, finding Tyler lying on his side beside me, his head propped on his elbow.

His free hand moves to my temple. "Shhh," he whispers, threading his fingers through my hair. Dumbfounded, I blink at him.

He gives me a tender smile and leans in to plant a gentle kiss on my startled lips.

"What are you doing here?" I scrape out.

"Waiting for you to wake up."

"Tyler."

"Couldn't sleep." He shrugs and kisses me again. "I need to talk to you. Why don't you get dressed? We'll talk on the way to the airport."

I blink at him again. Because . . . what in the?

Standing up, he offers me his hand. "Get ready. I'll get us coffees to go."

I let him help me get out of bed, where he steals another kiss on the way. "Tea for me, please." I eye him incredulously.

"Oh right, jasmine green tea?" he casually asks, as if he hasn't just sent my mind into a tailspin.

I need to talk to you. I couldn't sleep. I need to talk to you. His words keep reverberating in my head as I take a quick shower and get dressed. I lace my hair in a thick side braid, leaving my face free of makeup. Grabbing my tote bag and my kindle, I notice that Tyler has already taken the rest of my luggage downstairs.

When I walk into the predawn dimly lit kitchen, where Tyler waits for me with two travel mugs in hand, a wave of something wonderful, thrilling and frightening flows over me. *I need to talk to you. I couldn't sleep. I need to talk to you.*

Tyler steps over to me, hands me my tea, and takes my bag from my shoulder. I gape at him as he leans in to kiss my lips and continue gaping at him rather deviously when he says, "We'd better get going."

I remain in my spot, watching him as he makes his way to the double doors. "Tyler, what are you doing?" Every bit of confusion I'm nursing filters into my question.

Tyler, who's a few steps ahead, looks at me over his shoulder. "Taking you to the airport, Ivi."

"Tyler." My voice comes out a bit harder.

He turns to fully face me.

My eyes run over his glorious self. With jeans, a black hoodie, and red Chucks, Tyler looks like something I never want to leave.

"Ivi?" His voice is low and earnest, warmly spreading to every part of me, leaving me powerless to fight what I feel for him.

"What . . . are . . . you . . . doing?" I repeat, my emotions on overload.

With his eyes holding mine, Tyler takes a few steps to reach me.

"Wanting you."

My heart climbs up my throat.

Wordlessly, he takes my hand, leading us to the indoor garage.

Cranking the engine, Tyler puts his hand on my headrest, looking back as he rears the car. Still looking at the rear window, he says, "I shouldn't have let you leave my room last night."

Cradling the warm mug in my hands, tense with anticipation, I glance at his profile and turn to the window.

Looking at the road ahead, Tyler is quiet for some long beats. Clearing his throat, he glances my way and returns his eyes to the road.

I squint my stare his way, finding him lost in thought. His brows furrowed, his teeth sawing at his bottom lip. "I don't think that just because you're not able to have a conventional relationship that it forfeits the right of wanting to have someone you care about in your life," he says out of the blue as if he is talking to himself. But when his stare turns to me, his next words reach the roots of my heart. "I want you in my life, Kiisu."

"Tyler." His name is a whisper.

For the next long moments, I look out the window, anticipation building in me as I wait for Tyler to speak. When we pass the road sign for the airport, hope slowly leaves me.

Startling me, Tyler laces his fingers with mine, looking ahead. "I'm not sure how to make it happen." He chuckles humourlessly. "I'm still trying to figure it all out."

Tyler takes a turn to park the car when I ask, "What are you trying to say?"

Cutting the engine, he turns to me. Drinking me in for a silent beat, he checks his watch and says, "You've still got some time." Pulling his hoodie over his head, he steps out of the car, only to quickly get into the back.

I watch him as he extends his arm, gesturing for me to join him in the backseat. When I'm lying on top of him, confounded, with my heart almost beating out of my chest, Tyler cups my face. "This is what I'm trying to say. I want you to come back after you're done doing your thing." His eyes bore into mine. "Last night, I told you that you should find what you want to do, grow. What I failed to say is that I want to be by your side when you do that." His stare holds mine. "I want you to come back to me."

I'm choked up by his words, by what I'm feeling.

"Whatever we are; this thing that started between us . . . I don't know where it'll lead. But I know that it's too good to leave behind." His features edge. "I know I'm asking for too much, but well, I hope I got it right."

I bite on my lip, transfixed by his warm stare. "I'll be away on tour for all of next month. You'll be in Nepal. You have enough time to think about it and decide if you're willing to take this risk . . . for me."

"I'll come back and what?" I ask.

"You come back, and we give this a chance, a real chance. See where it'll lead."

Resting my cheek on Tyler's chest, I close my eyes and try to make sense of everything he's just laid on me. Processing everything he's asking of me raises so many questions I can't even begin to answer. Eli's words come back to me, and I can't help but wonder whether me being with Tyler is truly the best thing for *him*?

Coming back to L.A. Coming back to Tyler after Nepal means, in more than one way, abandoning my life as I know it. Leaving my family, leaving my country, and taking a detour from everything I know and thought was ahead of me. It's what I wanted and now that it is within my reach . . . it's overwhelming, and surprisingly, I suddenly feel . . . unsure.

I'm well aware of the fact that he could never do the same for me. I could never ask him to do that. He can't just leave everything he has.

But still, giving us a chance means changing my entire life completely . . . for him. There's nothing I want more than him, but then again, should I let my life be completely altered for him?

Tyler's hand brushes through my hair, resting on my neck. He draws small waves at the nape of my neck, saying, "I can't make you any promises. But what I can assure you is that the thought of letting you go physically hurts." The rhythm of his heart beneath me hastens. "I don't want to let you go."

I lift my eyes to him. "I don't want to let *you* go."

Tyler's hands trail to my waist, lifting me higher on his chest until his lips meet mine. I've never been kissed like Tyler is kissing me right now. At this moment of good-bye, in the back of the car with a future unknown to us both. It's gentle, and warm, and languid, and sensual, and consumingly powerful yet full of all the uncertainty, fear, and need we both cling to.

We slowly ease back, starving for more. Tyler heaves a sigh of surrender. "You need to go." His voice falls between us rough and low. We straighten to sit, our eyes never leaving one another. "Think about it, Kiisu."

I nod. Swallowing the swelling in my throat, I gravitate toward him. Blinking away tears, I grab his face and kiss him so hard, tasting him, breathing him, wanting him as I've never wanted anything before in my life.

The last stolen kisses and looks we share next feel like we're commemorating what we had. Feels to me like a seal, bringing to an end the best time I've ever had, giving a closure to my first, and too short, love.

I smile at him, a weak smile that somehow feels bereaved with loss. I haven't felt it yet, but the loss becomes tangible with every heartbeat.

Leaving the car, I never look back.

Boarding the plane, finding out I've been upgraded, and taking off to my new destination is a daze because I've just left Tyler behind. It's amazing how anything before him made sense because now, I can't imagine a life without him.

Even though promising words were spoken, no promises were made, leaving me with a bittersweet uncertainty that makes it hard to breathe. There's no way for us to communicate over the next four weeks. This is it. We are separate people living separate lives again.

The weight of our good-bye and its finality stays with me as my plane takes off, as I watch the ground slowly fade, as enveloping white overtakes my view. And it remains when finally the plane emerges from the clouds into the infinite horizon, as mockingly bright and indiscernibly vast as the hope and pain in my heart.

End of Book One.

UNPLUGGED II

CHAPTER
One

"Volunteering – our imbursement for living in this beautiful universe." A tattered plaque hanging in the volunteer camp kitchen.

I roll down the window and lean forward. Closing my eyes, I let the wind whip across my cheeks and deeply inhale the icy chill. Riding up the mountain in the rusty, rickety truck sends my stomach to churn on every turn and twist as it crushes over the gravel road. I stare out the window, a wealth of heavy thoughts seizing my mind.

"Ivi, you're coming to the bonfire tonight?" Pedro, a Brazilian volunteer and my instant buddy, asks from the backseat, cutting off my contemplation.

I turn to give him a confirming head bob followed by a thin smile. I met Pedro and his sister, Renata, the first day I got to the camp. They took it upon themselves to be my personal guides, what with their three days of seniority. Showing me around the village, they introduced me to the rest of the team. Twenty awesome people from all corners of the globe. A delightfully diverse group of like-minded people who immediately make you feel welcome, happy, and most importantly, useful. All joined together, here in this small village, which is both uniquely beautiful with its untamed nature and heartbreakingly damaged with its poverty and the destruction caused by the earthquake that recently hit. We have come together with one singular goal in mind: help make it better. It's not my first mission. I've been exposed to disasters and calamities that were both natural and manmade numerous times, yet each time anew, my heart breaks all over again when I meet the people who essentially get to live the aftermath.

My nausea mollifies when the truck finally rolls to a stop at the site, near where we are lodged. A shabby, ragged stone house with a kitchen, or better yet, an open cooking fire, and more than a few small rooms for joined sleeping. It belongs to one of the village's teachers, Miss Shristi. A diminutive older lady who, funnily enough, everyone calls Big Mom. She's always in colorful saris, with jingling bangles, a nose ring, a red bindi dot marking her forehead, and an ever-present motherly smile. Renata, Pedro, and I share a room on the second floor.

The driver, with a few missing teeth and a rolled cigarette held between his lips, walks over to the back of the car and drops down the tailgate. Pedro calls out for a couple of bulky guys to help him unload the truck, and I join the rest of the group. I pull my work gloves out of my back pocket and take a few more steps, dodging downed trees limbs, to reach Renata.

"Who's the new guy?" She tips her head at where her brother and the other guys unload log piles into a cart.

"There are two new guys, Re." I roll my eyes fondly at my gloves, shrugging them on. Every fresh day since we got here, she's been interested in a different guy. Pedro once said that Renata believes she's in The Bachelorette rather than on a mission trip.

"The one with the incredible pecs and the wild blond curls."

I give surfer dude a glance and turn back to my friend. "Kenny.

He's from England. You fancy?"

"Muito," she confirms in Portuguese, giving Kenny's rear too long of a stare to be considered innocent as he bends to drop yet another log on the cart.

Shaking my head, I link my arm in hers and tug her after me, toward the debris that once used to be a home of a lovely family of four. "Let's start this day, shall we? There'll be enough time to molest the poor boy at the bonfire."

Thus begins day eight of my mission trip.

Inhaling, I bend down to lift a large rock, my breath held with the exertion. By the eighth time I lift a heavy rock and walk over to set it in a cart, the process becomes robotic. Focusing on the music playing on my earbuds and the fresh, chilly air caressing my face, I ignore the smarting in my muscles and overall physical strain.

I halt with a block in my hands when I see Rajesh coming our way. Dropping the block back to the ground, I pull the earbuds out and smile at him. His big, dark eyes respond with amiability. His skinny arms flail as he hurries his steps toward me. "Hi, Raj." I rub his shorn head, greeting him. The little boy's smile brightens, but his eyes with their perpetual glum don't match that sweet smile. They never do. He gestures at the smaller rocks and branches, signaling he's going to help us. Renata, who's a few steps away, and I share an emotional stare.

We've all temporarily adopted Rajesh. A sweet boy who's sometimes afraid to go home at night to his pimp daddy and house full of men he doesn't know. The loss of innocence surrounding this area is heartbreaking and hard to bear.

I watch Rajesh as he takes a candy bar from Renata with a shy smile and sigh with mild sadness. It's hard to accept even though I know some things, we, the volunteers, can't fix. Perhaps, this is the hardest part of being a volunteer—the exposure to things you just can't fix. I wipe my face with the back of my sleeve and resume removing debris.

Nine hours later, we've cleared the rubble from fallen houses and built the frame for two new ones. Some of us are already laying down concrete floors and making the structure of wire, poles, and bricks for the school they started working on a couple of weeks ago. An hour of break is all we take for food and drinks; otherwise, it's hard work. Fulfilling work.

When four o'clock rolls around, not one part of my body doesn't protest. It's smarting all over from the physical exertion. I'm dirty and tired and exhausted but couldn't be more satisfied and content. Glancing at Big Mom's house, I cringe and decide to take a walk through the village instead. The house is by no means inviting or well insulated. A chilly breeze, insects, and spiders enjoy cruising around the rooms as they please. We all try to spend as little time in them as possible, given the conditions. What a glaring contrast to my lodging conditions at Tyler's. Feels like I've been teleported to a completely different universe. Hard to believe these two realities coexist on the same globe.

Adjusting the earbuds in my ears, I hit shuffle on my playlist and begin my stroll. Chautara, in the Sindhupalchowk region, is one of the most devastated areas from the quake that hit nearly six months ago. The village is mostly self-reliant, with every spare piece of land used for crops of corn, fields of beans and chilies, grazing goats, buffalo, and chickens with the occasional orange or apple tree. The scenery around the village is depressing. There's more than a lot of work to do to bring it back to an actual village condition. Just a few houses made it through the devastation that rises up in piles upon piles of wreckage. But if you just lift your eyes a little higher, the glorious exquisiteness of the Himalayas subdues everything with its wild, powerful grace.

Taking the path to the forest with a soft tune playing in my ears, it's just me and my thoughts, and immediately, Tyler takes center stage. Every passing day since I've arrived in Nepal has empowered the assumption that the day Tyler brought me to the airport and told me he wanted to give us a try was a product of high emotions with little, if not zero, thought behind them.

I can't deny the promise in his words, but I'm having a hard time holding on to it. It's hard to keep the hope alive when right up until this very moment, we haven't communicated. We never even agreed on the pragmatics of making anything between us work. We never agreed on anything to shift me coming back into motion. It was all up in the air. Nothing concrete to work with. Just like I ominously anticipated, when we parted ways over a week ago, it was a final good-bye rather than a promise for a reunion.

My musing makes my heart feel a bit heavier as I walk through the peaceful, stunning nature.

Even though more than a week has passed, I still carry the weight of our good-bye. The thought of Tyler is still a constant flame in my head. This place has helped to lessen it into a low burning ember, though. Breathtaking sunsets, spectacular nature, and a wealth of misfortune and poverty are bound to do that to you. It knocked sense and reality into me in less than twenty hours after my arrival in Nepal.

My fountain of self-pity has reduced to a drip. Real life and hardship have a tendency to minimalize, if not completely diminish, one's "little problems." If not put them to shame. It, if you will, smacks you upside the head, *hard*. Pummels some perspective into you. Because really, what does a bruised heart in need of nursing have on a child begging to simply live?

Coming back, I find the team setting up the camp for dinner. Eva and Jana, two mid-fifties ladies from eastern Europe, help Big Mom with making the staple Nepali dishes, daal bhat and daal roti. Day in and day out, it's rice or flatbread with lentils, and the occasional twist on these meals is with a few different styles of roti or rice pudding. If we're lucky, some potato and bean curry is served with the dish.

It hasn't been that long since I set foot in this place and already the physical changes in my body are hard to miss. I'm more toned, and my clothes feel a bit looser now.

I smile as I notice Renata and Kenny setting up the wood for the bonfire. Both looking more than happy in each other's company. Bet he's getting a rose tonight.

I head to the hose attached to a nearby tree to freshen up. A bucket and a hose, Nepali style bath for you.

"Ivi." Big Mom's voice reaches me as I wash my face for the second time, rubbing my hands over it to get all the dirt out. Or at least try to. Hygiene, to say the least, is not exactly a priority here.

Drying my hands on my cargos, I walk over to meet her. "You called me?"

"You box," she says in her limited English with an encouraging smile.

My brows bunch as I try to decipher her words. "Do you need a box, Big Mom? Do you need me to put something in boxes?"

She shakes her head, her hoop earrings swaying with the movement. Her expression coils with frustration. "You box, room." A little triumphant smile curls her lips. "Package! You package room."

"There's a package in my room?" She grins at me with a nod. "A package for me?" I ask again. No one has ever sent me packages during any of my trips so far. Perhaps, she's confusing me with one of the other volunteers.

"Package Ivi Kert," she says, reading my doubt. She drops her hands to either side of her hips, silently commanding acquiescence.

"Thank you." No point in arguing, Big Mom looks determined.

Indeed, on my narrow folding bed, on the itchy, tattered wool blanket stands a cardboard box with my name printed on a white label. Cautiously, I take the box in my hands for a closer look. Besides my name, there are no other indications of what it is or whom might have sent it. I bend to sit on the bed and put the box on my lap. My fingers itch to rip it open to find out what's inside. But they have nothing on my flipping belly and accelerated heart. I just know it. It's from him. It's from Tyler.

Shoving my hand into my thigh pocket, I feel for my Swiss army knife. We all carry one around. With our current line of work and the general conditions, it's elementary. Flicking the blade up, I run it over the middle of the box, cutting through the tape. I flick the blade back in and pocket the knife. Biting on my lips, I push the box flaps to the sides.

A giggle escapes my mouth to the packs of peanut butter filled pretzels lining the box. There's a black cotton fabric nestled amid the snacks. Picking it up, I realize it's a folded shirt. I hold it up and let it roll down. Another chuckle leaves my mouth, this one louder. Joyful and amused to find Tyler's face plastered over the front with a sexy smile. My own smile feels like it's coming straight from the center of my happy heart. I hug the soft fabric to my chest. When I turn to set the box aside and go join the rest of the group, I realize something else is at the bottom of the box. I cock my head, looking at the smaller black box before opening it to reveal its content.

I observe the cell phone in my hand with its thicker body and funny looking antenna. And the penny drops. I've seen this type of phone before. It's a satellite phone. Tyler sent me a satellite phone. One of the only options to communicate with the outside world besides traveling to one of the surrounding cities, which is at least sixty miles. That is if you're lucky enough to catch a ride there.

Besides being a source of communication to the world, I also know how pricey these calls are. I sigh, holding the phone in my hands. About to put it back in its box, I sense something attached to the back. It's a little note folded in half, taped to the back. I release the paper and unfold it. I don't know what it is, but seeing Tyler's handwriting here, in this place, is like a shot of energy to my spirit.

Call me, Kiisu.

Three simple words that mean the world to me right now.

Giddy, I leave the room, not before tucking my care package under my backpack. Opting to call Tyler once I figure out the time difference (we're on two different continents, after all), I join my friends.

Both volunteers and some of the locals had congregated around the fire by the time I join. Kenny's friend strums a guitar while two of the older ladies in our group give a whole repertoire of The Beatles. The younger local crowd keeps watching us like we're a newfound species. It's something you get used to quite quickly. They follow us a lot during the day. As a matter of fact, as soon as we leave the house, we have an audience staring at us. Especially those of us of Northern European descent. The fairer you are, the most fascinated looks and followers you get.

I walk over to help myself to some Chiya, a local tea with milk. Noticing Mike approach, a proud American veteran with whom I had an immediate click, I remain in my place. Cradling the metal mug with both hands, I bring it closer to my mouth and blow on it, waiting for Mike.

"Ivi." Mike tips his head, reaching for the thermos.

I grab a mug and hold it out for him to pour the steaming tea. "Erm, Mike, do you happen to know what the time difference between Nepal and the States is?"

Taking the full mug from me, Mike asks, "Where in the States, darling?"

"Oh." It takes me some beats to answer because I don't have one. I know that Tyler is on a mini tour across the States, but I have no idea where he might be right now. "L.A.?" Comes out as a question rather than an answer.

Taking a sip of his tea, Mike licks his lips. "Nepal is about fourteen hours ahead of L.A." Mike's mouth twitches as my mind drifts, doing the math. "It should be around six a.m. in the City of Flowers and Sunshine."

I give him a coy smile, which he returns with an amicable one. With our steaming mugs in hand, talking about the progress we made today, we walk toward the group. I share a boulder with Pedro, who brought us each a dish of daal roti. With a tummy full of warm, wholesome food and a content, easy smile, I watch the people around me, feeling utterly blessed to be a part of the group. Familiar tunes have me slice my stare to Kenny who's holding the guitar now, crossed-legged on the floor beside us. Longings explode in my stomach when he sings one of Tyler's songs. I hug myself, watching him, listening and counting the minutes until I make that phone call.

When the logs turn into burning coals and people start to scatter for the night, I volunteer to do the dishes. A way to keep myself occupied until another hour passes, and it won't be as early in L.A.

At ten, with my phone in hand, I make it to one of the swings suspended from a sturdy ficus with aerial roots to a moonlit corner away from the house. Away from the few who remain outside to chat and smoke. With a shaky hand, I dial Tyler's number. The ringing sound has my stomach coil with anticipation like a tight spring.

In lieu of a greeting, Tyler says, "I've dreamed about you nearly every night since you left." His voice surges right to my heart. He sounds tired and weary. His voice distinctively hoarse, not his usual husky cadence, like it was overly used, strained. But the emotions it brings, the butterflies it releases inside me. The sweet press on my chest.

Though all I want is to tell him that I missed him so much, I could hardly breathe, so I downplay it, going with a tease instead. "Is that a new sappy song?"

Tyler chuckles. I can hear something clicking at his teeth and then a deep swallow. "No, it's literally how my nights have gone since you left me." Another clink and a swallow. Probably the herbal candy he chews on whenever he's strained his vocal cords.

"Are you after a concert?"

He hums a confirmation. "Yep, last night."

"How did it go?"

He chuckles briefly after a short pause. "There were a few thousand calling my name and the only one I wanted next to me is far away."

"Where's that person? Can't you, I don't know, do the thing you do. Flick your fingers and have someone bring that person to you?"

"Can't do that. She's too busy saving the world." His voice brims with flirtation. His chuckle is an afterthought. "I don't want to upset the universe. You know what they say, Karma's a bitch." After another short pause, he adds in a low voice, clear of teasing, "Ivi, I meant what I said before you left."

My chest feels heavier.

"And now after not seeing you or talking to you for over a week, I'm more than certain. Come back."

"Needy, are we?" I joke, too overwhelmed to tell him I'm moments away from throwing everything to hell and jumping on the next plane to L.A. My soft chuckle dies to the extended silence on the line. "Tyler . . . you're quiet." I break the silence in a soft chord.

He takes a generous inhale. "Yeah. I'm waiting for you to really hear me." He exhales audibly. "Really listen to what I'm trying to say. I want to give us a chance, Ivi."

"I'm listening, Tyler." It's a choked whisper.

"I feel like I haven't been the same since the morning after . . . you. You're everywhere. All over my mind. All the more since you left."

"Tyler—"

He cuts me off before I'm able to say another word. "Ivi." He brings my wayward thoughts to a screeching halt. "It's simple, very simple, as I see it. What we had is too good to not at least give it a chance. It's about two people liking each other. That's it. I want you to come back and move back in."

Move back in? I thought . . . I don't know what I thought. But this is . . . "Are you serious right now?"

"The boxes you asked Eli to send to Estonia. I asked him not to. They are here, waiting for you."

"You are serious," I say on an incredulous breath.

"Yeah, I am. Come back to me, Kiisu."

For updates on Unplugged II release, sign up for my newsletter: http:// www.sigalehrlich.com/contact.

Or stay tuned for updates on my **FB page.**

Note from the Author

Dear Reader,

Thank you *so much* for taking the time to read Unplugged.

So, if you have any extra time, it would be great, REALLY GREAT, actually it would be more than fantastic, if you leave a review on Amazon, iTunes, Barnes and Noble, Goodreads, or anywhere else you wish. ;-)

Also, I more than love hearing from my readers, honestly, it's the best part of the whole writing process. So, send me an email at: author.sehrlich@gmail.com or chat with me on Facebook.

Thank you for allowing me to share my stories with you, and I hope to be re-invited to your bookshelf with my next releases.

Again, THANK YOU!

Loads of x's & o's,

Sigal

Acknowledgments

THANK YOU to every single person out there who read the book!

Big thank yous for those who helped, encouraged, and shared with me the fun experience of writing this book. Sima, Kiki, Sylvie, you rock.

Some gigantic, heartfelt thank you to my Liis for being an inspiration for this story, and for being such a beautiful human being in general.

Nicole Hornbaker, for your magnificent work and priceless suggestions. You always make the editing part so much fun.

Jenny, for making my words pretty.

Gal, as always, for making this thrilling journey called life as great.

My kiddos, for being as perfect and nutty and awesome as you are and still loving me unconditionally even with less mommy-time.

Olivia Luck, my favorite author, thank you for never judging, for making me smile with your emails and for listening to all my shiz. I adore you.

BLOGGERS, truly incredible bloggers. I'm forever grateful and humbled by your continuous support. You are simply the best.

And last but not least, my readers. Since Layers was released I've been constantly overwhelmed by your response. You guys are truly amazing and I could have not asked for better readers.

Thank you! Thank you, and then some. Thank you for reviewing, messaging, emailing, loving, liking, spreading the word.

Also by
SIGAL EHRLICH

About the Author

By teen age, Sigal already lived in three different continents where she was lucky enough to experience and visit varied places and meet unique people, which only helped fuel her overly developed imagination. Currently, Sigal calls Estonia home where she lives with her husband and three kids.

Not exactly sure where they will end up next ...

Sigal would love to hear from you, please visit her on her website, Twitter, and Facebook.

http://www.sigalehrlich.com/
@Sigal_Ehrlich
https://www.facebook.com/sigalehrlich.author
http://www.pinterest.com/authorsehrlich/
auhtor.sehrlich@gmail.com